Good 10

Another Woman . . . Another Life

John Lee braked to a stop for a light. "My mother lives up in Fall Creek. I mentioned her this morning. Pearl Jordan."

The green and white street sign dissolved in a dust storm of gray, eaten from the edges in. With a huge effort Abby took a breath and leaned back in the soft seat, falling, falling.

No more gray. The world went black and something pressed down on her like a second skin, cold and damp and heavy. She opened her mouth to gasp and tasted dirt, tried to scream, but there was nothing in her chest but old, foul air and it couldn't get past the lump of dirt in her mouth.

Falling.

A blast of cold wind swept over her, blowing the dirt away, and a warm pair of hands caught her and held her tight against the swirl of black and gray that tried to drown her.

When she opened her eyes, the world steadied around her, bright and sun-faded, and John Lee was kneeling in the open passenger door, hands on her shoulders. His face had gone pale under the Texas tan.

"Abby." He shook her, one convulsive jerk that traveled up and down her spine like lightning. "Abby, what the hell's going on?"

Copper Moon

by

Roxanne Conrad

AN ONYX BOOK

ONYX
Published by the Penguin Group
Penguin Books USA Inc., 375 Hudson Street,
New York, New York 10014, U.S.A.
Penguin Books Ltd, 27 Wrights Lane,
London W8 5TZ, England
Penguin Books Australia Ltd, Ringwood,
Victoria, Australia
Penguin Books Canada Ltd, 10 Alcorn Avenue,
Toronto, Ontario, Canada M4V 3B2
Penguin Books (N.Z.) Ltd, 182–190 Wairau Road,
Auckland 10, New Zealand

Penguin Books Ltd, Registered Offices:
Harmondsworth, Middlesex, England

Published by Onyx, an imprint of Dutton Signet,
a division of Penguin Books USA Inc.

First Printing, July, 1997
10 9 8 7 6 5 4 3 2 1

REGISTERED TRADEMARK—MARCA REGISTRADA

Printed in the United States of America

PUBLISHER'S NOTE
This is a work of fiction. Names, characters, places, and incidents either are
the product of the author's imagination or are used fictitiously, and any
resemblance to actual persons, living or dead, events, or locales is entirely
coincidental.

To Vin Richards, Keith McCarty, Mr. Shelton,
Mr. Sudduth, and all my musical friends and mentors.

Most especially, to Marcia McNiel Diehl and P. N. Elrod,
for being chandeliers in a world of bug zappers.

Special heartfelt thanks to my editor,
Jennifer Sawyer Fisher. She knows why.

Prologue and Fugue:
August 5, 1957

Sometime just around sundown, when the whole world turned red, she gave up. It wasn't any considered thing; she just got tired, and sat down where she was on the rough gravel at the edge of Texas State Highway 115 West, going nowhere or going to hell, depending on where you started from. One thing about going nowhere: you sure didn't know when you got there.

She thought about crying but she'd done that until she was sick, and anyway there didn't seem to be much to cry about anymore. The world was red, and she sat on sharp gritty rocks with sand blowing in her face, wearing a twenty-five-cent dress from a rag bin.

Her feet were all cut to hell.

I'm lost, she thought, and pulled up her legs to wrap her arms around them the way she had when she was little, when she'd wanted to make herself small so things would go away. *It's not so bad.*

Behind her, soft padding noises and harsh panting. Without looking away from the flat red horizon she said "C'mere, dog," and he whined and pressed his skinny body against her. She patted him on the flank, hardly noticing the stink anymore; he'd been roaming longer than she had, that was for sure. Hard to tell what kind of dog he was. Big and old, scarred on one side and one ear missing. He whined again and she scratched at the mass of fleas leaping on his coat. "Poor old boy. How's that?"

He slurped on her hand, then her face. She'd been scared to touch him at first, mean-looking beast, and then she'd gotten sick looking at all the ticks and fleas and God-knew-what crawling on him. Then it had all stopped mattering, things like ugliness and ticks and fleas. His stumpy tail beat against her leg and she scratched his patchy neck and stared at the sunset. Waiting.

Waiting for nothing.

"I ain't afraid," she said to the dog, as the world started going brown instead of red. "Used to be, but ain't now. Like you."

He licked his chops in agreement and settled down next to her, head on her lap.

They watched the world go black. She thought, right before the sun disappeared, *This is the best night of my life*, and she was right. On the far eastern horizon, the new moon rose like a fresh penny.

"See that?" She rubbed his flea-bitten ears. "Copper moon. Good light for traveling."

In the distance, like some wild animal growling, she heard a truck coming down the highway. She didn't bother to move; it was getting dark, and nobody stopped anyway, not for some stray starving mongrel and a skinny girl. She closed her eyes and listened to the truck rumble closer. It was making squeaks, like the springs were old. A song was playing on the radio. Nat King Cole. She'd always liked Nat King Cole. She caught the smell of burning oil on the thin hot breeze.

Lights splashed over her. The dog woofed and lifted his head; she kept her eyes closed because she didn't want to see the truck. Seeing it might make it real, and she was tired of real, she just wanted quiet.

The truck's rumble sputtered and died, and in the stillness she heard Nat singing, clear and cool. The tires made a smacking sound on the hot pavement as the truck rolled to a stop. The dog scrambled to his feet and let out a deep-chested, wet-sounding bark.

"Hush," she said. He didn't listen, just kept barking and barking, spraying her with hot spit and noise. A truck door creaked open and slammed. Footsteps crunched.

She opened her eyes and saw a man staring at her. He was big, rawboned, brown as an Indian and leathery from the sun. He wore old faded work pants and a greasy shirt and a straw hat with holes like rats had gotten at it.

Narrow light-colored eyes.

"Ya'll's on my land," he said tightly.

She started rocking back and forth, not so much scared as distressed. She didn't want to talk. Didn't want anything but quiet.

"We got law 'round here, missy. No trespassers. I could shoot you if I was of a mind to."

She knew the law enough to know the gravel beside State Highway 115 wasn't his land, but that didn't matter much, not out here in the dark. His land was where he said it was. The gravel stabbed sharp, but she didn't stop rocking, no, sir, the pain was good, it kept her from being scared.

"Shut that dog up," the farmer said. The dog barked louder, like he knew he was being talked about, and charged like a bull. The farmer backed up toward his truck.

"Hush, boy," she whispered. It didn't matter. She wished she could make the dog understand that, but for dogs it always mattered. Little things, like skinny girls in ragged dresses. Big things, like the farmer and his cold blue eyes.

The dog snarled and crouched, ready to spring. The farmer reached in the bed of his truck and pulled out a long rusted piece of iron pipe. He smacked his palm with it and grinned down at the dog.

"Well, you just come on," he said. She stopped rocking.

"Boy. C'mere, boy. Boy!" She slapped the gravel next to her. The dog's legs trembled with strain. He looked around at her and his snarling stopped. "That's it, boy. Good boy."

The farmer stepped up and swung the pipe like a bat, slamming it into the dog's side with a wet, thick crunch. She lunged forward, slipped on gravel, skinned her knees, tried to grab the farmer's arm. He shook her off and took aim again.

The dog whined and tried to crawl away.

It did matter, it did. The dog was right; it mattered.

She saw the farmer's eyes when he brought the pipe down again, and again, and again, until the dog wasn't moving any more and the night was quiet except for Nat King Cole, singing on the wind.

"Law says I can kill me trespassers," the farmer said. She knew she should get off her knees but the sticky warm tar of the road held her down. He grabbed her hair and raised her head until their faces were inches apart. Close up his eyes looked like blue marbles, cracked with white. "Guess that means I can do pretty much anything I want with 'em."

There wasn't any point in fighting him but she didn't want to leave the dog, not right there on the road where somebody'd run him over, he didn't deserve that, he was a good dog. The farmer hit her with the pipe until she couldn't breathe for the blood in her mouth and threw her in the back of the truck on top of old rusty pieces of metal and barbed wire. Blood dripped off her face like tears and above her the sky turned black, black as the tarry road, and all she could see was the fierce bright copper moon.

She just wished it was quiet, that was all.

And she wished he hadn't killed the dog.

Opening Movement:
December 3, 1994

Huntsville, Texas

He knew prison tradition, and he damn well knew it was custom for guards to stand at the gate and shake his hand as he left. Nearly thirty years in this place, hardly a breath of air or a look at the clean blue sky, and the only men waiting were the ones who had to be there. The two mangy bastards couldn't even crack a smile for him. They were wearing silvery sunglasses today, and he saw himself twisted like a hunchback in reflection, his hair gone thin and gray. The damn Salvation Army suit hung on him like a secondhand sack.

"Well, boys, any last words of advice?" He pulled in a deep breath of the morning. Pure free air, scented with pine and grass; he caught the stale smell of prison and knew he carried the reek of despair in his clothes. The guards' mirrored glasses shifted away from him and reflected the rising sun, the cool green tree line, the dull gray gun towers.

And they said nothing at all.

The outer gate squealed as it ran back on its tracks, like the jaws of hell pried open. He took a firmer grip on the secondhand duffel bag and took a step forward, coming even with the guards. They shifted away like he was tubercular.

"You want some advice, pops? Stay out," one of them said, he didn't know which. He backed up and grinned at the both of them.

"Surely do intend to." He tipped an imaginary hat to them with callused hands. "Ya'll have a nice day, boys."

They stood rock-still as he strolled out the gate, out into the cold Texas morning. Out into freedom.

Custer Grady was a free man again.

He walked to the road, where the bus would presently wind its way around the curve and squeal to a stop for him, where the bus driver would look at him like a rotten worm in a fresh apple but would take him on into town anyway. He had the bus fare in his pocket, jingling like Christmas bells. After that—

After that, he had things to see to.

He sat down on the rough concrete bench and scuffed his shoes in the winter-blasted grass. In the distance, at the foot the gentle hill, a freeway sliced through the trees, and cars moved along in a shimmering blur. Freeway, now there was a word. He was a free man on the freeway.

"Yes, sir," he continued. The blunt silver nose of the bus edged around the curve and blundered toward him. "It'll all be over soon."

Midland, Texas, same day

Abby's first thought of the day was *I'm going to be sick*, and then she was, violently, into the trash can she'd put next to her bed. It was a wide-mouthed trash can with two plastic liners, just to be sure.

Preparation paid off.

When the spasms were over she lay back and folded her hands over her rolling stomach and tried calming exercises. *Start with your toes.* Her toes had nothing to do with it, it was her *hands*, it was her goddamn *hands. Are your toes relaxed?*

Of course they weren't. She went on to her feet. By the time she'd reached her thighs she was tired of the whole thing and sat up. Sitting up was bad. Her stomach lurched, and she had to think about emptying the trash can. Better to do it now, while her stomach was still in shock.

The bed had been warm—not comforting, exactly, but warm. The floor was another story, chill sliding across the wood like invisible snakes to writhe around her ankles. She hip-hopped to the many-times-painted-over closet door and banged it back. Piles of shoes, none of them new. She dug until she'd located one frazzled gray slipper, shoved her toes in, and kept digging. The other slipper lurked under a discarded box of last Christmas's chocolate-covered cherries.

"Gross," she said gloomily. She rattled it. Full. It was probably a roach farm. She shuffled back to the trash can and dropped the box in from an arm's length away, got down eye level with the rim to pull the liners up and twist them shut. It was the ambush approach to cleaning.

The plastic bags gurgled like her stomach as she

quick-shuffled down the dark hallway toward the kitchen, holding the bags as far as possible.

"Maria?" she yelled. No answer. Her roommate knew her too well to be around for these little waste-disposal problems. Abby fumbled one-handed in the junk drawer and found a plastic twistee to secure the bags, then shoved the whole thing in a bigger green trash can with peeling biohazard stickers and smiley faces. She slammed the pantry door on it.

Mission accomplished.

Maria had taped a big note to the refrigerator door that said GOOD LUCK PUKEY, which almost made her smile. She opened the box and found a half-empty carton of chocolate milk. One glass left semi-clean beside the sink; she rinsed it out and poured sweet relief until the carton went dry. The first mouthful went down hard, but the second was easier. She drank until the glass was empty and rinsed it clean with a few halfhearted swipes of lemony detergent.

Carlton's doggie bowl in the corner was full, which was a blessing; opening a can of dog food would have been the end of the world. And where the hell was Carlton, anyway? He usually would have been whining at her door by seven, and it must be later than that.

Abby squinted out at the world through a slit in the blinds and saw a blank concrete walkway along with some sprigs of half-dead grass that winter hadn't managed yet to kill. Midland, Texas's ideas of landscaping. Maybe Maria had taken the dog out for a run.

As she turned she saw the clock hanging crookedly

on the kitchen wall. 9:30 A.M. *Five hours!* the beast in the back of her brain screamed. *Five hours! Five hours!*

"Shut up," she sighed. She negotiated through the maze of rickety tables and secondhand furniture—plaid earth tones and one enormous pastel chair Maria had found at some garage sale—and found an uncluttered spot on the couch. She curled up in a comforting ball and searched for the TV remote one-handed. She found it stuffed in the couch cushions and clicked it three times before the TV came awake, as sluggish as she was.

Maria had left her another note, this one in big black letters sitting on top of the littered coffee table. It said, GO GET YOUR MUSIC NOW!!! and the NOW!!! was underlined three times. Abby groaned and hugged a pillow close and tried to go back to sleep, but Maria's NOW!!! and the beast's *Five hours! Five hours!* ruined it. She shuffled back down the dim wooden hallway to her bedroom, gathered up her black concert folder—the expensive leather one Benny had given her last Christmas—and her instrument cases. She dumped them by the front door, right where she'd trip over them if she tried to leave without them.

Damn, it was cold on the floor. She frowned as she thought about the delicate wood of the clarinets, and set the cases on top of a table where the central heating could reach them. Then she flopped on the couch again and curled up to let the chocolate milk work its magic.

She'd left the nasty plastic sack full of stomach contents in the pantry. The thought brought her bolt upright and scrambling; she dug a robe out from under a pile of pillows, found her boots and coat, and retrieved the bag. She hurried outside, across the parking lot to the rusted gap-topped Dumpster, and tossed the bag in, retreating even before she heard it plop wetly inside.

The joys of housekeeping.

Back in the warmth of the apartment, she drifted off on the couch to the buzz of the TV and the beast screaming *Four and a half hours! Four and a half hours!* and came awake in a panicked fog, flailing, pillows flying like frightened chickens.

Somebody knocked on the door. She stumbled over Maria's cherished throw rug and cursed. Her music folder slid under her foot like a skate and escaped into the gloom. She had the door halfway open before she remembered that she was wearing thin pajamas with a button missing at the top.

Then she staggered back, arms full of struggling dog.

"Carlton?" She blinked away confusion and pushed the dog far enough away to see Carlton's grinning long-nosed face. "Damn, boy, where did you come—"

Words failed as she saw the man standing in her doorway. He was wearing blue jeans and a plaid work shirt and a straw cowboy hat. A narrow, intense, guarded face. Large dark eyes.

"Hi," she said lamely, and tried to get Carlton to lay off the slurping. "Uh, hi."

"Ma'am," he said, giving her a nod as he took his hat off. She realized that wrestling with Carlton had popped another button on her top, which gave him an unobstructed view all the way to her navel. She clutched at the fabric one-handed and got Carlton under control. "I guess that'd be your dog, then."

"I didn't know he was gone," she blurted. *Responsible pet ownership strikes again.* "I thought, uh, my roommate had him. She takes him out for runs, sometimes."

The stranger was staring at the floor to avoid looking at her cleavage—no, he was looking at Carlton's feet. She glanced down and saw that there were bandages on the dog's paws, too clumsy to have been vet-done.

"Found him at my mom's door before sunrise this morning. Looked at his tag and figured I'd bring him back, since I was coming to town anyway."

"What the hell happened to his feet?" She hung halfway between scared and mad, appalled that she hadn't been worried about the mutt, hadn't even thought much about him in the press of her own selfishness.

"He was at my mom's house," the man explained again, slowly. "In Fall Creek."

Carlton thumped his fluffy tail against Abby's leg hard enough to bruise. She scratched his head and he licked her fingers enthusiastically.

"Where?"

"Fall Creek. Thirty miles that way." He pointed vaguely toward the southwest. "Kind of a long way for a dog to run. He been missing all night?"

Thirty miles? She looked at Carlton for confirmation, but he thumped his tail on her and walked away, sniffing the furniture to make sure she'd taken no other dog before him. "Uh, no, I thought he was here last night—I was sick—look, would you like to come in?"

He nodded. She backed up to let him in and watched Carlton rub against his leg. It looked okay. Bad guys couldn't make friends with dogs, could they? Not big dogs. Not big *stupid* dogs like Carlton.

Now that he was standing in her home and blocking the door, she had no idea what to say to him. He wasn't much bigger than she was, compact and wiry. He looked strong.

"Coffee?" she asked.

He took his hat off, turned it in his hands, and nodded.

"Coffee. Uh—I'll just be a second." She flip-flopped at high speed to her room, pawed through an untidy pile of clean clothes, and found Maria's thick blue fleece robe. Perfect. She tied it tight on her way back down to the kitchen.

"No trouble. Least I can do when you bring me back the mutt." Maria kept instant coffee somewhere. Sugar canister? No, that was full of baking soda. She hit the jackpot in the tea canister and spooned black crystals into chipped blue mugs. "I'm out of milk. Black okay?"

"Fine." He'd stepped around the stucco divider to watch her. Didn't his face do any expressions? "Your name's Abby, right? Abby Rhodes?"

"Mom loved the Beatles." The explanation was re-flex, but he smiled. "Know what makes me feel really old? People ten years younger than you don't think my name's funny at all. So you're—"

"John Lee Jordan." He stuck out a hand. She caught a glimpse of scars crisscrossing his palm, felt the ridges press against her skin as they shook. He had cuts on the back of his hand, too. A few looked recent.

"Carlton didn't scratch you, did he?"

He saw her looking at the cuts and shook his head. "He was just fine. A real good dog."

John Lee Jordan was not a talker. She waited for the microwave to do its thing and jittered her slipper nervously. He turned his hat in his hands and set it down on the countertop.

The microwave dinged. As she took steaming cups out of it, he said, "You ever live in Fall Creek?"

"Never been there." She felt something when he said the name, though. A surge of adrenaline. Fear. She stirred both cups of coffee until they were the correct brown sludge and handed one over to him. "Why do you ask?"

"Sometimes when dogs run away they go to old homes, places they remember."

"I can definitely say he never lived in Fall Creek."

He kept staring at her face like he knew her. She wanted to stare back but didn't dare; she blew on her coffee instead, using the steam like a modesty veil.

"Well, maybe you know my mother," he said. "Pearl Jordan."

If she hadn't been holding onto the counter she might have fallen; her knees went weak and the world went gray and she heard a voice say, from a great distance, *Pearl? My Lord, Pearl,* and the next thing she knew her heart was hammering hard enough to hurt and John Lee's hands were guiding her to the big pastel chair and he did have another expression, this one worried. She felt dizzy again and put her head between her knees and gasped for breath. Carlton, ever helpful, tried to lick her face since it was within reach. John Lee nudged him firmly back.

"Sorry," she mumbled. His hands massaged her shoulders.

"Deep breaths. Keep your head down." He pinched tension out of her neck. "Abby? Can you hear me? You want a doctor?"

"No." She sat up and leaned back. Her shoulders felt hot where he'd rubbed them. He backed up a couple of steps, still watching her. "I—I've got this thing. This, uh, nausea thing. It'll go away."

He looked guarded. She reviewed the sentence in her head and said, "Oh, no, it's not morning sickness or anything. It's performance anxiety."

He cocked his head like she'd said something in a foreign language. *Oh, God,* she thought, *that didn't sound too good at all.* She rushed on.

"See, I'm a musician, and I get these shakes before I play. It's nothing, really. I'm okay."

The beast in the back of her brain, taking no notice at all of Carlton's disappearance or rescue or a strange man sitting in her living room, announced that she had *four hours* until curtain, and expressed some intention to throw up the chocolate milk she'd appeased it with.

"Whatever you say." John Lee reclaimed his coffee cup from the kitchen counter and leaned against the counter, sipping and watching. "So, you don't know my mother? Pearl Jordan?"

The name still stung like a wasp. "Never met her," Abby said sharply.

"Then maybe old Carlton there just wanted a long midnight run. You'll probably want to get those paws seen to by a vet."

Now that the excitement of the reunion was over, Carlton was definitely limping as he surveyed his domain; when Abby snapped her fingers he hobbled over and draped himself at her feet, panting and pleased. She dug her fingers into his thick warm coat and scratched his neck under the collar, which sent him into spasms of doggy ecstasy.

"Mutt," she murmured. "What the hell were you doing, running all over creation? Chasing a girl?"

"You didn't get him from a pound, did you? Maybe found him?" John Lee was still obsessing over his dog-returns-home theory. She wondered whether she was going to have to sign something to convince him.

"You think he was going back to a previous owner?"

"Never know."

"Well, I know. I've had him since he was small enough to fit in one hand, haven't I, baby?" She got up, tested her balance and found it more or less adequate, and took the coffee cup from him on the way to the door. "Look, Mr. Jordan, I can't thank you enough for what you did for Carlton. It was really sweet. I wish I could pay you but—"

She gestured around at the secondhand apartment,

as if that was all the explanation she needed. He gave her one more look, the intense kind, put his hat on, and went out the door she held open for him. His eyes went the color of dark beer in the sun.

"I don't need any money, Miz Rhodes. But thanks for the coffee. Carlton, you be a good boy, hear?" He held out his hand and the dog licked it one more time, politely. As Abby started to shut the door, John Lee put one hand flat on it and stopped her. "What kind of music?"

"Excuse me?"

"Performance anxiety. What kind of music?"

"Classical," she said. "Clarinet. I'm playing at the Civic Auditorium at two-thirty today. Mozart."

"Mozart," he repeated, and smiled. It was startling how much of a difference it made in his face, his eyes. "I always liked Mozart."

She found herself watching him as he walked away and was entertaining a cautious, half-hazy fantasy when the beast in the back of her brain screamed, *Four hours! Four hours! Four hours, you dumb talentless bitch!*

"Oh, perfect," she breathed, and eased the door shut. "He likes Mozart."

She got mascara in her eye, cursed, and dabbed at the tears with a scrap of tissue. Her hands were shaking. *Maybe I scratched my cornea. Maybe I can't go on.*

Any port in a storm. She blinked against the burn and tattooed black dots from her eyelashes to her eyelids. As she dabbed them with the damp tissue, she took off half the eye shadow.

Another typical performance.

Outside the bathroom window, a car horn honked part of Beethoven's Fifth. Great. She abandoned her makeup and put her glasses back on. Deep breaths, right from the diaphragm. Her black dress, a relic from her college recital days, looked fine. She'd twisted her hair back into a motherly-looking bun. No necklace or bracelet. Only one ring, a little jade circle from her mother.

The uniform was correct. She left the bathroom, gathered up her music folder from the floor, checked to be sure everything was there. It was. Purse. It was hiding under a chair. Her instruments—A, B-flat, E-flat—were all bundled together in one unwieldy carrying case. She checked the latch to make sure it wouldn't open when she picked it up and spill a fortune all over the floor.

The door vibrated under a staccato of knocks. Carlton limped into the living room and whoofed half-heartedly. Abby opened the door and squinted through burning eyes.

Benina Wright lit another cigarette from the butt of an old one, blew a thick lungful of smoke into the air, and said, "Land shark. You ready?"

She crouched down to pat Carlton's head. Abby stared at her, speechless with amazement. When she'd gotten control of her tongue again, she sputtered, "What happened to your hair?"

Benny looked up, tossing tiny braids over her shoulders like snakes. Black and white braids, the Bride of Frankenstein gone reggae. She looked like an industrial accident.

Yesterday she'd been a *redhead*.

"You like it? Black and white," she pointed out, rubbing Carlton's head. "Very formal."

There was no sense at all in pointing out to Benny that she was supposed to be *invisible* as an accompanist at a recital. Benny had never been invisible in her life. Today, she wore skin-tight black tuxedo pants with a glittery silver stripe down the side, stiletto heels, and a spangled vest that featured Bugs Bunny and Daffy Duck. And the braids, of course.

Abby gave up and turned away to take inventory again, wondering what she was missing, wondering if it would even matter. No one would notice her, with Benny's hair onstage. Her instrument case was where she'd left it. Her purse—

"You don't like the vest." Benny's voice had gone small and quiet.

Abby sighed, closed her eyes, and turned back to her. "The vest is great, Ben, and whatever you do with your hair is your own business. Anything else?"

"Well—there's my nails. What do you think? Too Liberace?" Benny held out her hands for inspection. She'd been to an adventurous manicurist—glitter polish, red and black notes drawn on top of the enamel. Abby gave them a long, serious look.

"Amazing," she said truthfully. Benny smiled. "What am I missing?"

"Reeds?"

"Shit, I think they're around here somewhere. What time is it?" Abby turned to search through stacks of magazines. Benny hip-bumped her aside and slid bright purple sunglasses down her nose to look over the mess.

"Time is an illusion of the working class," she said, and fished a flat wooden reed case out from under a *National Geographic.* She popped it open one-handed, like a cigarette case. "So you thrown up yet?"

"No." Abby took the case and closed it. The three reeds nestled on glass inside looked fine. "What am I missing?"'

"Sedatives? Ligature? Barf bag?"

Abby ignored everything but the serious question. Ligature. "I picked the Bonade, it's in the case."

"Which mouthpiece?"

"Charles Bay."

Benny tilted her head to one side, braids rustling like corn husks, and asked, "Why did you put socks on your dog?"

"They're not socks. I'll explain later."

"Because if you're going to put socks on him at least make them lime green or something. I mean, if I was a dog I wouldn't want to run around in white athletic socks. It's like wearing knee-highs with Bermuda shorts."

"They're not socks, Benny, they're bandages. Carlton ran away last night and tore up his feet. A guy brought him back this morning. Damn, where's my music? Do you see my music?"

"What guy?"

"Damn it, do you see my music?"

Benny plucked it from where it was hiding under a chair and flipped through the pages like a punk auditor. She nodded, slapped it shut, and tucked it under her arm.

"About this guy—"

"Later," Abby said tightly. She swung the door wide and kneed Carlton back as he tried to limp outside. "Out. Out."

Benny ambled casually out to the walkway, where she glittered like a chandelier in the harsh winter sun. Abby rubbed Carlton's head for luck and locked the door behind her. She hefted the instrument case and frowned. She'd forgotten something, she was sure of it. Purse, keys, instrument, reeds, music—

"Abby?" Benny puffed her cigarette, eyebrows cocked. "I'm not the fashion police or anything, but did you mean to wear the fuzzy slippers?"

Abby looked down, closed her eyes, and said, "It's going to be one of those days, isn't it?"

"It's always one of those days."

Midland was having a sunny winter, cold and clear and dry. Benny drove with the windows down on her beat-to-hell Gremlin, flicking ashes out into the air and admiring her nail polish. Abby watched the road—somebody had to—and concentrated on breathing. In. Out. In.

"Truck," she said. "Truck. Truck!"

Benny looked up and twisted the wheel just enough to slide by. The salvage truck was big and half-rusted, squeaking on its springs; the faded letters on the side said, JESUS SAVES, WE RECYCLE. The driver was a hunched old Hispanic man with a face that looked eroded. He gave them a toothless smile as they passed.

"You don't like my driving, get your own damn car out of the shop," Benny grunted. "Uh-oh. Traffic jam."

There were two cars at the light ahead, one late-model Ford pickup with smooth decolike styling, one decaying Mustang with a missing left quarter panel. The Mustang farted black smoke in a steady stream. Benny eased the Gremlin in behind the truck.

"So, you live out here in the country, you'll know the answer to this. Why do they bother to make pickup trucks aerodynamic?" she asked. She flicked the butt of her old cigarette out to the street. "And how come he has an empty gun rack? If you were going to be macho enough to have a gun rack, wouldn't you put something in it? Was he cute?"

"Cute?" Abby repeated blankly. "Who?"

"Him." Benny waved her newly lit cigarette vaguely, leaving a ragged scarf of smoke. "You know. The guy."

"Oh, John Lee. Yeah, I suppose. In a cowboy kind of way."

"What else is there out here? Intellectual professor types? Sensitive artists?" Benny rolled her eyes. "John *Lee*? Not a guy with two first names."

"Hey, watch it, everybody out here has two first names except you and me." Abby found herself smiling and didn't know how it had happened. Benny had that effect on people. "John Lee Jordan."

"Classy. But before you marry Joe Bob—"

"John Lee."

"—Bubba Lee . . . come to Dallas with me and meet some guys with real first names. Bob. Steve. Duncan." Benny took a meditative drag on the cigarette and drummed fingernails on the steering wheel. "Duncan's a babe. You'd like him."

"What does he play?"

Benny grinned. "Okay, guilty. Guitar."

"You're kidding."

"Classical guitar."

The light changed. The pickup ahead of them cruised cautiously out into the intersection of Main and Parker. The hat brim of the driver moved right to left as he scanned the sides of the street. Benny hissed smoke and popped the clutch. The Gremlin vibrated uneasily as it picked up speed.

Almost there. The Civic Auditorium was only four blocks away, a squat square building that looked like a prison except for the ample parking. Abby felt a spasm of dizziness and put her head back. Why did she do this? Why? Not for the adoration of her fans, that was for sure. If she was lucky, she'd have twenty-five people and most of them would be her clarinet students. Probably a few college kids from UT Permian Basin fulfilling recital credits. Maybe, if she was very lucky, a reporter from the local Midland paper would fit her in between garden and gun shows.

Benny's hand slid over hers and squeezed.

"You'll do great," she said with a sigh. "What gives with the program? I thought you said you were sick of doing the Concerto."

"I am, but half my students will be playing it at a

region contest. And most of them don't have any idea what it's supposed to sound like." Abby swallowed hard and closed her eyes. *Not that I'm likely to show them how Mozart ought to sound.* "Did I tell you I've got one kid doing Debussy?"

"No kidding? Total bitch of a piano part. You got anybody decent for it?"

"I was kind of hoping you could give it a try."

Benny patted her hand. "Of course you were, you slut."

Abby opened her eyes as they pulled into the parking lot. The brakes squealed as Benny parked; she jerked the hand brake, killed the engine, and fished a pack of Marlboros from her blue satin jacket. She tapped one out and lit it, sucked smoke like most people sucked air.

"I thought you were quitting," Abby said.

Benny shrugged. She blew a wiggling halo of smoke, then another. They blew apart against the windshield.

"I tried aerobics, but it wasn't as much fun. You sick?"

"Not yet," Abby lied. She popped the door of the car and stepped out into the cold air, adjusting her long skirt around her. The world looked grainy and drab, the sky dust-orange. There were three other cars in the parking lot, and one of them was missing a tire. "I'll go warm up."

She collected her instruments and music. As she closed the door, Benny punched the radio buttons and found Black Sabbath. She wiggled in the seat, grinned, and blew another smoke ring.

The world wasn't drab. Benny was too bright for it.

The auditorium's lobby felt chilly and dead when she entered, too cold and far too dark. There was an easel in the lobby with her picture on it—well, a glamorized approximation, anyway. Underneath, the sign said, ABIGAIL RHODES, MOZART CLARINET CONCERTO. Underneath, in smaller letters, BENINA WRIGHT, PIANO.

Abby's stomach lurched. She darted for the bathroom and made it to one of the stalls in time, emptied her already empty stomach, and sat on her knees admiring the tan and orange tiles of the wall. The room smelled of Lysol and mildew. When she was sure it was over, she flushed the evidence and went to the sink to brush her teeth and gargle. Travel-sized toothbrush, toothpaste, Listerine. Like a Boy Scout, she came prepared.

"You can do this," she told her pallid reflection. Her blue eyes looked as faded as old denim. Gray strands in her black hair. She'd put on a few pounds in the last two years, not enough to bulge the dress but enough to soften the sharp bones of her face. She wasn't sure she liked it. "You can do this. You know you can."

She knew. But knowing wasn't enough.

She picked up her instrument case and headed backstage. The stage manager was messing with a light board and a roll of electrical tape; he jumped as if she'd caught him with a *Playboy* and a towel.

"Miss Rhodes, so nice to see you again. I'm looking forward to hearing you play. You know where the dressing room is—"

"I know, thanks, Paul." She should. She'd been in

the theater hundreds of times in her high school years, had performed with the Midland Symphony at least thirty times since. She avoided the skeletal remains of a ladder and turned right down a narrow concrete hallway. The tap of her footsteps chased on ahead. The door of the women's dressing room was propped open with a block of wood; she left it open and laid her instrument case on the makeup counter.

Ritual. When panic shut down her brain, at least she had ritual. She took out the bottom half of the A clarinet and fitted it to the top half with a decisive twist of her wrist. The bell went on the bottom, the barrel on the top, the mouthpiece atop that. She took precise care in aligning her dampened best reed on the mouthpiece, checking from the back and front before screwing the slender silver ligature tight.

Ready. She put the instrument to her mouth and, all by themselves, muscles worked. Her diaphragm, pushing air. Her lips, falling naturally to a proper armature. Her fingers, finding the keys.

The notes echoed from the walls, satiny-warm, round, alive. It was there.

The music was there, after all.

She played, eyes shut, listening as her body produced the music her soul heard, and her mind had nothing to do with it at all.

When she opened her eyes some endless time later, she saw Benny standing quietly in the doorway, listening. Behind her shoulder, Paul the stage manager suddenly found someplace else to be. Benny's sharp, angular face softened into a gentle smile, the blue eyes warm and fond.

She only asked "Ready?" but Abby could tell she already knew the answer, and before she could say it Benny turned and walked away, shoulders straight, braids swinging, down the hall toward the stage.

Rondo:
December 3, 1994

Playing left her with an empty place inside, a sense of loss as unnerving as the anxiety. She came out of the quiet place in her head to hear the last notes die away. It had almost happened this time—a tiny click of a second when the music had almost broken free and soared, incandescent. So very close.

Applause swelled, thin but enthusiastic, and the shadows in the audience turned to smiling faces. She remembered to bow and stepped aside to indicate Benny, who acknowledged her fans with both hands in the air, vest glittering like diamonds. God, it was like appearing onstage with a rock band. *Tonight, ladies and gentlemen, Abigail Rhodes backed up by Aerosmith!*

Maybe she'd get a bigger audience.

Benny followed her offstage into the dusty velvet shadows behind the curtain, and before she could bolt out for a cigarette Abby grabbed her arm and said, "The tempo was off on the third movement, wasn't it? Too slow?"

"No, I thought it was fine." Benny frowned and fidgeted. "You were great. The second movement was about the best I've ever heard you play. Why? Was I setting too slow?"

"No, I—"

That was all she had time for because Paul came forward, beaming, to deliver a bouquet of roses tied with red ribbon. He kissed her hand awkwardly, flushed apple-red in his cheeks, and backed off as a swarm of junior high and high schoolers entered from the stage door waving programs.

Benny pulled away and beat it for the alley and the haven of a Marlboro. Three of the kids cut her off. One of them was Delilah Kimble, Abby's star student—Delilah, habitually quiet and self-contained, had a glow of hero worship in her eyes. Abby shrugged off a petty jab of disappointment and smiled at the other kids crowded around her, picking out fragments of compliments like thrown roses.

Roses. She frowned down at the flowers and dug a card out of the center.

Best wishes, it read.

John Lee.

She glanced up, startled, and saw him leaning against the raw brick wall next to the stage door. He smiled to her and nodded.

A girl tugged on her arm and said, "Miz Rhodes, I don't want to play *Mozart*, I want to play what *Delilah's* playing. I like it better, can I play that one?"

"Like you could," a younger boy sniped. "You can't even do the slow parts."

"The slow parts aren't easier," Abby chided, and tore her gaze away from John Lee's face to look down at them. "Jen, I think you should stick to the

Mozart, don't you? You've practiced it so hard. And
the Mozart is something everyone wants to play, especially the professionals."

Jen looked stubbornly down at her own feet. "You
said we could play anything we wanted. My *mom*
said I could play anything I wanted or I could get a
new teacher."

Abby bit back the impulse to tell her to get another
teacher, and good riddance. Jen wasn't a bad kid,
really, she was just spoiled. Who was she to criticize
when she'd been on her knees in the bathroom half
an hour before curtain? She patted the girl's thin
shoulder and said, "We'll talk about it Wednesday,
okay? Carl, did you like it?"

"It was really good," Carl said with just the right
touch of teenage superiority. Over his shoulder she
glimpsed Charlie Harris—*Mr.* Harris, the band
guru—waving and smiling as he tried to stop two
junior high students from hanging on the dusty velvet curtains. The gang was all here.

"Thanks." She looked around for John Lee again.
He was gone, and the musty-sweet smell of his roses
was making her dizzy. Maybe he hadn't been there
at all; maybe she'd imagined him. Was she that desperate for admiration?

Of course she was. Why else would she go through
the horror of performing?

The kids wandered off, duty done, making plans
to cruise the Sonic drive-in restaurant and hang at
the mall. Delilah was still in earnest conversation
with Benny, who shifted from one foot to the other
like a kid interrupted on the way to the bathroom.

"Friend of yours?" said a voice from behind her, close enough that warm breath touched the back of her neck. She turned so fast she wobbled on her high heels. He moved back a polite step but the feeling of his presence stayed with her, a hot space in the chilly air.

"Benny. She was my roommate in college." *Say something intelligent*, her brain urged. "Thank you for coming."

"What college?" He asked it like he wanted to know.

"Texas Tech in Lubbock. Then Cincinnati Conservatory, Certificate of Performance." She had to stop herself from bubbling over like a pot left too long on the stove.

John Lee's gaze slid over to Benny as if magnetized. A smile crinkled the corners of his lips, and he said, "I guess conservatory must not mean conservative. She always looked like that?"

"Mostly." Abby became abruptly conscious of the roses cradled in her arms, shifted them with a springy rustle of leaves. "Thanks for the flowers. You didn't have to do that."

He held out his hand. She felt awkward taking it but not taking it seemed worse, so she juggled clarinet and flowers and let him fold his fingers over hers. She was unprepared for the warmth of his touch, the strength of his grip. He didn't seem willing to let her go. He had fascinating eyes, full of secrets, and she couldn't tell anything about what he was thinking. Like Benny, she had a tendency to date within the musical faith. She didn't know a thing about cowboys, except that he made her nervous. Maybe he played pedal steel.

"You were good," he said. "Third movement could have been a little faster."

She stared at him, stricken.

"I'm kidding. You said it to your friend, remember? You were great, Abby."

The sound of her name from him came as a shock. It fluttered her pulse and sent heat screaming into her cheeks. She pulled her hand free and used it to hold the roses and clarinet between them, crossed swords.

"Thanks again for Carlton. I really appreciate it."

He folded his arms over his chest, rocked slightly back and forth, heel to toe. He took a long time to answer, as if he'd chosen the words carefully. "I feel like I know you."

Before she could stop herself she said sharply, "You don't."

God, where had *that* come from? His eyes widened. He kept staring, a frown grooved between his eyebrows.

"No, I guess I don't," he admitted. "But I think I might want to. That a problem?"

I'm hopeless, she thought in despair. As soon as she twelve-stepped her way out of one phobia there was always another one, coiled like a rattlesnake under a rock.

"You want me to go?" he asked.

"No."

In the long silence that followed, she listened to the normal workday sounds of the stage lights clicking off, the curtains hissing shut, the retreating footsteps of her escaping audience. The stage door slammed. Benny must have made it to the alley for her cigarette.

John Lee hadn't moved when she finally had the courage to look up at him again.

"Abby, look, you can tell me to go to hell if you want to." He had the oddest way of turning things back on her, of seeing into her head. "I do something wrong?"

"Nothing." *Everything.* "It's just a bad time. I'm sorry."

"Hell, if you wait for the good times you'll die waiting." He gave her a long, level stare. "We don't get but about three perfect minutes in our lives, but that doesn't mean all the rest is a waste."

Her lips parted, wanting to say something, but her throat wouldn't cooperate. After a second or two the pressure eased. She didn't need to say anything.

He was right.

"Hi." A hand slid between them, long fingers outstretched. Glitter polish blinked in the dim light, and Benny angled in like a wedge behind it. "You must be John Ray."

"John Lee. John Lee Jordan," he said, and pumped her hand with exaggerated enthusiasm. "All your people have hair like that?"

"All the ones that lived." Benny stepped over to wrap a proprietary arm over Abby's shoulders. "What do you think of her? Pretty good, eh?"

"Real pretty music," he said. He'd done something to his posture, rounded his shoulders, bowed his

legs. His accent had steamrolled. *Ree-ul purty.* Abby
didn't know whether to laugh or slap him. "Not
much of a beat, though."

"Not like Garth Brooks," Benny agreed.

"I was thinking more like Lyle Lovett. You ever
two-step, ma'am?"

Benny laughed from the gut. "You ever been in a
mosh pit at a GWAR concert?"

He gave her a wicked grin. "Not this month."

Benny punched Abby in the shoulder, said "I like
him, he's stupid," and walked away.

Abby stared after her. "Hey! Where are you
going?" she called.

Benny turned, a chandelier of glitter, and held her
arms out in an extravagant shrug. She kept walking
backward, a feat of balance that left Abby speechless.
"Back to the hotel, hang out in the bar, watch some
wrestling. Oh, hey, cowboy?" She looked directly
into John Lee's face and winked. "Would you mind
giving her a ride home?"

"Nope." He tipped an imaginary hat to her.

"She's always mopey after a good concert." Benny
executed a perfect showgirl high-heeled spin and
clicked away down the hall, speckles of colored light
following her like a fan club of Tinkerbells.

"That," Abby said when she could speak again,
"wasn't fair. Was it?"

"Nope." John Lee reached out and took the flowers
out of her arms. "I guess you'll want to put that
thing away."

The clarinet. It felt so natural in her hands that it
was a shock to realize she still had it.

"And after that?" she asked.

John Lee cocked his head and shrugged. "Dinner?"

Right on cue, her stomach growled.

Drive-through fast food had never tasted so good. The hamburger was deliciously perfect, the french fries the ideal mix of Idaho potato and Georgia peanut oil, the chocolate shake a thick smooth caress on her tongue.

"See those kids over there?" she asked, and pointed with a french fry at a slow-cruising primer-gray sedan. John Lee, busy sucking on a vanilla shake of his own, nodded. "Those are my kids."

He inhaled ice cream and had a coughing fit; she pounded him on the back after cramming the fries in her mouth.

"My *students*," she corrected when they could both breathe again. "Sorry. They're cruising because they're waiting for me to do something crazy."

"Like what?" he asked, and reached for the last french fry at the same time she did. They both pulled back. "Go ahead," he said.

"No, you go ahead." They waited. The french fry remained in the lonely no-man's-land of the checkered paper tray.

"You're going to disappoint them?" he asked.

She felt a little nervous at the glow in his large, dark eyes. "I . . . maybe. No. I don't know."

He picked up the french fry and held it out, pinned between his thumb and forefinger. She looked at it doubtfully. He cocked his head and raised his eyebrows, silently daring her; she knew without looking that her students were cruising closer, craning their necks to see. The spectacle of Old Miz Rhodes dating a cowboy at the Sonic drive-in was irresistible.

Just for the hell of it, she leaned forward and bit into the french fry, biting close enough that her teeth grazed his fingertips. The taste of him was startling. It tingled salty and vivid on her lips.

For a second he sat frozen, and then he grinned and ate the half inch of severed french fry himself. She couldn't decide what the look in his eyes was, exactly.

"You," John Lee said, and started the car, "are dangerous."

"You didn't think I'd do it."

"Hell, no."

He backed the car out from under the aluminum shelter into the white winter sun; she shaded her eyes with one hand and twisted in her seat to watch drive-in and students disappear behind them.

"That's the problem," she said, and turned back to face the front. The immediate shopping district was full of drab brick buildings with neon sale notices in the windows. Furniture sales flamed on the right. Rent-to-own advertised NO CREDIT REQUIRED in English and Spanish. "Everybody underestimates me."

He smiled and shifted to a more comfortable position in his seat. She decided she liked his car, new and maroon, seats as soft as kid leather. He kept the backseat clean, a habit she envied. She'd once gone an entire year in college without ever excavating the trash from the floorboards.

"What about your folks?" he asked. He drummed

his fingers on the steering wheel, no particular pattern, and she noticed that he had nice hands, large and square and long-fingered. He had three or four irregular dark scars on the back of his fingers, finer dark lines that looked like cat scratches.

No wedding ring, she was relieved to notice, and no sign that there'd been one recently.

"Abby?"

She looked up, startled, and saw him watching her. Heat bloomed in her cheeks and she turned her head to look out the passenger window. Nothing to see. A few stores with Christmas sales on the sidewalk, some constipated-looking shoppers. More battered, sun-baked cars parked slantwise in front of the stores.

"They live in Dallas," she said quickly, to get it over with. "My dad's an electrical engineer. My mother passed away seven years ago."

He gave that the appropriate moment of silence before asking, "Any brothers or sisters?"

"A brother. Eddie. He's an actuary."

"A what?"

"An actuary. He calculates numbers for an insurance company. Look, don't ask me, I didn't get a degree in it. How about your family?"

John Lee braked to a stop for a red light, and she leaned forward to look at the faded street sign. Spargus. They were only about a mile from her apartment. If that was where they were going. She supposed she ought to ask.

"My mother lives up in Fall Creek. I mentioned her this morning. Pearl Jordan."

The green and white street sign dissolved in a dust storm of gray, eaten from the edges in, and with a huge effort she took a breath and leaned back in the soft seat, falling, falling.

No more gray. The world went black and something pressed down on her like a second skin, cold and damp and heavy. She opened her mouth to gasp and tasted dirt, tried to scream, but there was nothing in her chest except old foul air and it couldn't get past the lump of dirt in her mouth.

Falling.

A blast of cold wind swept over her, blowing the dirt away, and a warm pair of hands caught her and held her tight against the swirl of black and gray that tried to drown her. She swallowed and swallowed and tasted metal and blood.

When she opened her eyes the world steadied around her, bright and sun-faded, and John Lee was kneeling in the open passenger door, hands on her shoulders. His face had gone pale under the Texas tan.

He tried twice to speak before he got her name out.

She looked past him to the sidewalk, where a couple of curious Mexican women clutched shopping bags and whispered.

"Say that again," she said. Her voice sounded strange and distant. He wet his lips and looked puzzled. "Say my name again."

"Abby." He shook her, one convulsive jerk that traveled up and down her spine like lightning. "Abby, what the hell's going on?"

She shook her head, too weary to be afraid, and

scrabbled for a discarded Sonic napkin. She rubbed her mouth with it, then her tongue, until the taste of dirt was gone.

He insisted on taking her to the emergency room, and they waited in a cramped, overheated treatment room while two doctors discussed her in the hall. They frowned a lot. Abby didn't like the look of it.

"This is a waste of time," she said for about the tenth time. John Lee had heard the accusation before and didn't bother to respond. He'd settled himself comfortably on a chair near the door, elbows braced on his knees, arms dangling. There didn't seem to be a tense muscle in him.

Abby could not make the same claim. She had a panicked fear of hospitals, doctors, and needles, and she'd experienced all three in the hour since John Lee had delivered her to the ER door kicking and screaming. She sat at the very edge of the treatment table, legs dangling in space, and practiced the fingerings for the Debussy *Clarinet Concerto*, which was the first that came to mind. The flutter of motion soothed her, a little. She tried to hear the piano part, *there*, a cascade of notes like a rainstorm.

The music broke off in midmeasure as the treatment room door opened.

"Abby, I think we've found the problem," her doctor said without a glance at John Lee. He breezed forward to lay a chart on the treatment bed next to her. She shifted nervously away from him and hated the dry crackle of paper underneath her. "Your blood sugar crashed. Now, you did the right thing eating, that was fine, but you need to be more careful about what you eat and when you eat it. You *do* know you're hypoglycemic?"

"I know," she sighed. "But this didn't feel like—"

"You did experience disorientation? And a gray-out?"

She shrugged. He beamed, satisfied, and handed her the ubiquitous healthy menu. His lecture was longer than she was used to, so she passed the time by staring at John Lee. His dark hair hung straight near his face, escaped into rebellious waves at the ends. Red where the fluorescents caught highlights.

He looked up around the time the doctor's lecture was winding down, and their eyes met.

"I'll do that," she said to the doctor, who was clearly waiting for a response. "Can I go now?"

"I don't see why not. Go home and rest. Make sure you're following the menu every day."

He didn't insist on a promise, which was good, and he left without any more fuss. She slid off the table and wavered on her high heels, less from dizziness than from unfamiliarity with the shoes. John Lee jumped to his feet and braced her with an arm around her back, one hand holding her forearm.

"I'm fine," she said. "See? Low blood sugar. Gets me every time. First my dog and now me. You must feel like you're running an ambulance service."

He must have known that she didn't need the support, but he didn't let go. She felt the heat of him all along her back, down her arm. It felt like they were dancing, but they were standing very still.

"It wasn't blood sugar," he said. She felt his pulse

through the tips of his fingers where they rested on her skin. "I saw your face, Abby. You weren't sick, you were scared to death."

Tears welled up in her eyes, carrying with them a tide of fear she hadn't known was there. She didn't know where the feeling came from, or why, but suddenly she could put words to it.

"I felt dead," she said. "Dead."

Maria had left another note on the coffee table. This one said, *Heard it went great, gone to Memphis, see you Thurs. next.* Below that, in tiny script, was, *Took C. to vet. What happened to feet?*

Carlton licked Abby's hand, chocolate eyes woeful, and she cheered him up by scratching his neck. He lost interest in her and limped around the couch to sniff John Lee's blue jeans. John Lee crouched to give him a good-dog shakedown, and Abby couldn't help but notice that he had one of those great cowboy butts, minus the usual can of chewing tobacco in the back pocket. The back of his belt didn't spell out his name, either. Another plus.

"My roommate's gone," she announced, and immediately regretted it. "Uh, I mean, I can make some dinner if you want to stay. Would you?"

John Lee looked over his shoulder and gave her a warm, lopsided smile. "I don't think that was what the doctor meant when he said to rest. How about I take you someplace?"

Abby kicked off her high heels and resettled her black skirt around her, picking at the folds while she considered.

"John . . ."

"Just dinner."

Damn him, she'd never met anybody who read her mind like that. "Another drive-through?"

"Doctor didn't exactly recommend it."

"Screw the doctor!" she snapped, and covered her mouth with her hand, just like she had in high school. John Lee looked mortally amused.

"Do I have to?"

"I . . . sorry. I have this thing about doctors. My mother kept taking me to doctors when I was a kid, first this and then that, nothing wrong with me but they kept giving me tests. Painful tests." When she dreamed, which was often, she wasn't chased by demons or closet monsters, it was always doctors in white coats, holding syringes.

"The man was right, you've got to eat." He stood and leaned against the back of the couch, looking down at her. "Here or someplace else, whatever you want."

She picked up her shoes and started down the hall, careful of the smooth wood in her stockinged feet. "Wherever we're going, I'm pretty sure I don't need a long black dress," she called over her shoulder. "Ten minutes."

Once she'd shut the door behind her she leaned against it and breathed, deep diaphragmatic breaths like an opera singer. She was being stupid. Rushing headlong toward destruction.

She tossed the high heels in the corner near a drift of other mismatched shoes and yanked open the top drawer of the dresser. Cotton underwear, sports bras, where the hell . . . under the dowdy flowered undies she found what she was looking for, the emergency underwear, teal blue satin high-cut panties and a teal-blue satin bra. She struggled out of the concert dress and the matching dreary underwear and stood, naked and shivering, looking at the gleaming Victoria's Secret arsenal laid out on the bed.

"This is a mistake." Her voice echoed hollowly off the cold wood floor. She reached out to touch the satin with a tentative fingertip. "Right?"

Satin glided cold over her skin, raised goose bumps where it passed. She took a second to stand in front of the mirror, cataloging the faults, and stopped before she lost her courage completely. From the back of her closet came a pair of tight blue jeans and a sweater soft enough to pet. From the litter of makeup on the dresser she found lipstick and applied it, had to do it twice because her hands were shaking.

Then the perfume. Not too much, nothing *desperate*, just a hint. God, was she doing this right? What was missing? Shoes. She found a pair of flat slip-ons and paused by the door again on the way out. More opera breaths.

When she opened the door she found John Lee standing in the hallway, just coming out of the bathroom. She hadn't expected to see him there and wasn't prepared for the way he looked at her, the leap of pleasure in his face.

"Nice," he said, which somehow was the most genuine compliment she had ever received. "You the one with the subscription to *Playgirl*?"

Maria insisted on keeping a magazine rack next to the toilet, stuffed with a haphazard mix of *Ladies' Home Journal* and *Weekly World News*. The *Playgirl* subscription had been a birthday present from Benny. Trust Maria to stuff them in with the other reading material.

"Sorry," she sighed. "I only read it for the centerfolds."

He held the door open for her on the way out, a strange little smile on his lips. As she passed, he leaned over and said, "Me, too."

His grin was as good as a laugh.

"You're not, are you?" she asked after they were safely in the car. He froze in the act of hooking his seat belt. "I mean, it's okay if you are—"

"Are what?"

Her voice didn't want to come right out and say it, so the word came out small and doubtful. "Gay."

He moved far enough to finish fastening the seat belt, to turn the ignition key, then relaxed back in the seat. "No. I'm not."

She was reminded of the falling sensation earlier, the taste of dirt in her mouth. The confidence beast, frustrated by her lack of failure at the concert, chimed in with a litany of all the things she was doing wrong, how unattractive she was, how big a mistake it all was.

John Lee asked, "How bad am I screwing up here?"

"Excuse me?"

"Seems like everything I've said to you since you

opened the door this morning's gone wrong. You want me to go to hell?"

She folded her hands carefully in her lap, swallowed a surge of relief so strong it almost choked her, and said, "Kind of a long drive for dinner. Plus I don't like spicy food."

Adagio:
December 4, 1994

Benny slid her round purple sunglasses down her nose, blinked against the glare of morning, and said, "So?"

"So?" Abby took a bite of eggs with more than her usual amount of glee. "Nice weather we're having."

"Fuck you, you—" Benny froze in midcurse. The clean-cut church crowd sitting at the next table had stiffened like mannequins. She cleared her throat and lowered her voice to a raspy, precoffee whisper. "—bitch, I hate the goddamn morning, so don't screw around. Did you?"

"Did I what?" Abby took a frothy, pulpy sip of orange juice. "Eat your bagel."

"Oh, for Christ's—Ab, you're killing me here." Benny morosely examined her breakfast. "Jesus, what is this thing? A Texas donut?"

"It's a bagel."

"Not on this planet. Was he good? He looked good."

"How was the dating game at the Holiday Inn?"

Benny leaned back in the leatherette booth and considered her gravely over the top of the sunglasses.

Abby peered back intently. Benny had dressed in her morning clothes—tight black T-shirt, black leather jacket, tight black jeans. It was a severe jewelry day. She only wore three necklaces, all silver. One of them had a pentagram.

"I wore the thigh-high red boots," she said.

"And?" Abby prodded.

"And I got lots of drinks. *Lots* of drinks. Where the hell is my coffee?" Benny glared at the waitress, who strode past holding an empty pot. "You know, I am not in a very good mood."

"I noticed." Abby took a bite of egg. "If you'd stop glaring at her she'd probably bring you coffee."

"I hate West Texas. People are so damn sensitive. You aren't going to answer me, are you?"

Abby leaned across the table and gestured. Benny met her halfway.

"Not a chance," she whispered, and held out her half-eaten piece of toast. "Want a bite?"

"Serve you right if I throw up on you, you—"

"Coffee?" the waitress—a no-nonsense lady in sensible shoes and stiff hair—elbowed them apart and splashed Benny's cup without waiting for an answer. She dumped creamer and sugar packages on the table and strode away toward a knot of other waitresses, all babbling excitedly.

"They think I'm a rock star," Benny said wearily. "Perfect."

"Actually, they probably think you're a satan worshiper, but, whatever. We had a very nice evening and ate Chinese food. He brought me back home and was a perfect gentleman. There. Now you know."

Benny picked up her bagel and nibbled half-heartedly at it, took a sip of coffee and grimaced.

"Perfect gentleman. That means—what? He brought his own condom?"

Abby sipped orange juice and smiled. Benny glared and ate her bagel in tiny tasteless strips.

"What about your new guitar player? Duncan?" Abby raised her eyebrows. "Anything exciting to report?"

Benny waggled her hand palm down. "He plays jazz sometimes."

"Oh."

"Well, maybe there are a few fun details but the church crowd's already throwing a rope over a light pole. Listen, kid, I've got to hit the road, got a six-thirty rehearsal." Benny dug in the huge patchwork leather bag she called a purse and found an ancient wallet held together with duct tape. "Are you okay?"

It was said in the casual Benny way, but Benny's eyes were serious. Questioning.

"Yeah, why?"

A frown grooved between Benny's brows and spread ripples to her forehead. She shook out a cigarette, eyed the NO SMOKING sign on the table, and tapped it thoughtfully on the Formica table.

"I don't know," she said. "I don't know. You want me to run your cards?"

"Oh, God, Benny, not your New-Age crystal-gaz-ing—"

"Tarots are a very reliable, ancient method of focusing psychic energy," Benny said primly. "Heathen slut. Anyway, it's just . . . I don't know."

"I do," Abby said. "It's morning, which you hate, and you haven't had enough coffee, and you're dying for a cigarette. And you're jealous as hell that I had a good time last night. Anything else?"

Benny grunted. "You left out the eight-hour drive home." She slid out of the booth and waited for Abby to join her, ready or not. Abby grabbed her purse and fanned bills out next to what Benny had left, looked up, and found her friend strolling through the bright yellow restaurant toward the door. Heads turned in her wake like flowers toward the sun. Benny had already lit up a Marlboro by the time Abby joined her on the sidewalk. They strolled quietly toward the lime-green Gremlin, close enough that their elbows brushed. Benny swung open the driver's-side door and paused in the act of climbing inside to give her one last look.

"Past-life analysis," she said.

Abby blinked. "What?"

"You know, regression? Anyway, I did it and it's just fabulous. I mean really—way cool what you can find out about yourself. I've always been afraid of the ocean, you know? Come to find out I drowned on the *Titanic*."

Abby rolled her eyes. "Spare me, Benny, please."

"You wound me. Hey, I mean it," she said. "You be careful."

"You, too." Abby leaned over to embrace her. Benny's warmth and startling floral perfume clung to her for a few seconds after they'd pulled apart. Benny slammed the door and cranked the engine to a roar.

The whole car shuddered like a wet dog. "Especially you."

Abby watched until the Gremlin was out of sight, then stuck her hands in her coat pockets and walked the two blocks back home, to Carlton. The wind was cold and spiced with fireplace smoke, a good winter smell, clean and fresh. She was feeling the usual post-concert euphoria, she decided. Any day she didn't have to face a demanding crowd was a good one.

She felt positively great by the time she turned the key in her door. Her next-door neighbor, a squat, round-shouldered guy with freckles, waved good morning as he went out for his morning run. She waved back and thought about taking Carlton out for a good walk, stretching both their legs. Of course, walking with Carlton was a chancy proposition—one minute he'd be dragging her along at a gallop, the next stopping to rain on somebody's bicycle tire.

She opened the door of the apartment and stepped in, prepared for the doggy assault. Nothing. She listened to the chilly silence and shivered; it was colder than usual, though she'd left the heat on. Could the damn heater be broken again?

"Carlton?" she called. She shut the door behind her and turned a slow circle, looking the room over. "Carlton?"

Nothing looked disturbed; it was the same cluttered mess she'd left. She took a tentative step forward and felt a cold breeze touch the left side of her face. She turned her head slowly in that direction, toward the dim reflected light of the hallway.

"Oh, no. No."

She dropped her purse on the floor next to the couch and pelted down the hallway. The bedroom door was wide open.

She stood in the doorway and stared at the broken window next to her bed, the thin curtains blowing in the breeze and making a quiet, whispery sound. The wind had blown over a picture of her father on the table next to her bed. It lay on the floor, facedown.

After a second or two, she realized what was wrong with the broken window. There wasn't any glass inside the room.

It was broken *out*.

Carlton was gone.

"Hello?"

John Lee sounded almost exactly the same on the phone as he had in person. Abby closed her eyes tight and said, "Hi, it's Abby."

"Abby." His voice relaxed and went deep, like a cat's purr. "Nice to hear your voice. You're not thinking about canceling on the movies, are you?"

"I—" She'd just taken a breath but he had a way of making her need more air. "I just—you haven't seen Carlton, have you? Around your place?"

"No." The warmth drained out of his voice, replaced with concern. "He gone again?"

"He broke a window in my apartment. I don't know where he's gone, I looked at the pound and I've been out walking for hours but—"

"He hasn't been here," John Lee said. "If I see him, I'll bring him back, you know that. But he wasn't here before, he was at my mom's place. I'll swing by there on my way over."

"Over?" she repeated blankly.

"Figure you'll want some help."

She wrapped a finger in the stretched-out phone cord and curled closer to the warmth of his voice, the memory of his smile. The apartment seemed so lonely without Maria, without Carlton. Even though her neighbor—Craig, she found out, a civil engineer—had taped the window shut, she didn't feel safe. Or warm.

"Please," she admitted, and forced a smile into the shaky structure of her voice. "I'll buy the burgers."

"Tell you what, we find Carlton and I'll fix you the burgers. That a deal?"

"Deal." She pressed a shaking hand against her forehead. "I'm so sorry to bother you, John."

"No bother. I'll be there in half an hour," he said. "Dress warm."

She sat for a while with the phone held close to her chest, thinking, and finally got up to put on her coat for the third time that day.

Carlton was hurt, maybe dying. The jagged glass caught in the window frame still had blood on it. What the *hell* had made him run away like that?

Somehow it had to be her fault. Somehow.

She waited on the couch, fingers tightly laced, for the sound of John Lee's car door slamming. When it came thirty minutes later it brought a surge of hope that surprised and frightened her—he was just a *guy*, for heaven's sake. She unlocked the door in time to interrupt his knock.

A gust of cold wind fluttered his brown hair into untidy curls. He had a serious expression but the light was still in his eyes, warm and welcoming.

"Figure we'll start out toward Fall Creek. Maybe we'll run into him, if he's going that direction," he said. "Weather channel says there'll be snow tonight. We need to find him fast."

She nodded and stepped back to grab her purse and coat.

"Where's your friend with the hair?"

"Gone back to Dallas," Abby said, and frowned as she sifted through her purse for keys. She came up with them and flipped through choices to find the door key. "I came back from breakfast and Carlton was gone. I've been out looking ever since but my car's in the shop and I could only go so far on foot."

She locked the door and followed him out to the car—he'd left it running, and the sound was a slow smooth purr on the window. She climbed into the warmth and had herself buckled in before he got his own door open.

"Hot chocolate," he said as he settled himself, and gestured to two cups in the holders between them. "Figured you probably hadn't stopped to warm up much."

"You're right there." She took one of the cups and peeled the top back. The liquid was hot and smooth, dark, spicy-sweet. Some of the tension left her. "I can't understand why he would do this. He's never run away before, not even as a puppy. It just doesn't make any sense."

"Nope," John Lee agreed, and sipped his own

chocolate while he backed out into the drive. "I want to do a little experiment. You ready?"

She eyed him doubtfully.

"Put the cup down."

She secured it in the holder and waited. He signaled a left turn and waited until they were on Grand Avenue before looking at her.

"How do you feel when I say Fall Creek?"

A subliminal rush of heat under her skin. Fear.

"What do you mean?"

"How do you feel?"

"I don't feel anything." She shifted her weight away from him and looked out the window. Afternoon was fading toward evening, the sun already misted with clouds. "Why? Should I?"

"You got some mighty strange reactions for a lady who's never been there before. How about if I say my mother's name?"

She shrugged, still watching the darkened windows glide by outside. The town had a sepia look.

"Pearl Jordan."

She gritted her teeth hard enough to feel her jaw muscles crack. Gray swam over her but she fought it back, fought hard, and blinked away tears.

"I don't feel anything," she said. He threw her a look of sheer disbelief. "I *can't* feel anything, can I? Because I've never *met the woman*! I've never been to Fall Creek in my life! How the hell can I feel anything—"

Her voice sounded ragged and hysterical. She swallowed the rest and concentrated on slow, quiet breathing. *Look for Carlton. Just look.*

"I don't know," he said slowly. "But you do, Abby. You know you do."

She shoved the subject away with a wave of her hand and picked up her hot chocolate, drew comfort from the warmth and sweetness.

John Lee turned right on State Highway 115 West, and they left the weak sepia-toned lights of Midland in the distance. Behind that, the sister city of Odessa glimmered like the richer, prouder stepsister. They headed into growing darkness, into a flat vast horizon of tawny sand and black twisted Joshua trees and the round spiky skeletons of tumbleweeds drifting over the road.

No Carlton.

Half an hour later it was dark enough that John Lee turned on his headlights; the white stripe in the road caught fire and made the road dead black, like a burned-out cinder. The car shuddered as headwinds pushed hard. Behind them, Midland had disappeared into the sand, only a glimmer on the clouds marking it, and ahead there was nothing. It was like driving into space.

"Maybe he's already made it to town," John Lee said quietly, bringing Abby out of her miserable roadside watch. "Might be laid up someplace warm in a house, some nice folks feeding him steak."

"Do you really think so?"

He shook his head and looked over at her. "You okay? You feeling okay?"

They passed a shield-shaped road sign that said TEXAS 115 WEST, words almost obscured by scouring dirt and rusted pitting from an ancient shotgun blast.

The reflective paint was old enough to have a soft yellowish tint to it.

"Where are we?"

"About ten minutes from town. My house is over that way." He pointed off to the left into the dark. "Hard to find, but I like it that way. Keeps down the Jehovah's Witnesses and vacuum salesmen."

"And over there?" She pointed to the right. An old house bulked black in the distance, more shadow than substance. John Lee glanced over and quickly away, face gone blank and closed.

"Just an old house. Lot of those old wrecks out here. Couple of years and the desert pretty much takes them back."

He wasn't lying, but she was sure he wasn't telling the truth, either. She twisted to look over her shoulder at the dim outline of the house.

"Farm?" she guessed.

"They're all farms out here. Cotton farms, mostly. Or ranches."

"How long has that house been—"

"Look for your dog." His voice had a hard edge to it that surprised her. She turned to face forward and caught sight of another house, set farther back from the road. Windows glowed dull yellow against the night.

The gray hit her again, a riptide of emotion, things clutching at her shaking and screaming. She pressed one hand flat on the car window to block out the sight of the house but it seemed to be burned into her eyes, like an image of the sun.

She'd seen it in the daylight. Dusty broken pansies

struggling out of harsh heat-dried ground. Wood gone gray from the relentless sun. The rusted screen door, squeaking on its hinges. The shock of darkness after the blaze of sun, a hot, close, diseased darkness—

Pearl. A man's voice, whispering and distorted. *You know what to do.*

"Stop!" she screamed. John Lee slammed on the brakes and the car fishtailed to a stop. She couldn't get her breath against the weight on her chest. "Carlton. Carlton!"

A rush of cold air on her face as John Lee opened his door and got out. She watched him walk in front of the halogen glare of headlights and he seemed taller, thinner.

He turned to look at her and his face changed. His eyes became hell-blue.

He mouthed her name, but she heard him say, through a mist of years, *Missy.*

She fumbled for the door and got it open. The cold breeze steadied her a little. John Lee's eyes went dark again as he moved out of the headlights to stand in the shadows by the roadside.

Carlton lay on his side on the sharp tarry rocks of the shoulder, chest heaving. He lifted his head as Abby came closer, licked his chops and whined unhappily. She dropped down next to him and cradled him in her lap. His fur was matted with blood where the glass had cut him. He'd run the bandages off his feet.

"Oh, God," she whispered. She buried her face in

the warm thick comfort of the coat. "Oh, sweetie, why? Why'd you do this?"

Carlton licked her hand and whined. When she tried to pick him up he got shakily to his feet and limped off, toward the glow of windows in the distance.

"Jesus God," John Lee said, and shook his head. He picked Carlton up and lifted him like a baby. "Open up the back door."

Abby ran ahead to hold it open as John Lee eased the dog inside.

"No, wait, the blood—" Abby struggled out of her coat. "Here, put him on this."

Carlton buried his nose in the arm of her coat and watched her with great, dark eyes as she shut the door. She leaned against the cold metal and looked at John Lee, at the blood on his hands. For a flash of a second John Lee's eyes were blue again.

"He was going back to my mom's place," he said, and jerked his chin toward the glowing windows. "Again."

Carlton howled, a long, lonely, frightening sound.

The vet wanted to keep Carlton overnight for observation, though none of his cuts seemed serious. Abby was secretly grateful. She didn't think she could stand staying awake all night with him, and she wasn't sure if she could trust the dog to stay put, even sedated as he was. If he squirmed out of the window again while she slept—

"Dinner or home?"

She looked over at John Lee and smiled slightly,

which was more than she'd felt capable of ten minutes earlier. Something about that road, the dog, the house—no, the *two* houses. He was right, there was something strange going on. Something she could no more explain than Carlton could.

"Dinner," she said. "Oh, God, yes. Dinner."

"Fair enough. I said I'd make the burgers if we found him." John Lee put the car in gear and pulled out of the animal hospital parking lot, heading for darkness again, only the brilliant white line for a guide. "You like beer?"

"A little," she said, cautiously. A *very* little.

"I got a buddy that brews his own. Very good. You'll like it. Hamburgers okay with you?"

"Fine." She traced a treble clef sign on her jeans with a fingertip. "You were right about . . . the feelings I get."

He nodded. "I know."

"When you say Fall Creek, I feel—I don't know—uneasy. Afraid." She drew in the sharps for the key of A next to the treble clef. "When you say your mother's name I feel something else."

"What?"

She shrugged. "Fear. Anger. I hear voices. God, do you think I need to see somebody?" She added in two or three bars of notes, painstakingly drawn.

"Thought you were seeing me, at least tonight." He smiled. "Look, I admit, maybe you should talk it over with somebody who knows about stuff like this. Tomorrow."

"Tomorrow." She let her head drop back against the seat. "God, I feel so drained."

He reached over and rested his hand on top of hers, a warm, unexpected contact that made her shiver.

Ten minutes later, they turned down a dark, barely visible road. She opened her eyes to see a stretch of jet-black with red reflective markers on either side. The road stretched off into the distance like an airplane runway. John Lee took it fast, maneuvering around the small curves with expert care. They pulled up in front of what looked like a small weatherbeaten barn. She tried to make out the sign hanging above the door but the angle was wrong, and then John Lee was out of the car and ushering her into the cold, biting air.

"Snow," he said, looking up. She raised her face and felt the feathery brush of flakes. "Better get inside."

As she went up the steps she looked up again at the sign. It said JORDAN GLASSWORKS. She pointed up toward it, a question on her lips, but John Lee was holding the door open and the wind was bitterly cold.

"Whew!" He shook the chill out of his coat and brushed flakes from his hair as he shut the door behind her. "Hold on a second, let me turn off the alarm."

"Alarm?" She unzipped her coat and followed him out of the entry hall into a pitch-dark room where her footsteps echoed up toward a distant roof. "Out here?"

"Hold it. Don't move." There was unmistakable

tension in his voice. She stopped where she was, swaying. "Wait until I get the lights."

She heard several soft beeps and a longer, lower tone, and then the lights came up, flickering in banks toward the back of the room.

She was standing in the middle of fairyland.

The sign outside lied. John Lee didn't make glass, he made beauty. What stood on the workroom floor were moments of time, frozen—a bird, launching into flight with its feathers gleaming iridescent behind it. A dragon breathing gold-green fire, the eyes winking red. An unfinished stained-glass window of a young woman reaching toward the sun, the colors as vivid and beautiful as grass and sky. She let her breath out slowly, afraid to breathe. Everywhere she looked, there was more. Tiny, casual pieces of beauty sitting on worktables. Glasses and bowls as thin as soap bubbles.

John Lee touched her arm. She reached out and grabbed his hand and held it tight.

"This . . ." Her voice failed. She took a deep breath and tried again; the air tasted of the sawdust that covered the floor. "It's amazing. It's yours? You did all this?"

"Well, yeah. All this is in production. Got to deliver that window next week, don't know when I'm going to finish it." He frowned at the girl reaching for the sun. "Don't have it right yet."

"Right!" She laughed aloud. "My God, John, it's beautiful!"

"Go ahead and look around if you want. I'll make

us something to eat." He hesitated, watching her face; she focused on him with difficulty. "You okay?"

She nodded. He squeezed her fingers and let her go. She watched him as he ambled around pieces of glass and through a door in the far wall.

She sat down in the middle of all that beauty and stared.

He came back carrying two frosted mugs filled with clear amber; as she took hers she realized that the mug wasn't the smooth, store-bought, machine-made kind. These had been hand-blown, thick enough to knock out a drunk in a bar fight.

She took a cautious sip of the beer. It tasted deceptively light, but when it hit the back of her throat it turned hot and thick as fermented honey. She coughed and swallowed two or three times before she was sure she'd gotten it down.

"Good, huh?" He clinked mugs with her and draped himself over a handy battered recliner that squatted nearby. She'd chosen a padded camp stool that had seen more camps than the Boy Scouts. "Burgers coming up."

"Is this what you do full-time?"

"Make burgers?" He gave her his quirky smile.

"Make . . . all this beauty." She felt a little foolish saying it, but the embarrassment faded when she saw the pleasure lighting his face. "It is beautiful, you know."

He glanced around at it, taking stock. "It's just a hobby. I put in a hell of a lot of windshields and storm windows."

"Hobby?" She stood up to run her fingers gently

over the cool curve of a glass lily. "No, no way. This has passion."

His eyes were fixed where her fingers rested, and she realized with a warm rush of embarrassment that he was probably worried she'd break it. She stepped away, ducking her head apologetically, and he immediately reached over and picked up the lily. He set it in her hand and folded her fingers around it. The glass felt heavy and strong and strangely alive.

"I can't . . ." she began, and looked away from the glitter of its beauty to stare at his face. His fingers lingered on hers, just for a second, and he let go and sat back without breaking the stare. She cradled the lily in both hands, the curves of it fitting naturally to her skin. "God, John, are you sure?"

"Reminds me of you," he said. She looked down at the strong, feminine curves of it and felt a bright, daring thrill of pride. "I've been carving glass since I was seventeen, learned glassblowing out in San Francisco a few years ago."

"And the stained glass?" She nodded at the window. He cocked his head and looked at it ruefully.

"Just learning, and not too damned good at it yet."

She put the lily carefully aside and looked at the window, the angelic perfection of the girl, the glowing warmth of the stained-glass sun. She backed up until she was next to his chair and tried to see it with him. Tried to see the flaws.

"But it's perfect," she breathed, and sat down on the arm of his chair, still staring. "Absolutely perfect. I've never seen anything like it."

His fingers closed over her arm. She turned to look at him.

"Not much market for it out here," he said. "Most of it's done to special order or I ship it out of town to Dallas and Houston. People around here think it's pretty strange stuff for a grown man to do."

"You mean art?"

"Whatever you do, don't call it art in a small town. It's a craft, like painting sunsets on rusty saw blades. Craft's a manly word. Art's something ballet dancers do, and they better not do it around here." He smiled, but she saw something dark flickering underneath it.

"You could move," she suggested.

He rubbed his hands together and stared down at them as if they were strangers. "Could. Don't think I will, though."

"Why not?"

"Must be about time for those burgers," he said, and drew her to her feet. They were so close together that it made her breath catch. Still smiling, watching her eyes, he eased her coat—his coat, really, he'd insisted she wear it—off her shoulders and draped it over the back of the recliner.

Liquid warmth flooded down through her. God, he had beautiful eyes, amber-gold, ringed in dark brown.

"Stay awhile," he said. "Please."

She watched him walk away toward the kitchen and sank down in the chair he'd abandoned, feeling the warmth he'd left behind like another touch. There was too much beauty in the room; it overwhelmed her. She closed her eyes on dizziness and searched for some sense of balance. Instead, she saw an image.

A two-story farmhouse, weak-stemmed purple pansies nodding by cracked concrete steps. All the windows were open against the fierce summer heat. Torn sheer curtains waved in and out, as if the house breathed.

Up the steps.

Rusted screen door, squealing as she pulled it open. Inside, darkness, furniture dim and dusty.

Hands holding her wrists behind her. She blinked sweat out of her eyes.

No sound, but she knew she was crying. Hands shoved her forward, through the tangled maze of furniture, past open doorways, into a filthy kitchen with a peeling yellowed floor.

At the end of the kitchen, a door. It opened and yawned into blackness.

She fell, screaming.

"Abby?" Another hand on her, shaking her. She came awake with a violent shudder and found John Lee bending over her. "You all right?"

"I . . . yes. Yes." She tried to slow the pounding of her heart. "Dinner?"

"Thought we'd eat like civilized people at the table. Bring your beer."

She fumbled for the mug and found it blessedly solid; *this* was reality, not a dream. She'd never had a dream like that before, never. All her dreams had to do with doctors and hospitals and performing naked in front of ten thousand people.

She shoved the vision away and followed him

through the glass room and another door, into a room that smelled like apples and vanilla.

He had a small table, barely big enough for four chairs to fit around it, and he'd taken two of them away to leave them elbow room. The table itself was black wood, smooth as glass, with matching chairs. On the other side of the raised serving bar was a white kitchen, not antiseptic but clean. John Lee set her plate on the table and turned toward the stove.

"This is nice," she said awkwardly. He handed her another plate, this one loaded with lettuce, tomatoes, onions, pickles. She put it in the center of the table. "You live here, too?"

"Saves money." He shrugged and pulled out her chair for her. She sat and waited until he'd taken his seat before she started garnishing her steaming hamburger.

Not that it needed much. It was a big, thick, delicious-looking thing, nestled in a toasted onion roll. Conversation lagged while they ate, sipped beer, listened as the wind rattled around outside. There was a window on the other side of the kitchen and it showed falling, swirling snow. Somewhere in the kitchen a radio played softly, golden rock 'n' roll oldies. She heard a Beatles song and glanced up, smiling, saw him looking back, sharing the joke.

Good old Mom. *Abby Rhodes.*

"Not as bad as it could be," he said, as if he'd read her mind. He sat back, sipping beer. His plate was clean except for two lonely-looking potato chips and a dusting of crumbs. "I got three friends named Misty, Sunny, and Wendy Rainey."

"No way." She laughed. He grinned.

"Yep. One, maybe it's just a spur-of-the-moment thing. Three times, you got to figure their parents knew what they were doing."

She chuckled and nodded. He continued to look at her, just look, with a light in his eyes that made her blush and look away.

"It's coming down pretty hard," Abby said. John Lee glanced toward the window and nodded. "I guess we should start back pretty soon. Before the roads get too bad."

He broke a potato chip in half, dusted his fingers, and said, "Yeah, I guess you're right."

Another long silence, this one uncomfortable. She got up and carried her plate into the kitchen, concentrated on rinsing it off.

He came in behind her, stepped up, and took the plate away. As she turned, he put the plate in the sink, shut off the water, and put both hands on her shoulders. He bent his forehead to touch hers.

"I don't know how to do this, so I'm probably going to screw it up. Abby, you said you never saw anything as beautiful as what I do out there; but you're wrong, I saw it myself when you were on that stage, playing. Something so beautiful it made me shake. And I don't want you to go away not knowing that."

She didn't move, couldn't move. His fingers squeezed, gently, and slid down her arms. Off her arms, to fold around her waist.

"Tell me now," he whispered. "God, Abby, if you don't feel it, tell me now."

Her hands drifted up to touch the beard-rough skin of his cheek, to bury themselves in the warm curls of his hair. She leaned into him and loved the way his body burned hers through their clothes, the way his lips trembled when she kissed them. A long, warm, sliding kiss.

"Stay," he whispered, mouth pressed against her ear. His tongue touched her earlobe and drew a moan out of her. "Please, Abby, stay with me."

She kissed the line of his jaw, down his neck, feeling muscles tense and blood beat just under the skin. His breath escaped into her ear.

"Absolutely."

She leaned into his kiss again, into the warm circle of his arms. He touched her neck and traced a hot line down her collarbone, farther down, until his fingers caught in the fabric of her shirt. She reached up and undid the button stopping him.

His fingers continued to explore, tracing the satin top of her bra, unfastening the other buttons. By the time he'd opened them all she'd loosened his shirt, bared his chest, traced the smooth lines of muscle there. She put her own skin against him and he held her there.

"You have another room to this place?" she asked, brushing the hair back from his face.

He made a purring sound deep in his throat. "Got a living room with a couch."

"Interesting."

"Nice big bathroom."

"Hmm." She tried to distract him from the home tour by nibbling on his neck.

"Closets." He refused to be distracted, and anyway what he was doing to her wasn't keeping her mind on conversation, either. "Got three or four closets."

"Anything else?" she asked. He started walking backward, drawing her with him toward an open doorway at the far end of the kitchen.

"Well, I've got this bedroom in the back . . ."

"Mmm?"

They passed under the doorway, bumped into the end of a sofa. Living room.

"But I don't think I'm going to make it there," he said.

Mezzopiano:
December 5, 1994

The burglar alarm went off.

Abby flailed wildly and froze as John Lee caught her wrists and held them tight. He was looking away from her toward the bedroom doorway, the darkness in it.

"Stay here," he whispered, and slid out of bed. On the way to the door he found a pair of fleece pants on the floor and pulled them on, gathered a shotgun from the closet.

"John—" she hissed.

He shook his head. "Stay here. I'll be back."

The dark swallowed him. She threw the covers back and tried to remember where she'd left her clothes. On the floor by the couch—in the hallway—damn. She opened John Lee's closet and threw on the first thing she could grab from a hanger, a long-sleeved shirt barely long enough to hang to her thighs. She found something else in the closet, too, a baseball bat. Not as good as John's shotgun, but it would do. She shouldered it and crept cautiously toward the doorway.

The deafening scream of the alarm cut off, leaving

echoes like angry ghosts. Lights clicked on somewhere near or in the workroom, washing reflections
from the wood onto her bare feet. She paused in the
living room to wrestle on her discarded blue jeans,
lost her balance and took an unplanned seat on the
rumpled sofa.

"Terry." John Lee's voice echoed from the workroom. It was a completely different voice than she'd
become used to in the past hours—flat, cold, unwel-
coming. "Guess you got a reason to be in here."

"You might call the cops," said Terry. He had a
deep, drawling voice and an ugly edge to it. He had
an ugly laugh, too. "Sheriff Hayes'd be real damn
sympathetic, specially when I tell him how I saw
prowlers creeping around in your workroom. Didn't
wake you up, did I?"

"Get to the point, Terry."

Something shattered in the workroom. Abby felt
sick at the thought of all that breakable beauty, gritted her teeth, and edged toward the door. Through
the kitchen she saw part of John Lee's naked back,
muscles tensed, shotgun pointed at the floor. Facing
him stood a big linebacker type, muscular, wearing
a khaki police uniform. In spite of the hour, he
looked well-pressed. His grin looked as sharp as the
crease on his trousers.

"Oops," he said. At his feet lay shards of glass.
"Damn shame, you having all this breakable stuff in
here. Prowlers surely could cause you a problem."

Terry stirred the remains of the glass with the toe
of a polished shoe.

"I'm just deliverin' a message," he continued.

"From Sheriff Hayes. He says the old man walked out of the gates of Huntsville two days ago, eight A.M. sharp. Warden there says the old bastard's got a notion to come home to Fall Creek. Guess you wouldn't be too damn happy about that."

As Abby watched, John Lee raised the shotgun. The muscles in his back were so tense they jumped.

"Go on, do it," Terry invited softly. "Show me you got the guts."

"Get the hell out of my house. *Now,* Terry."

"Got a guest, John Lee? Some little artsy-fartsy faggot in your bedroom?" Terry sneered, and kicked at the worktable nearest him. Glass shivered. A blown-glass goblet fell and smashed. "Bring him on out. I want to pay him my respects."

Abby put the baseball bat down and stepped through the doorway, walked slowly to John Lee's side, and stood there while Terry stared at her.

"Want to introduce me to your friend, John?" she asked. He didn't take his eyes off Terry. The shotgun stayed on target.

"Not a friend," he said. "And he's just leaving, weren't you, Terry?"

She'd expected to see Terry get angry at being wrong, but he looked her up and down, up and down again. A complete, insulting inventory. At the end of it he gave her a sour smile and nodded.

"Ma'am," he said dryly. "You ought to be more careful who you pick up at closing time."

"Weren't you leaving?" she snapped. He tipped an imaginary hat to her and sauntered toward the door.

John Lee followed. Terry gave her one more toothy grin before swinging the front door shut as he left.

"You should've stayed in the bedroom," John Lee said, and grabbed a piece of wood. He braced it under the front doorknob where the lock was broken and jammed it tight. His face looked ashen, his eyes too bright. "Could've gotten ugly."

"It did," she said, and put her hand on his arm as he turned. "God, John, who the hell is that guy?"

"Nobody," he said. "Thanks."

"For what?"

He met her eyes. "For trying. Don't really matter. Terry'll make up whatever he damn well pleases. Wouldn't matter if I had the Rockettes in my bedroom, he's been saying I was gay since I was twelve years old."

"You grew up with that guy on your back?" Abby shivered. "Is everybody in Fall Creek like him?"

"Nope, but he's my personal cross to bear. Sheriff Hayes ain't a bad guy but he's basically lazy. He'll let Terry slide because it's just easier that way. Besides, Terry saved his life a few years back, so Hayes'll never turn on him now."

He opened a closet near the entry hall and took out a broom. She watched as he methodically swept up the remains of the broken glass.

"So you just let it go? Let him break in here and destroy things?"

He found a piece of cardboard and used it to scoop up the glass.

She tried again. "Who's the old man?"

A slight hitch as he was bending, like she'd

stabbed him in the back. He finished and tossed the shards in the trash.

"My father."

"And he's been in prison?" she asked. He put the broom away and turned to face her.

"Yep." He let out a sigh and reached for her, folded her in his arms. "He killed four people they know of. Buried 'em out in his own fields."

The house, the one looming black in the darkness next to the welcoming glow of Pearl Jordan's window. She didn't know why she knew, but she did. And she knew his name, as surely as she felt John Lee's warm skin against hers.

"Custer Grady," she whispered.

Shock rippled through his body.

She looked up into a face she didn't know but remembered, a tough, seamed, leathery face with ice-blue eyes. As she opened her mouth to scream, it faded into John Lee's sharp-boned face, his dark eyes, his frown. He watched anxiously. "Abby . . ."

She shook her head and buried her face against the satin warmth of his chest, listening to the whisper of his heartbeat, the river-rush of his breathing. After a while he relaxed and held her tight.

"Never mind," he said, and rested his chin on top of her head. "It's okay."

"What time is it?"

"Damn early. You want to go back to bed?"

"Do you want me in your bed?" She raised her head to look at him again and saw the dark preoccupation in his eyes melt away. He gave her a wry, one-sided smile.

"I ain't done with you yet, lady."

"Is that a yes?"

"I was thinking about that sofa in there. Closer than the bed." He trailed a finger down the side of her face, ringing the collar of the shirt she wore. "I like that shirt."

"It's yours."

"I'd like it more off," he said, and started unbuttoning. His lips found skin underneath. She slid her hands down to his waist and undid the string tie on his fleece pants. "Better be careful, you might get something started."

"With any luck," she murmured. Her fingers teased the pants down. "Hmm, looks like I already did."

"Yeah," he whispered, voice gone husky and deep.

She woke at eight A.M., alone in the warm wrought-iron bed, wrapped in thick quilts. Her skin smelled of John Lee. She buried her face in the pillow and drank it in, flashes of memory and sensation that trailed fire like comets. It had been a long time. A *long* time. The aftershocks of pleasure left her with a shivery, wickedly liquid sensation inside.

The shower started in the bathroom. She yawned and stretched and slipped out of bed to look in the open door. John Lee had clear glass walls on the spacious shower stall, and she stood watching him for a while, hungry for the sight of him, the way his back flexed as he bent his head under the hot water, the way that water trailed down his legs. She could still taste him, musky at the back of her throat.

She stepped forward and knocked lightly on the glass. He turned and tossed water out of his eyes. His hair, wet, hung long on his neck.

"Want me to go away?" she asked. He opened the shower door and stood there, dripping.

"I was just thinking about you," he said, and reached for her hand. "And you going away wasn't in it."

She stepped into the spray of hot water. He backed her against the tile wall, braced himself on out-stretched arms, and kissed her, hard.

"Good morning," she sighed when he came up for air. "Oh, God, what a good morning."

"It's starting to be one of my favorites," he said. "Want me to wash your hair?"

"Mmm." She twined her arms around his neck. "Later. What time do you have to open your shop?"

"Oh—now."

"Now!"

"Whenever I get ready to open, I'll open." The smile faded out of his face. "Guess I got to take you home, too."

The seriousness in his eyes touched her almost as much as the smile had. She reached up to trace the solemn set of his lips.

"Yes, I guess so. Kids to teach today."

The water beat down on them, hot as sunshine, but suddenly she felt a chill of separation. He felt it, too; she saw it in the crooked smile, the gentle light in his eyes.

"Can I call you later?"

She traced the smile, kissed it. He tasted of warm water and clean male skin, beautiful, so beautiful.

"You better," she murmured, lips still on his. "I'm getting pretty fond of you."

"Turn around," he said. She raised her eyebrows. "Please."

She turned and braced herself against the wet tile. He put both hands on her shoulders and rubbed. Her muscles twinged, and she sighed and pressed back against him.

"Feels good," she said. "You aren't going to do anything outrageous to me, are you?"

"Thinking about it."

She pressed her hips back and made contact. He returned the favor.

"Keep thinking," she said.

Back in Midland, later, she found the teacher's lounge abuzz with the news that Mr. Henderson, the new shop teacher, had been spotted buying beer at the local Quick-E-Mart outside of town.

"Six-packs of Heineken," said Mrs. Graham as she inspected the selection of junk food in the vending machine. She chose a candy bar and took a seat between Abby and Mr. Harris, the band director. Her candy-bar-a-day habit was clearly having an effect; her face had taken on a shiny, overstressed look like the skin of a microwaved sausage.

"Well, he's toast," Mr. Harris said. He was busy counting squares on a marching band layout grid. "They would have let him get by with American beer. Imported, forget about it."

"Oh, come on, they wouldn't really fire him for that, would they?" Abby asked. Mrs. Graham regarded her with narrowed eyes behind her thick glasses and broke her Mr. Goodbar into precise bite-sized pieces. Mr. Harris sighed and drew X's through six squares. "You're kidding, right?'

"I'd watch out about inviting your friend with the hair back to town, too, if I were you," he said, and looked up to give her a second's glance from sky-blue eyes. He had a deceptively innocent quality that she wasn't quite sure she bought anymore. "People will talk."

"About her hair? It's not *my* hair."

"Guilt by association. Listen, if you're going to buy beer anywhere in a hundred miles, wear a wig and dark glasses. If you're going to buy hard stuff, get somebody to bring it in from out of town for you. Hell, half the people in town probably think your friend brought you drugs."

"Charlie, do you know anything about Fall Creek?" she asked. There was a long second's pause while he mapped the conversational curve.

"Little town to the west, isn't it?"

"I think so. On 115."

"Alpine Highway? No, don't know anything. Cora?" He cocked an eyebrow at Mrs. Graham. She looked thoughtful and ate a square of chocolate.

"Well, I've driven through it but I don't know much about it. They have their own school out there." Her expression turned prim and sour. "You might ask Mrs. O'Rourke if you just have to know.

Lord knows, that old biddy knows everything and everybody from New Mexico up to Big Bend."

As the bell rang for the second lunch period, the lounge door opened and Mrs. O'Rourke breezed in— a well-kept woman over fifty, devoted to the beauty shop and the latest in local Dress Barn fashions. Today she was wearing a navy skirt and magenta blazer with an anchor on the pocket. At the sight of her, Mrs. Graham covered up her chocolate bar with a stack of papers.

"Doralee!" she said with overdone joy. "Why, we were just talking about you. How *was* your Cancún vacation?"

"Dreadful, honey, just dreadful. Poor Floyd was indisposed the whole time. I told him, foreign countries are just no good. Why, Cora, dear, you haven't been sick, too, have you?"

Mrs. Graham's smile switched off. "No. Why?"

"Well, I— Oh, no reason, honey, never mind. Abby, you are just the talk of the town, aren't you? Having your little friend in for the concert and getting flowers from that mystery man, how exciting." Mrs. O'Rourke had eyes that looked too green to be real, and probably weren't. They scanned with the cool precision of a computer.

Abby kept smiling through a cold stab of fear. "Benina's very well regarded in music circles. She's a concert pianist."

As she'd feared, Mrs. O'Rourke got right to the point. "I'm sure she's wonderful, dear, but do tell us all about your new *man*."

"Actually there isn't much to tell. He's just a friend."

"An out-of-town friend," Mrs. Graham contributed. "I didn't recognize him, and I'm *sure* I would have if he'd been from Midland."

"There are a lot of people in Midland," Harris observed mildly.

"Well, I certainly know all the *good* people."

"He's from Fall Creek," Abby said quickly, hoping to end the discussion. No such luck. Mrs. O'Rourke's eyes took on a predatory gleam of interest.

"My, my, Fall Creek. If *that* doesn't bring back memories. Fall Creek had quite a reputation, back in the fifties." Mrs. O'Rourke stirred her tea and stared contemplatively at Abby. "Scandalous."

"Scandalous?" Mrs. Graham chirped, happy to be on the receiving end of gossip she wasn't part of. "Well, do tell."

"Some farmer out there committed murders, or so I remember—buried the bodies out on his farm. I think they sent him to prison for it."

"Do you remember his name?" Abby asked. Mrs. O'Rourke sipped tea and frowned.

"Grady, I think. He was carrying on with some farm woman out there, I can't remember her name. All but killed her, too. An ugly business, all the way around." She shuddered delicately. "What some women will do in the name of love."

She speared Abby with a cold, knowing glance. Abby looked down at her spinach salad.

In the silence, Mr. Harris said casually, "Considering how well you did with the Mozart, I told Sheryl

Patterson over in Odessa that you'd probably be willing to do a concert there, too. Different program, if
you want. She said to call her."

Her stomach was not prepared for the thought of
another performance, not so soon; she gave him what
felt like a pale smile and nodded. An all-new audience. Joy.

As he got up from the table to dispose of his lunch
trash, he added, "Nice roses you got. I saw them in
your dressing room."

She looked up to find Mrs. O'Rourke and Mrs.
Graham both spearing her with laser eyes. With one
stroke, he'd implied a secret lover and his own visit
to her dressing room. Good God.

She mumbled a hasty apology and left so quickly
she was out the door ahead of him. She turned to
face him as he walked by, grinning.

"You did that on purpose," she accused, keeping
her voice to a whisper. Their footsteps echoed flatly
over the wide linoleum hall; early afternoon spilled
warm liquid gold over her scuffed black shoes.

"Guy's gotta have a little fun every now and then.
Heckyl and Jeckyl in there need something new to
talk about, might as well be you." He gave her a
toothy grin. "Better you than me, anyway."

"Oh, thanks a *lot*, Harris, you're tons of help. How
do I get them off my back?"

"You don't," he said, and stuck his hands in his
coat pockets. They walked down the empty locker-
lined hallway toward the music hall. From the classrooms on either side came the muted buzz of voices
and laughter. The hallway had a lifeless feeling to it,

as if the kids took all the excitement with them when they entered the classrooms. "Better not be doing anything naughty, Abby, or you'll find it nailed on the announcement board in there."

She blushed hotly, feeling the imprint of John Lee's body on hers like a sunburn. Harris shot her a sideways look.

"I have a one-thirty with Carla Jane," she said, and lengthened her strides to leave him behind.

Carla Jane was waiting in the practice room, fidgeting her lace-tied lemon-yellow tennis shoes in impatient circles on the floor. She hadn't even gotten her clarinet out. Before Abby could even sit down, Carla had excuses ready.

"Miz Rhodes, I have a sore throat." She tried hard to make her voice raspy, even gave a pitiful cough at the end. Abby opened her own instrument case and let her hands go to work assembling the clarinet.

"Do you? Did you see the nurse?"

"No." Carla's woeful face perked up. "Should I? Now?"

"If you don't feel better in a little while, we'll see. Let's go through some of the Rubank exercises first."

Carla sighed and kicked the floor and, finally, opened her case. She had a beautiful instrument— her parents had paid a mint for it—but the wood hardly saw the light of day. It took all of Carla's concentration to remember how to put it together. Abby waited patiently. Carla sucked on her reed as enthusiastically as if it were a cough drop. It was the one part of the setup process that seemed to appeal to her, and she dawdled over it until Abby pointed to the open book and the exercise she'd marked in red.

"I assume you practiced it," she said. Carla nodded, eyes fixed somewhere around her lemon-yellow sneakers. "Then we can get it right out of the way. Go ahead."

Carla fumbled her way through it, honking like a goose with a cold. It was miserable. Worse than miserable. Abby sighed and played the exercise with her, slowly, over and over, fingers automatically finding the easiest path to the music while Carla's searched the air blindly.

Harris had told her at the start that Carla was hopeless. She was starting to believe it.

Someone knocked on the practice room door, and Abby looked up to see Harris's unsmiling face framed in the window. She motioned to Carla to continue—which Carla didn't, of course—and got up to answer him.

"Somebody here to see you," he said. His face was carefully blank. "In my office. Hey, Carla Jane, keep going. I'll take over until Miz Rhodes is back."

Carla Jane looked devastated. Abby hesitated in the doorway, a question forming on her lips, but Harris closed the door on her. She took a deep breath and crossed the huge green-carpeted band hall to the closed door that said DIRECTOR. Harris had stuck a NO DIVING sign on the door. She turned the knob and looked inside.

Vice Principal Orwin Prather stood in the center of the room, hands clasped behind his back, shoulders slumped. He was a short, dumpy man but his round-shouldered body language always reminded her of Richard Nixon, and so did his eyes—narrow, dark, calculating eyes. He looked her up and down without comment and indicated the battered visitor's chair in front of Harris's littered desk.

She sat, legs gone suddenly nerveless. He had a smile on his face. He *never* smiled unless someone was in trouble.

"I got a call this morning," he said. His voice had the disconcerting habit of rising at the end of his sentences, as if he were asking a question. She gave him a hesitant nod. "Miss Rhodes, this kind of behavior is clearly unacceptable. It reflects badly upon the faculty and the school, and it can't continue."

"I beg your—" She took a deep breath and started over. "Who called?"

"The Fall Creek Police Department," he said, and picked lint from his suit lapel. He needed to keep doing it, she thought; the suit looked like it might be shedding. "An officer there clocked your car speeding out of town this morning. He said he'd let the whole incident go with this warning, but I, Miss Rhodes, am hardly as forgiving. If you want to make a practice of—"

"Excuse me?" she blurted. *Terry.* Somehow he'd found out her name—found her concert program in John Lee's car, maybe. "I didn't."

"Didn't what?"

"Didn't speed through Fall Creek this morning," she said, and breathed a deep sigh of relief. "My car is in the shop—Hernandez Transmission, if you want

to check. It's been there for three days. I'm not sched-
uled to pick it up until tomorrow."

The Principal of Vice did not like being thwarted.
He gave her a beady-eyed frown and said, "So you
were not in Fall Creek this morning."

"Would you like to call Mr. Hernandez? I'll be
happy to give you the number. In fact, I was planning to call him myself to find out if—"

"No, I'm sure I've kept you long enough," Prather
interrupted. "Shouldn't you be getting back to your
lesson? I have a two o'clock appointment with Mr.
Henderson."

He didn't wait for her reply. She sat staring at the
open door, listening to the distant squeaking anguish
of Carla Jane's latest finger exercise, and felt a deep
stab of fear.

Officer Terry had put out a lot of effort to cause
trouble.

She caught a ride home with Harris, which was
probably a mistake, considering the presence of gossip twins Graham and O'Rourke, who lingered near
the parking lot, the better to watch you, my dear.
She imagined she saw O'Rourke's lips moving even
before she'd closed the pickup truck door.

'Well?" Harris asked. She balanced her instruments
more carefully on her lap. "Don't keep me in sus-
pense. What was the beef? Prather find out you
posed nude for *Penthouse*?"

"*Playboy*," she said. "Better clientele."

"Not around here. Don't worry, he gets everybody,
sooner or later. We all get the 'reflects badly on the

faculty' speech. Or the 'high moral character' speech. Which one did you get?"

"Option A. It was all a mistake, anyway. He apologized."

Harris, in the process of turning onto Main Street, almost lost control of the truck. "Apologized? Did you see his lips move?"

"Come to think of it, it wasn't so much an apology as a retreat. Did he get Henderson?"

"Mr. Heineken Man? Oh, yeah. Smoke detectors went off. Could have been worse. We once had an assistant director who took a bunch of seventeen-year-olds to a bar in Dallas on a band trip. Almost lost the whole music program over that one. Before my time, of course."

"Of course."

"You're damn lucky to get off with Prather, mistake or not. Once he smells blood, it's all over." Harris fished a package of Camel cigarettes out of the glove compartment and lit one, savoring the smoke. "My one vice per day. Verboten at the concentration camp."

"Could do it at home," she suggested, and waved away gray tendrils that undulated toward her.

"I think they've got the place bugged. Hell, they paid for the house to get me here. How do I know they don't have video cameras in the walls?"

She couldn't tell if he was joking. He flicked the half-smoked cigarette out the window into the snow-slushed street and made the turn into her apartment complex.

John Lee was sitting in his car by her door, reading

a book. She took too long staring at him; when she looked over at Harris to thank him for the ride he had a demonic light in his eyes.

"Friend of yours?" he asked blandly. "Never mind. I don't want to know you're having more fun than I am. Have one for me."

"One what?" she asked as she stepped down from the truck. "He's here to fix my broken window."

"Oh, yeah, sure. Tell me another one, Rhodes. Wait'll I tell—"

She slammed the door on the threat and watched him drive away. She felt John Lee's approach, shivered when he trailed warm fingers across the back of her neck.

"Afternoon, ma'am," he said. She closed her eyes and leaned back into him, fitting perfectly. His arms went around her waist. "Have a nice day at school?"

"Very . . ." She turned to face him, close enough that their lips brushed. Not quite a kiss. Not quite. "Very educational. So, you're here to fix my window, right?"

Amusement ironed creases at the corners of his dark eyes. "Damn straight. Among other things."

"You in the mood to be dog taxi later?" A cold, sly breeze teased his hair back and combed it into waves. She let her fingers follow and the soft, feathery brush of his hair made her smile. "The vet's approved Carlton to come home. That would be after I pay you for the window, of course."

He leaned into her touch like a cat, watching her eyes. "I might be willing to do a little extra work on the side. Ma'am."

"Mmmm." She had a deep, hungry need to kiss him, but the temptation was almost as satisfying. "Better hurry, mister, I'm not paying you by the hour."

He laughed and let her go. The wind crowded in between them like a jealous stepchild. She ran to the door and unlocked it, missing Carlton's welcoming bark but obscurely glad to have John Lee all to herself, then turned to watch him unload tools and plywood from the trunk of his car. He'd have an orderly trunk, she was almost sure. Nothing there but clean space and a spare.

He carried the stuff inside and set it carefully on the floor next to the couch.

"The window's in the bedroom," she said helpfully. He froze in the act of straightening.

"That sounds like an invitation."

"It's information." She grinned. "What you do with it is your business, mister. Straight down the hall—"

"Oh, I remember where it is, don't you worry. I stood there in your bathroom and listened to you get dressed."

"What? You rat! And I thought you were looking at *Playgirl*."

"Couldn't keep my mind on the damn thing," he said, and picked up the tools again. "Maybe you'd better come with me, make sure I don't get lost."

He measured the window while she sat on the end of the bed and watched him. He made careful notes on a pad that went back in his toolbox. The whole process took about a minute.

"Want me to nail some plywood over this for to-night? Keep out the wind and prowlers?" he asked.

"Is that it? All the maintenance I get?"

"I'm a craftsman, lady, I don't just slap glass in a frame. Besides"—he raised his eyebrows—"don't you want me to keep coming back?"

She reached out and grabbed his belt buckle, reeled him closer.

"What do you think?" she asked.

And the phone rang. She jerked as if it had stabbed her in the back—which it had—and gave him an ex-asperated look before rolling over the rumpled cov-ers to grab the receiver.

"So," Benny said brightly on the other end of the line before she could even say hello. "There I was, driving back to a dull evening of Grieg and Dvorak when—wham!—all of a sudden it hits me."

"Hello, Benny," she said, and threw an arm over her eyes. The bed creaked as John Lee took a seat at the end of it. "I hope it wasn't a truck."

"A narrow escape, but no, it wasn't. I'm thinking about old Professor Courier—you remember—he's got a retirement party this weekend down at the Meyerson, and I was thinking since you were his prize student you'd better just hop a puddle jumper and stay with me for the weekend."

She refused to answer while she wrenched her mind—violently—away from John Lee and followed Benny's convoluted logic.

"I don't know if I can make it," she said cautiously when she thought she had it. "I'm kind of in the middle of something right now. Can I call you back?"

"Is the something live and breathing?"

"None of your business, Benny. When's the party?"

"Saturday night. The hot, hip crowd'll go out to scope out the night life later. You, me, Duncan—well, scratch Duncan. What about it?" When the hesitation grew too long, Benny's voice took on a sharper, more interested note. "You weren't *really* in the middle of somebody, were you? Like, some cowboy or something?"

"Ben—"

"Oh, man, I knew it. Listen, too much passion messes with your head. Get on the plane and get your butt up here on Saturday, or else." She hung up before Abby could answer. Abby strangled the receiver with both hands, violently, before putting it back in the cradle.

John Lee got up off the bed and positioned plywood over the window. He was one of those guys who took two blows of the hammer to put a nail in—one tap, one solid hit. A professional. Abby watched him work with a lazy appreciation. The bed seemed to have acquired extra gravity since she'd laid down on it.

"Done," he announced, tossed his hammer like a twirling baton, and caught it behind his back. "Have your new window for you tomorrow, ma'am. Anything else I can do for you?"

"Take me to pick up Carlton from the vet," she

said. He leaned over her, so close that a deep breath would have made their chests touch.

"You mean right this minute?"

"Well . . . not right now."

"Anything else you can think of you need?" His lips brushed over the smooth skin of her collarbone, breath blowtorch hot.

She said, "I could think of one or two."

"Do tell."

She did.

Largo:
December 10, 1994

"Pearl Harbor Day," said Benny's mother from the backseat as Benny floored the car and pulled out into Love Field traffic. "Pearl Harbor Day's always been very special around our house, hasn't it, Benina?"

"Yeah. So how was the flight? Skinny flight attendants and salted peanuts?"

Benny's question dragged Abby away from a sweet, tactile memory of John Lee's mouth on her skin and made her blink. The conversation, which had been an ongoing sniping match between the two Wright women, had just fired a shot in her direction. "Oh. Fine, thanks. One of my seatmates talked about his business meeting the whole time except when he was complaining about airsickness. The other one might have been dead." She turned in her seat to offer Mrs. Wright a smile. The sweet little elderly woman had dressed up in honor of Abby's arrival in a cherry-pink flowered dress. She'd had her hair done, too. The gray curls and creases looked razor-sharp. "Special how, Mrs. Wright?"

"Well, Henry—that's Benny's father, dear, you never met him—Henry was very patriotic. He always used to hang our American flag outside every Sunday, remember, honey? He was just beside himself when the Japs bombed us. Went right down and enlisted." Mrs. Wright nodded twice for emphasis, cupid's-bow mouth drawn up tight. "Pearl Harbor Day has always been remembered at our house."

"He only tried to enlist, Mom," Benny said in a quick, bored monotone. "They didn't take him."

"That doesn't make him any less patriotic, now, does it? Abby, dear, how is your father these days?"

"Fine," she said, and made a guilty mental note to find out. "Benny, aren't we going to stop for lunch?"

Benny gave her a look of pure betrayal.

"Oh, I'm sure Mom wants to go home in time to see *Days of Our Lives*, right, Mom?"

"No, that's just fine, I'd love to hear Abby talk about all her little students. You know, Benny's father was a teacher, and he never seemed to have good students. I just couldn't understand it. Do you think children are more intelligent today?"

All Abby's thoughts just now seemed to have to do with John Lee or the barbed-wire gossip circle at the school. And she didn't think the kind of things that she was thinking about John Lee would make suitable lunchtime gossip, at least not with Benny's mother. God, she missed him with a physical intensity that surprised and distressed her. What was it he'd told her that first day? *We don't get but three perfect minutes in our lives.* She had the awful feeling that by leaving him, she was missing out on at least two.

"How about Mexican food?' Benny interrupted brightly.

Mrs. Wright leaned forward, brushing invisible crumbs from her dress. "You shouldn't eat such spicy food. Gives you gas. How about some nice American food?"

"It's Tex-Mex, Mom, it *is* American. Okay. Okay. Chicken-fried steak? Mashed potatoes? That all right?"

"Fine, dear." Mrs. Wright began humming off-key, smiled secretively, and broke off to say, "Abby, dear, don't tell me you have some nice young man waiting for you back in Midland?"

"Excuse me?" Abby blurted, and twisted around to get a good look at her face. Benny wouldn't—no, from the shocked look on Benny's face, she clearly *hadn't*. "Ah—no, I'm afraid not. Not just now."

She wasn't sure why she was lying, except that maybe it wasn't *lying*, exactly—he was hardly pining away waiting for her; he was busy doing his work and living his life and *damn* she was already regretting the trip and that wouldn't do at all. Benny deserved better than that.

"Well, you really ought to find one, neither one of you girls is getting any younger. I'm not saying your hobbies aren't nice, but you really need to find some direction in your lives soon." Mrs. Wright fanned herself with a battered leftover program that had Benny's picture on the back, looked out, and said, "Lord, I do wish we'd just get on with winter. It's always worse when it waits until February to let go."

Benny, face gone rigid, said, "Suddenly I'm not

very hungry. I really need to take Abby to do some shopping for the party."

A taxi driver swerved in front of them, forcing Benny to brake; the driver turned to glare back at them as if *they'd* cut *him* off. Benny glared back, cornrows bristling. The taxi slowed to thirty and the car pitched and jerked as she tried to get around him but he leisurely changed with her, sliding from lane to lane and taking no notice at all of the other cars honking their alarm like frightened geese.

"If that's what you want, honey," Mrs. Wright said. She continued to gaze out her window, eyes fixed on the distant horizon. "I'm sure you girls have more important things to do than eat lunch with me. Just drop me off at home, Benina, and let me know when you'll want some dinner. I have my shows on tonight, so I have to be done with the dishes by seven o'clock sharp."

"Of course, Mom," Benny said. She refused to look in Abby's direction, even though Abby waved to attract her attention. "Can't miss those shows."

It was a long, mostly silent drive through winding tree-lined neighborhoods. Abby had made the trip a hundred times before but it still managed to surprise her how suddenly and visibly the price tags of homes changed—overblown mansions crouched behind spiked iron gates, then down a tax level to rambling brick homes for corporate executives, doctors, and lawyers. The Wright home was several blocks farther, in a gently seedy neighborhood where the Christmas decorations were desperately festive. Mrs. Wright had a herd of plastic reindeer grazing on the dead

grass of her lawn, with a dyspeptic-looking Santa
lurking near the bushes like a Peeping Tom. The
large front window featured an oversized diorama
manger scene. Mary had a round-faced, wholesome,
fifties sort of beauty. Jesus was the size of a toddler.

"Door-to-door service," Benny said as the Gremlin
lurched to a stop in the driveway. She got out and
folded down the driver's-side seat and helped her
mother out. Mrs. Wright offered her daughter a lukewarm limp hug and came around the car to offer a
much more enthusiastic one to Abby. Abby squeezed
very gently, aware of the woman's crepe-soft skin,
the frail bones beneath. She smelled of powdered
gardenias and fresh hair spray.

"Don't let my daughter get you in any trouble,
now," Mrs. Wright patted her hand, bird-quick, and
marched up the sidewalk to her bright-red-foil-pack-
aged front door. Benny waited until the door was
open and the plump cherry-pink figure had disappeared inside before turning to the Gremlin and
banging her forehead off the roof two or three times.

"She means well," Abby offered. Benny stopped
pounding her head and looked up. After a second or
two of speechless staring, she pounded her head
again. "Don't take it so personally, Ben, she really
doesn't mean to hurt your feelings."

They got in the car. Benny, tight-lipped, started up
the car and backed out into the street with a little
too much speed. The sign at the corner was big, yellow, and said DIP on its diamond-shaped surface;
Benny stepped on the gas.

"It's her new thing that's getting to me. The 'when

are you going to quit this hobby and settle down'
thing. I mean, she's sitting on top of programs with
my picture all over them, and she's still calling it a
hobby!" Benny sucked in a deep breath, and so did
Abby as she spotted the wide black ditch that the
city of Dallas called a DIP. "Whoops. Hang on."

Abby grabbed the handhold on the door. The
Gremlin went airborne and came down with a slam
that she felt in her tailbone like a kick.

"Sorry about that. Anyway, enough about my
problems, let's talk about yours. What disgusting
habits does he have? Chewing his toenails? Eating
raw meat? Kissing with chewing tobacco in his
mouth?"

"He's not a problem," Abby said, and smiled. "Far
from a problem."

"Oh, sure, you say that now but just you wait,
baby." Benny shuddered. "Is he circumcised?"

"Ben!"

"Well, is he?"

"Mexican food sounds just fine to me." Abby
sighed and turned to look out as winter-ravaged
trees flitted by the window. Some of them were putting out cautious green buds, fooled by the mild
Texas winter. They'd learn. After a few minutes of
silence, she said, "He's not."

"Didn't think so," Benny said serenely, and turned
toward Margaritaville.

Eating lunch with Benny was, as always, an adven-
ture. She could hardly help but attract attention, but
it wasn't just the stares; Abby always felt invisible in

Benny's presence, so the stares didn't bother her at all. It was the *people*.

Benny knew everybody. Everywhere.

She knew somebody standing in line at the restaurant. She was neighbors with the maître d'. She'd been there, done that, dated him. Abby felt as if she'd been through a formal reception by the time she'd gotten her seat at the wide terra-cotta-tiled table and been handed her menu. She scanned it while Benny discovered a common interest with the waiter.

"That's very annoying," Abby said, and glanced up as Benny folded her menu and sipped her lime and water.

"What?"

"The last time we went to the movies the person sitting ahead of you was your long-lost babysitter."

"Well . . ." Benny tilted her head to consider it. Her black and white cornrows made a shocking contrast with her plaid jacket. "That only happened once."

"For God's sake, she was from *Cleveland*."

"Am I to blame for that? So, what'll it be? Margaritas and tacos?"

"Sounds good." Abby gave up on the menu while Benny relayed the order, at length, to her new friend the waiter. "Tell me about the new show."

"New show . . . oh, that one. Blah. Pit orchestra for *Cinderella*. I've got the worst conductor in the world and I can't understand a damn thing he says." Benny shoved braids back over her shoulders with a theatrical flourish. "Ze douf ez non parsed."

"What?"

"That's what I said. I still don't have a clue, I just play it the way the guy wrote it. Anyway, enough about life in the pit, tell me about *him*."

"Is that all we talk about? Sex?"

Benny pretended to consider. "So what's your point?"

She was saved by the arrival of margaritas, thick, lime-green mush. Abby licked salt and vacuumed up a slushy mouthful. It shimmied down her throat, ice-cold and tequila-hot.

"I think this thing might actually last," she said, and scared herself. She scared Benny, too; her friend paused in the act of straw-stirring her drink to blink several times.

"I hope to hell you're talking about the margarita."

"I know. I know."

"Last time you ended up calling me at four in the morning to tell me all about what a miserable jerk he was. Remember?"

Abby nodded dutifully. She had, after all, made Benny promise to remind her about what's-his-name. She *did* deserve it.

"It's just that—I know you're not going to believe this—he's different." Abby laughed nervously and wiped cold sweat from the side of her glass. "I feel like I *know* him, Ben. Like I ought to know him. Is that nuts?"

"Deeply. It's hormones, baby, not karma. Six weeks from now . . ."

"I don't think so." Abby stared down into the cool pale surface of her drink, the pebbly green curve of the lime wedge. "Something strange is going on. I

know I always sort of laughed about it, but . . . I'm
getting these, these *visions*. Not like déjà vu, worse.
I *know* I've never been to Fall Creek but I *know* I've
been there. I *know* I've never seen those houses but
I *know* them. I know what's inside them. Sometimes
when I look at him I feel like . . . like he's somebody
else, and I'm somebody else, and things are all different. Am I making any sense at all?"

She looked up to see Benny staring at her, drink
neglected. No amusement in her face at all.

"Should I not use the 's' word?" Benny asked.
Abby frowned in confusion. "Psychic."

"I'm not psychic. I don't even believe in psychics."

"Yeah, I forgot." Benny licked hot sauce from a
tortilla chip and took a small, neat, catlike bite. "So
what exactly do you call it when you know things
you don't know?"

Abby pushed her silverware around and shook
her head.

Benny's voice turned soft. "You're not jazzing me,
are you? You're scared."

She nodded. Benny's hand reached across the table
to cover hers, and in spite of the sudden weight of
misery she felt, Abby couldn't help but smile. Benny
had chosen a different color of polish for each finger,
shading from red to blue.

"Tell me all about it," Benny said.

Abby took a deep breath, and started.

"I thought we were going to go shopping," Abby
said doubtfully. Benny drove past the edgy, glittery
gloom of downtown and into another neighborhood

that featured clapboard and chain link as prominent design features. The cars were all Midland models, Abby thought—old, dented, sun-damaged. Left unlocked in the hopes of attracting a less choosy grade of thief. The Christmas decorations here were simple strings of lights, usually draped unevenly over sharp-leafed pyracantha bushes.

'Yeah, we will, Later."

"Where are we going?"

"I told you, to see somebody. Somebody *special*." Her voice held a unpleasant amount of glee. *Special*, translated from Benny's vocabulary, usually meant *strange*. Benny was taking her to a crystal-gazing, tarot-reading gypsy psychic with a fringed shawl and finger cymbals. Abby gave a heartfelt groan.

"Are you finished?" Benny asked. She didn't sound sorry.

"It's starting to look that way."

"I promise, nothing strange. You have a glass of tea, nothing bizarre will happen, it's all very calm. And you'll like him, he isn't weird or anything." Benny visibly hesitated. "*Too* weird. And he's very cool. You'll like him, I promise. And he's been wanting to meet you."

There didn't seem to be any point in asking why. They stopped at an intersection while a glitter-blue low-rider sedan cruised by, blasting Tejano music. The driver, a waiflike teenager, drove with one hand on a chrome chain steering wheel barely bigger than his palm. Around the interior of the car, orange fringe shifted and shimmied in time with the beat.

He had a skull-and-crossbones laminated on the back window.

"Gotta love it," Benny said, gazing after the car. "Great neighborhood."

Abby made a sound low in her throat that could have been taken for agreement.

Two blocks farther on the houses gave way to cheaply built 1940's houses that had become shops. REDUX RAGS competed with VERA'S HAIR STYLING, identical buildings with only different-colored trim and signs to distinguish them. Benny pulled into the curb at the next house. The sign said COSMIC JOE'S TEA ROOM AND COFFEE HOUSE, and, in smaller script, MASSAGES, HEALTHY FOODS AND PSYCHIC SERVICES.

"I don't think this is a very good idea," Abby said. Benny ignored her and got out of the car. Abby stared at the dashboard stubbornly, picking where the plastic had split and spilled out white fiber. "I don't have to do this. I really don't."

"Sure you do," Benny said, and opened the passenger side with a limousine driver's flourish. "One cup of tea. What can it do, kill you?"

Inside, the shop smelled of cinnamon and ginger and fresh bread, the scent so strong she swallowed and thought she could taste it. It was jam-packed with aisles of packaged foods, a tiny corner grocery carrying no-fat, no-salt, all-natural products with herbal seasonings. The special of the day, stacked in a neat pyramid of cans, was vegetarian black bean soup.

Beyond the shelves, where Benny went, was the coffee and tea bar—a long polished wooden affair, stools to fit, small nondescript chairs and tables filling the rest of the space. Earnest-looking college students who wore their hair too straight nursed foamy cinnamon-topped cappuccinos with their bran muffins. Older, harder-faced intellectuals drank straight black coffee, disdained muffins and pastries, and made notes on legal pads while they argued in whispers. A weary-looking aging hippy looked frankly glad to be back in the womb again.

Benny hitched a hip on a barstool and tapped her fingernails in a drum roll on the bar. A short, whippet-thin man in black and white T-shirt and jeans came out of the back room. He had a whippet's face, too—a sharp pointed nose, large close-set eyes, receding chin. He broke into a wide, enthusiastic grin when he saw Benny.

"New hair," he said, and reached across the bar to feel the cornrows. He had a lyrical, low voice, smoothed with an accent that she thought sounded European. "Very nice. Kaneesha's work?"

"How'd you know?"

"I have my ways. Tea?"

"Yeah, with lemon and honey. Abby, you want tea or coffee? He makes really great cappuccino here, too."

"Tea's fine," Abby said, and perched uneasily next to her. The bar felt cold and slick under her fingers. The thought of cappuccino warmed her but it might take longer and she didn't want any excuse to wait around. "Darjeeling. No lemon, just honey."

He nodded pleasantly and turned away, pulling china cups from a rack where other bars would have had wineglasses or beer mugs. His thick black hair was braided into a neat club that reached halfway down his back.

"That's Miklos," Benny said, nodding at their server. "Miklos Azapolous. Used to be a dancer, right, Mik?"

"Still a dancer." He shrugged, deftly pouring with his left hand while his right stirred honey into the cups. "But not so much now. Benina and I, we met when she was in the pit orchestra for *Giselle* six years ago, yes?"

"I try not to count. Miklos was choreographing. He did this great temper tantrum with Old Cross-Eyed Henry, the conductor—what was it—" Benny leaned back on the barstool, assumed her most theatrical expression, and affected a mock-Greek accent. "I never had to put up with this kind of bullshit when *Bernstein* was conducting!"

"Really?" Abby looked at the man with new respect. He put her cup on a delicate white saucer, handed it to her, and raised an eyebrow like an exclamation point. "Bernstein?"

He smiled and gave Benina her tea.

"Old Henry looked like a bullet train had just run over him," Benny continued. "From that point on everything was 'Yes, Mr. Azapolous; No, Mr. Azapolous; What do you think, Mr. Azapolous?' Heaven. I decided right then and there this was one guy I *had* to meet, so I offered to buy him coffee and he told me he owned this place. So we had cappuccino for free." Benny squeezed her lemon wedge into pulpy submission and stirred her tea. For a fraction of a second she looked at Miklos and he looked back and there was something there, raising the temperature of the room by several degrees. Abby raised her eyebrows.

"You just had cappuccino?"

"World-class cappuccino." Benny shrugged elaborately and her layers of chains jangled like wind chimes. "How's the tea?"

Abby dutifully sipped. The tea had a strong clean taste, sweeping away the Mexican food and leaving a pleasant tingle behind. The honey was a hidden reward on the back of her tongue.

"Wonderful," she said. "So, Mr. Azapolous—"

"Miklos," he interrupted. "To any friend of Benina's, Miklos."

"I guess you danced in New York."

He nodded gravely, eyes bright as a crow's. "When I was young and foolish, before my knee was plastic. A beautiful, terrible town, New York. Here is much better and much worse. Not as much dirt but the rich are too loud and the poor see them too much. It makes for bad feelings, don't you think?"

"I don't know," Abby said, and sipped tea. "I don't live here."

"Yes, I know. You are from Midland," Miklos agreed with a quick, firm nod and a soft smile. "Maybe it's Midland that brings on your bad dreams."

She shot Benny a look of panic. Benny raised her eyebrows and developed an interest in the contents of her teacup.

"It's nothing. Imagination, I guess." Abby fumbled

her cup as she tried to set it down, and hot liquid sloshed, amber-gold. Miklos' hand shot out to steady it. Their fingertips brushed.

Miklos' eyes went wide and black, a whirlpool sucking down the light, and she fell.

The sun squatted on the horizon, shivering in the heat. Pearl kept looking at the sun, checking it, making sure it hadn't gone sneaking off without her, leaving her in the dark.

"You ain't scared, are you, Pearl?" Tommy Burline sneered, and poked the shoe box in her face again. It was his momma's shoe box because it was pink and had some long name she couldn't read. His momma was gonna whip him stupid when she found out what he'd done with it. "Go on, if you ain't scared. Go on!"

Nobody else had done it, not Carleen Boggs nor Evvy Dodermann nor even Big Gordon Kingston, who wasn't afraid of nothing in this life. Evvy had messed her panties and run home crying. Carleen hadn't run but she had that quivery look to her face, like she might sit down in the dirt and wail but hadn't decided when.

Wouldn't be the first time Jimmy Burline had got the best of them, no, sir. And it didn't much matter if any of them turned yellow. But she wasn't one of them, not really, and it mattered, all right. They all thought she was touched in the head, on account of what her momma had done and her daddy not letting anybody in the house anymore, not even Brother Threadgill.

Jimmy Burline, ginger-haired, gap-toothed weed of a boy, held the box out to her again and shook it. Inside, something shifted and slithered.

"Go on!"

She looked over her shoulder. The sun was still there, shivering, old, tired, ready to die. The dark was going and it would get all over everything, even her, and she couldn't stop it just like Daddy couldn't stop it, even though he kept all the lights on all the time.

"I ain't afraid," she said, and put her hand in the box. She touched something muscular and alive that felt cool on her fingers, like rainwater, and grabbed it hard and pulled it out of the box.

It wasn't a rattler, after all, just some dusty-looking milk snake, not even poisonous. It tried to wiggle out of her hand and she squeezed tighter, feeling its muscles work under her fingers. Jimmy Burline's mouth dropped open in astonishment.

"I ain't scared, Jimmy Burline," she said, and held the snake out to him. "Here."

Before he could reach out, even if he was going to, the snake whipped back on itself and buried its teeth in the fleshy part of her palm and hung on while she tried to shake it loose. It sawed its jaws like it was trying to eat its way into her. Carleen ran away, blond curls bouncing, screaming like her head would bust open. Jimmy Burline dropped his momma's pink shoe box and ran, too, white-faced.

She shook the snake off and threw it away into the spiky brush outside the white rail fence. It slithered off into the sand, into the dark. She sat down in the dirt and held her bleeding hand close and rocked, back and forth. She didn't cry because she never cried, never cried at all. After a while she heard the front screen door squeal and looked up. Daddy was a shadow-shape on the porch.

"I ain't afraid, Daddy," she said. Her voice sounded scratchy and old. "I ain't afraid of nothing, Daddy. Not ever again."

"Come in the house, Pearl," he said, and she started to shake all over.

Miklos' eyes. Dark.

The cup warm against the palm of her hand.

Miklos' fingertips just brushing hers. She pulled in a deep breath and rocked backward, eyes filling with tears that made the room into rainbows. Around them, voices continued to murmur.

Miklos slowly drew his hand back and cocked his head to one side, birdlike, never blinking.

"Are you all right?" he asked. She swallowed hard and nodded. "You looked ill for a moment. Not the tea, I hope."

The world looked real, felt real, but so had that *other*, the sun shivering on the horizon, the dust storm twisting in the distance. She looked down at her hand and rubbed trembling fingers over the fleshy part of her palm where she remembered blood.

She couldn't get her breath. Panic squeezed her chest and she opened her mouth to drag in shallow, painful, cinnamon-dusted breaths. A warm hand covered hers where she gripped the edge of the bar. She looked up to find Miklos watching her intently, something warm and soft in his eyes.

"Come with me," he said. "Come. Please."

She found herself moving, slow dreamlike steps

that felt weightless. Dreaming, that was it, it was all a dream. Dreams inside dreams.

Miklos' hand touched her elbow, gently guiding. Benny followed and she was asking questions but Abby couldn't quite get the sense of the words, only the music of concern. He steered her behind the bar and into the back room.

"Sit," he said. There was a chair underneath her, soft and springy. She had a quick impression of a dark, masculine sort of room, a Persian carpet cool blue at her feet. "Put your head down. Breathe."

"What happened?" Benny's voice asked from behind her, finally in focus; Abby kept her head down and closed her eyes and tried to breathe evenly. "Mik, is she okay?"

"That depends," he said. She felt his presence, very close, and opened her eyes to see him kneeling in front of her. He put his hands on either side of her head and stared into her eyes, frowning. "Yes. Yes, I think so. Better now, yes? The breathing?"

"Yes," she whispered. *I'll wake up soon now.*

"Then sit up, put your head back. Relax. Benina, bring me the blanket—yes, that one. Thank you." She sat up and let her head fall back against soft cushioning. Miklos tucked a thick, warm cover around her. She met his eyes for a second and couldn't hold the stare, not without remembering the panic. "This was like the other times?"

She gave him a nod that changed to indecisive denial once she realized what she was admitting to.

"Yes. No, I . . . it seemed so real. Like I was there."

"Perhaps you were there," he said, and patted her knee. "Something from your childhood?"

"No." She knew that much, at least. She'd never had that childhood, that terrible shadow-father. "Maybe I just . . . imagined it or something."

He floated gracefully back to his feet, a startling and sensuous movement, and pulled another chair close to hers, this one upholstered in threadbare fleur-de-lis. "How many times has this happened?"

"Two—no, three—I don't know." She took a deep breath. "It has something to do with Fall Creek."

A touch of cold stroked lightly down her spine. *Fall Creek.* She saw a sepia flash of dusty streets, of rusted 1950s cars neglected on the streets, of sun and heat and faces relentlessly staring. Miklos nodded and steepled his hands together.

"Benina, would you wait outside, please?" No movement from behind Abby's chair. Miklos' stare altered trajectory upward, and his lips quirked into a smile. "I'll give you a cappuccino, on the house."

"Do you want me to go?" Benny asked, leaning over. Abby reached up and grabbed her hand hard.

"I don't know. I don't know what's happening to me anymore."

"I'll be real quiet," Benny said, and sat down on the floor next to Abby's chair. Her chin lifted as Miklos continued to stare at her. "Forget it, Mik, I'm not going."

He abandoned the battle and turned his gaze back toward Abby. "Wait one moment."

He got up and went out to the bar again, had a muffled conversation with someone outside. When he came back he had their teacups, which he handed over before seating himself again.

"Fall Creek," he said, watching as Abby drank her tea. Her hands trembled. "Tell me about it. Everything you remember."

"I don't *remember* anything. I met a man named John Lee Jordan and my dog ran away and John Lee lives in Fall Creek."

"Carlton ran away twice," Benny reminded her. "Both times to Fall Creek."

"So? Is my dog haunted?"

"Perhaps your dog is reacting to the same thing you are," Miklos said, frowning. "A feeling. A memory. A ghost."

"I don't believe in ghosts."

"What was her name?"

"Pearl—" The name slipped out before she could catch it; she watched his face, appalled. She'd never known a Pearl in her life.

"Who is Pearl?"

"I don't know."

"Pearl lives in Fall Creek?"

"I don't know!"

"Tell me the last thing you remember."

"I don't know what you—"

"Sunset. The snake. What else?"

"What—"

"Dark." His eyes were wide and black, big enough to fall into. "I see the house, cracked steps, purple flowers wilting in the sun. Hands pushing you forward, a kitchen, a door, darkness, stairs into darkness, falling—"

"Stop it!" Abby cried out, and put her hands over her ears. She couldn't get her breath. "It's not true—"

"Death." Miklos said softly. Her breath stopped in her throat and turned thick and dark. "You see her die, don't you?"

She shook her head, hands still covering her ears, thinking over and over, *This is a dream, just a dream, I want to wake up now, I want to wake up.*

"Abby, my friend, there is something here. Something terrible. You must listen to it." Miklos looked flustered now, distressed, clearly out of his depth. "You *must*, don't you see that?"

"No!" she said sharply. It didn't sound like her voice at all. It burst out of her like a bullet and she saw the impact of it as he pulled away from her. His face went very pale. She was shaking uncontrollably, ready to hit something, ready to cry. "You just leave me alone, you hear me? You quit!"

It didn't sound like her voice at all. She fought her way free of the clinging hold of the blanket and stood up. When she swayed, Benny reached for her arm to help her, and she slapped her hand away. The sound of that, and Benny's gasp, echoed in the small dim room.

People just couldn't leave it alone, could they? Always prying, poking their noses in where they didn't—

"You, too," she said, and pushed past Benny's shock, out into the restaurant and the staring faces.

People always stared. Why was that?

Tarantella:
December 10, 1994

"We don't have to go to the party," Benny ventured as they drove back toward the hotel. Abby turned her head away toward the failing twilight, the gray shadows of buildings. She swallowed hard and shook her head.

"I came for the party, I'll go to the party." Her voice had a hard, uncontrollable edge. She wanted to stop it, but there was something bitter and black in her stomach, and she couldn't get on top of the anger. No reason to be angry, but she was, angrier than she'd ever been in her life.

She knew it hurt Benny, but she couldn't bring herself to care.

"Look, I know you're upset—"

"I'm not upset," Abby snapped. "I'm just fine."

Benny missed third gear and cursed. Her voice sounded fragile.

"Don't you ever do that to me again," Abby said over the grinding of gears, and turned to look at her. Benny's blue eyes skimmed away from hers uneasily. "I mean it. No more psychic bullshit, Benny, no goddamn more, ever. Don't you ever let me see him again."

"You won't."

"I better not."

"I said you won't!" Benny's eyes glittered with tears. Her jaw trembled. "Jesus, Abby, ease off. We never wanted to hurt you."

"Yeah, I'm sure." She clenched her fist hard on her knee. "Five more minutes and he would've been asking me for a thousand dollars to fix my problem, right? Psychic therapy? How close am I?"

"Miklos would never—"

"Right. Just don't do me any more favors, Ben, okay? Leave your gypsy voodoo buddies out of my life."

Benny wiped at her eyes with the back of a hand. She blew through a red light and turned right at the next street. Abby's hotel loomed out of the sunset, a haven of blinking neon and prepackaged cheer. Benny braked under the lobby overhang and looked over at her, lips parted. Abby stared at her a second and then opened the door and got out.

"What time do I pick you up?" Benny asked, leaning over to lock eyes with her again. There were lines in her face that Abby didn't remember, weary, pinched creases that were out of place with the desperate coolness of the cornrows and mismatched clothes. Her blue eyes begged.

"Nine," Abby said shortly, and walked away. When she looked back from the lobby Benny was still parked, idling the Gremlin, staring straight ahead toward the sunset.

She looked so alone, so lost. Abby bit her lip and tried to remember why it was she was so angry, but the feeling slipped around like cold mud. It *had* been Miklos' doing, hadn't it? Some damn hypnosis game. He had Benny buying in, but he was *not* getting her, too. Sadistic bastard. How *dare* he suck her in like that?

She paced her hotel room for a while, heels digging into the thick carpet, staring out at the jewel skyline of Dallas. The city gave her an unsettled feeling— too many people, too much anger. Her skin crawled watching the slow flood of car headlights on the freeways. She liked small towns, liked the easy pace of them, the feeling of knowing everyone, even if she didn't really know them at all. Better to be the subject of gossip than to spend her whole life alone in the glitter.

She lay down on the bed and closed her eyes and in a few minutes had slipped into a confused half-dream of old dusty rooms lit by yellowed bulbs, of a voice screaming in the distance. She remembered the feel of the couch, rough against her cheek as she huddled in the corner of it, under the glare of the lamp. It smelled like it had been stuffed with dust and when she moved it made uncomfortable groans like a living, hurting thing.

She jerked herself awake and off the bed, went to the bathroom and stared into the mirror at her reflection. She felt disconnected from the pale, strained face that looked back at her, as if it weren't her face, not really. She reached up to comb her fingers through her disheveled hair but for a terrifying second it felt like a wig, loose on her scalp.

The message light blinked a slow, steady rhythm

on her phone. She circled it warily, as if it might trigger some bomb, and slowly picked up the receiver and listened while the pleasant operator read her a phone number with an 806 area code. She wrote the number down in neat block letters on the hotel pad with the hotel pen, and wrote his name after it. *John Lee Jordan.*

Maybe there was no Pearl. Maybe that had been Miklos' fabrication. LSD in her honey tea.

Oh, God, but it had seemed so *real.*

She dialed the number without really knowing she was doing it. The phone clicked and buzzed and on the other end his voice said warmly "Hello?" and she closed her eyes and instead of John Lee's smile she remembered someone else, cold blue eyes, leathery face.

"Custer?" she said, and covered her mouth with both hands as memory slammed over her. *The house, dusty and decaying, her face pressed to the rough fabric of the couch, a voice screaming in the distance, fingers trailing cold over the back of her neck and she turned to look up at him, at the cold smile, the harsh skin.*

He climbed on top of her, pressing her face hard into the gritty fabric. No words. Never any words.

She collapsed sideways on the bed and drew her knees up to her chest, breathing deeply against a crippling flood of panic. The receiver lay on the pillow next to her, chirping half-heard words. She fumbled it up and put it back on the cradle and turned her face to the pillow, unable to cry but desperate to let out the anger.

It's not true. It's not true. She couldn't pretend it

was a dream, not anymore, she'd never had these horrible dreams, never felt the rage that seemed to come whenever Pearl did. She'd had a normal childhood, a quiet unexceptional life except for her dedication to her music. She'd had comfortable love affairs with men she still counted as friends, no emotional bonfires, no tragedy, no rage.

Pearl was so very different.

It had to be Miklos' doing. But she couldn't work up the proper load of resentment, because she knew it had started before Miklos, was continuing without him. It wasn't Miklos. It was her.

Only her.

Someone in the next room over was making love; she heard the misty cries and felt the vibrations of the headboard at her back. She closed her eyes and concentrated desperately on John Lee in the shower, the long smooth glide of his back, the sweet taste of his skin. So different from Pearl's memories. This was *hers*, all *hers*. John Lee was a good thing in the midst of all this devastation, she had to believe that, she had to.

She built him up in her mind, pushing away anything that might bring back Pearl—the way he'd smiled as he'd turned, blinking water from his eyes, the glitter of drops caught in his chest hair, the way the water had chased her hand down the curve of his hip. She felt the pressure of his lips, traveling down from her collarbone.

Even the memory triggered heat. She settled herself more comfortably on the pillows and slowly unzipped her blue jeans.

The phone rang. She sat up and grabbed for it, breathing hard. Pearl was gone, all right. Right out of her head.

"Abby?" John Lee's voice, gentled by miles but still slightly rough, a voice like a day's growth of beard. She remembered the thick rasp of his chin under her hand. "Hey. You just call? I think we got disconnected. How's the big bad city?"

"Big and bad," she said, and felt muscles relax she hadn't even known were tense. "Stupid. I want to come back." *Home,* she meant. *Home to you.*

"The sooner the better, that's my view. Tomorrow, right?"

"Right." She closed her eyes and took a deep breath. The bad things were going away now, chased by the sound of his voice.

"I was thinking, Abby . . ." He hesitated and let the sentence die. She made a questioning sound in her throat. "Uh, you tell me if it makes you uncomfortable, okay?"

"As long as it doesn't involve videotaping."

He laughed, but she heard the tension hanging on. "Nope, none of that. I was just thinking that tomorrow we could go over to my mother's to eat. That okay with you?"

Something went cold inside her stomach, heavy as a bullet. Pearl was trying to speak. Abby pushed it hard into the darkness and slammed a lid on it, clinging to the simple memories of him, the smell of his skin, the way he'd whispered her name, rough and hard and breathless as his body moved on hers.

"It's okay," she said. It was pale and quiet, but she said it. John Lee sighed in her ear.

"Only if you want to. She can't get out much, so I try to spend some time with her on the weekends. Thought you might like to meet the lady your dog's so much in love with."

He meant to get a laugh out of her but she couldn't laugh. The silence stretched until it was raw.

"I miss you," he said. Her fingers felt numbed with strain where they gripped the phone. "Picking you up tomorrow morning, right? Ten-thirty?"

"Yes. Ten-thirty." She focused on the memory of his beard rasping her skin. "I can't wait to see you."

"Yeah," he murmured. "I need to get in your apartment and check on that window tomorrow."

"You finished the window days ago."

"Well, I like to be sure about these things. Might take a while."

"How long?" She curled in closer to the phone as if it were the only warm place in the world, feeling him ghostly against her back the way he'd been in the shower.

"Oh, hours." His voice dropped an octave and stroked her like a hand. "Gotta put these things in just right. Make sure you're satisfied with the work."

"I'm a pretty tough customer, you know."

"Well, I'll just have to try harder."

She trailed her fingers down the smooth cool plastic of the phone. She was not quite trembling now.

"John Lee?" she murmured. "Where are you?"

"In my car in the middle of goddamn nowhere. On my way to a job way the hell out in Geiger. That's why I left you the cell phone number. I didn't want to miss your call." She could almost feel his smile. "Wish to hell you were here."

"I want you to do something for me," she said, and closed her eyes. "Pull over."

"Now?"

"Pull over to the side of the road and stop."

"Any particular reason?"

"Please."

"Okay." A few seconds later, he said, "I'm stopped. What?"

She unbuttoned her blouse and slid it off her shoulders, reached around behind to unsnap her bra catch.

"I want you to close your eyes," she said. "And unzip your pants."

"Damn, Abby, you're not serious." A pause. "Are you?"

She wiggled out of her blue jeans, taking a breathless, frantic pleasure in the feel of the bedspread along the back of her legs, the cool air on her thighs. She slipped her fingers into the elastic of her panties.

"I miss you," she whispered. "I'm thinking about pulling down your pants—"

"Oh, Jesus, Abby—"

"—kissing my way up your thighs, inch by inch—"

"They teach this in music school?"

"I'm a woodwind player."

His breathing was labored, raspy in her ear. The pressure of her hand was suddenly John Lee's hand, sliding slowly down the soft skin of her belly. She listened to him say her name in whispered groans.

"Oh, my God, I can't believe we're doing this," he said. But his voice was unsteady and breathless. She whispered his name and started to tell him things, things she'd never believed she could imagine, let alone say, things she wanted and needed and in the middle of it she heard him holding his breath, heard the creak of the car as he moved.

And then a long, whispering moan, uneven and gusty. She closed her eyes and could almost taste him, could feel his hands on her like ghosts.

The orgasm caught her by surprise, building like a tidal wave, hot blinding flashes clenching her thighs and trapping her fingers.

"Oh, God—" she gasped.

"Are you coming?" His voice stroked her. "Tell me you're coming."

"Yes. Yes. I'm coming. Yes."

"I want to see your face. I want to watch you." His voice went deeper, touching her spine, her thighs. "I want to be with you, Abby. Can you feel me?"

"Yes. Oh, God, yes." She collapsed into breathless laughter, muscles aching from the force of it, and curled on her side with the phone close. Tingles of heat rippled through her body like bright aftershocks. "Tomorrow," she promised. "First thing."

"In the car?" he asked.

"You want to do it in the car?"

He chuckled, tickling her deep inside. "Don't know about that. Could get us arrested and you know what they do to schoolteachers who disappoint the school board."

"Tar and feather us."

"Burn you in the town square."

"Okay. I can wait until we get on the road." She rolled over on her back and stared up at the ceiling. "John Lee?"

"Yeah?"

"You better hurry or you'll be late for your job."

The memory of his laugh warmed her even after the phone was back on the receiver, and his ghost stayed with her, warm at her back.

She was too drained to go to a party, but she'd promised, after all, and as she looked at the clock she realized that she'd have to hustle to be dressed when Benny arrived.

Still, she took another five minutes, holding the memory of him close.

Her dress was the most partylike thing she owned. It was short, black, and had a neckline that plunged nearly an inch lower than she usually wore them. She tried to creatively fluff her hair, always a mistake, and managed to salvage the experiment with hair spray. As she was considering the merits of coverstick and pale purple eye shadow, a crescendo of knocks announced Benny's arrival.

For a Saturday night party, Benny was positively funereal—a black pantsuit, for one thing, with only a little neon green piping and a huge matching green bow catching her cornrows into a ponytail at the base of her neck. She looked like George Washington on acid.

Abby stepped aside to let her in.

"So," Benny said, and sat down on the bed and bounced lightly. "Cool dress."

"Thanks." Abby leaned against the door and crossed her arms. "Nice bow."

Benny nodded and looked around the room without any real interest but great enthusiasm. "Nice place." She nodded again, eyes fixed on a pallid fake-Monet print hung over the bed. "So, are we still friends?"

"Still," Abby agreed. "I'm sorry, Ben, I guess I got a little freaked out."

"*You* did." Benny blew out her breath and flopped back on the bed. "Hey, I been to a lot of psychic readings and séances and past-life regression self-realizations, and I *never* saw anything like what happened to you, no shit. You got something big in there, Abby. I wish to hell you'd listen to Mik. He knows what he's talking about. He's not some Gypsy telling fortunes in a circus, he's—"

"I don't want to talk about Miklos," Abby said flatly, cutting through Benny's speech like a knife. "I don't want to talk about any of your psychic friends or your tea leaves or your tarot readings. Clear?"

"Yeah, clear. You ever looked at a hotel ceiling?"

Abby blinked and tilted her head up. Spackling.

"What about it?"

"Sometimes they put hidden messages on them. You know, like, *Sleep here more often, Buy our souvenirs*, that kind of thing. Subliminal advertising.

Works great because it's the last thing you see before you go to sleep and the first thing when you wake up."

"You're kidding," Abby said, and shot her a look to be sure. Benny's lips twitched. "You are kidding."

"Made you look." Benny sat up on the edge of the bed, hands braced on either side, and bounced up and down. "Come on, Abby, I'm not the enemy. Really."

"I know." Abby crossed over to the closet and pulled out her coat and the thin black evening purse she'd inherited from her mother. "I just don't want to talk about any of that again, okay? Just let it go."

Benny said doubtfully, "I will if you will."

"I already have."

The Meyerson Symphony Center had been built with the specific intention of making Dallas a world-class performance site. Abby couldn't help but feel that the building had a kind of calculated, desperate hipness, like designer grunge. She entered the huge glass doorway and the cold tap of her heels on marble made her shiver. The marble was, of course, genuine. The grimly classical lighting had inch-thick frosted glass shades. Overhead, chandeliers sparkled like the showroom of Cartier's.

And this was just the foyer.

"Some joint, huh?" Benny dug a sharp elbow into her side and raised her eyebrows. "Typical Dallas. Spend more for the frame than the picture. Musicians never get paid for shit, no matter where they play."

"Well, it's certainly expensive," Abby said. She

couldn't imagine what it must be like to play someplace like this. God, she'd have to buy a whole new
wardrobe. Benny crooked her finger at her and led
her to one of the sets of dark wooden doors that
marched along the marble walls.

"Wait'll you see this," she said, and swung the
door open. Abby stuck her head cautiously inside
and looked.

Inside was Europe, only bigger. Inch-thick carpet-
ing, graceful velvet seating, tiered boxes and balcon-
ies layered like jeweled pastry up to a confectioned
ceiling. And the centerpiece—stiff, glossy choir seats
above the stage, framing the golden spires of a huge
pipe organ as much art as instrument. Everything
gleamed like new gold. Abby let out her breath and
stepped back, shaking her head.

"It's so goddamn elegant it makes your teeth
hurt," Benny said, nodding. "C'mon. The party's
upstairs."

The Meyerson had been built to be a civic facility
as well as concert hall, and the Courier party had
been booked into one of the large ballrooms with
windows overlooking the foyer below. Of course,
Benny knew people. She always knew people. At the
top of the sweeping, *Gone With the Wind* stairs, she
knew the woman lounging artfully against the rail—
a plasticized, aerobically toned model with a professional look of boredom. She greeted Benny with
chilly, artificial glee.

"Ben-*in*-a," she cooed, a shark's calculation in her
aqua eyes. "Wherever have you been keeping
yourself?"

"Oh, hi." Benny offered a thin smile. "Renata Harhuis, meet my friend Abigail."

Renata offered a limp cool hand, palm down. Abby wondered if she should genuflect and kiss the large diamond ring glittering on the woman's middle finger.

"A pleasure." Renata's voice matched her skin, cool and pale. "I suppose you would be one of Max's students."

"I was," Abby answered. "And you?"

"Renata's a stand-up comic," Benny said, and grinned at Renata's obvious glare. She captured Abby's shoulder and propelled her down the hall, tossing an offhand " 'Bye" over her shoulder.

"That was rude," Abby observed, and concentrated on making sure she didn't catch her heels in the thick, mushy carpet.

Benny sighed happily. "Wasn't it? I usually save the Queen Bitch for later in the evening, like dessert, but I couldn't resist. Oh, don't worry about offending her. She's just a string player, you know how they get." Benny craned her neck and her face lit up. "Oooh, there's Alexis. Man, he's delicious. Want to meet him?"

"Not really. Benny, can we just—"

Alexis, a relentlessly gorgeous male model with perfect cheekbones and a genial air of vacancy, yielded fifteen minutes of gossip about a trombone player who was having an affair with the wife of an assistant conductor. What details he didn't know he apparently was willing to make up. His faux-European accent kept slipping to reveal flat Midwest vowels—farm boy, Abby guessed, looking for the cover of *GQ*. Also, apparently, a singer, which was why Benny thought him worth the time of day.

After a good thirty minutes more gossip, gleaned from six different people, they achieved the actual doorway of the party. The room was crowded with fashionably dressed people in various styles of formal black; the few exceptions—one adventurous, terminally sexy size-three woman in a tiny red dress, and one incredibly large woman in sea-green chiffon—stood out like M&Ms on black velvet. Onstage a string quartet packed up their instruments, chatting idly as if they'd just finished a practice session and not a performance.

Benny snagged a passing waiter and relieved him of two bubble-thin flutes of champagne. Abby took hers with a doubtful frown that disappeared as she tasted the vintage. No wine-in-a-box, not for this crowd.

"Max is in the corner—see him?" Benny pointed her glass toward a knot of people to the left; at the center, nearly invisible in the crush, stood a short, neat little man with white hair and a vivid, mobile face. Abby couldn't help a smile at the sight of him, the man who'd harassed her, through jokes and cajoling and silly, ridiculous threats, to excel in what she loved. She didn't know of any student who didn't love him, and wouldn't miss him, and although she held him in special regard she thought that he probably didn't much remember her—he'd had thousands of students in his long career, many of them far better than she'd ever been.

"He's busy," she said, and sipped champagne. "Wow. So who are all these people?"

"Well, of lot of the symphony folks, of course—and the major symphony contributors, of course, because we can't leave the money out of a party. Phi Mu Alpha. His relatives. His students. Folks who just wandered in off the streets." Benny shrugged elaborately and, for once, didn't jingle. "Anyway, it's a freebie. Hey, you ever heard these people?"

The string quartet was gone from the small raised stage at the far end of the room, and three young women—all red-haired—and a young dark-haired man were taking over. No instruments, Abby noted, except for a single guitar in one of the women's hands.

"Never," she admitted. "Singers? That's unusual, for a crowd like this."

Benny knew what she meant, of course—classical crowds generally preferred quiet chamber music, familiar tunes, nothing too distracting. If they had a singer, it was usually a refugee from the opera, doing one or two numbers. This looked . . . interesting. Different.

Without any visible signal, the young woman with the guitar started playing, but the music was lost in the babble of conversation. Until the voices began.

The only thing Abby could compare it to was the chandeliers glittering overhead—pure, cool, crystalline, perfect. Their voices blended seamlessly, not into harmony but into something that couldn't be separated into individual notes, not even by trained ears. All around the room, people fell silent—even the notoriously jaded society patrons. The song sounded old, older than classical, with a kind of alien beauty that Abby couldn't identify.

"Like them?" Benny asked, fox-sharp face bright. She already knew the answer. "They call themselves the Ravens. Miklos asked them to sing. Trust him to find something really cool."

Mention of Miklos drove all of the pleasure away, brought with it an irrational surge of fear and rage. Abby didn't want to think about him, about what had happened to her in his coffee shop. She turned away from the stage to look Benny in the eye, or try to, because Benny seemed suddenly fascinated by anyone and everyone in visual range.

"He's here, isn't he?"

"Well, fuck, Abby, I can't help that. Mik's popular. He's invited *everywhere.* Be nice, okay?"

"So what do you think, Benina, are they superb?" Miklos' voice came from just behind Abby's shoulder; she spun and backed away at the same time, nearly upsetting a passing waiter's tray of glasses. Miklos immediately held out his hands in apology, frowning. "Forgive me, please. I didn't mean to frighten you. Are you feeling better, Abby?"

"She's just a little jumpy," Benny said in a desperate rush. "Come here and say hi, big boy."

Miklos stepped into Benny's warm, intimate hug. He kissed her neck and, apparently inspired by her laugh, worked his way down to the notch of her collarbone. Benny pushed him back, face flushed, eyes bright. It was comical, and designed to take some of the edge off of Abby's resentment.

It didn't work.

Miklos turned to Abby, smile fading, and offered her his hand. She didn't take it. After a moment he lowered it to his side.

"Feeling better?" he asked. He looked surprisingly elegant in his loose white shirt and black vest. His eyes held regret.

"I'm just fine." She heard a sharp edge of Texas accent in her voice that wasn't usually there. She took another step back. "Excuse me if I don't want to discuss it right now. We're supposed to be at a party. Or are you working? Got a table set up in the corner with a crystal ball?"

"Abby!" Benny protested. "Hey, Mik, she—"

"Didn't mean it," he finished, and inclined his head. "I understand. It must be upsetting for you. It will take time to get accustomed to the idea."

"What idea?"

Miklos shot Benny a look. She spread her hands helplessly and shook her head.

"What idea?" Abby demanded.

"I thought you didn't want to—"

"What idea!" She was talking too loud, heads were turning. She felt a moment of regret for disrupting the Ravens' perfect harmony, but her anger wouldn't go away, and her fear wouldn't let him have the initiative.

Miklos studied her carefully. "What you are remembering must be a past life. The woman Pearl you remember, she is you. Was you. You see?"

"That's bullshit." The people closest were giving her quick, nervous glances, aware of the violence that lurked just under her words. Miklos' eyes turned wary. "You're a fake. All you want is money."

He shrugged and turned his hand as if pouring something out of it. "I will not try to change your mind. But if you remember this woman's life, and her death, perhaps it is meant for you to put something right."

Around them, the Meyerson glittered like an over-decorated Fabergé egg. The Ravens sang on in their heartbreakingly pure voices; the people nearest her stared and stared. People always stared, didn't they?

"Right?" Abby repeated. "What do you mean, put it right?"

"I mean that perhaps Pearl wants you to bring the truth to light. Perhaps her murder has never been solved. It is even possible that it has never been reported. Have you thought of that?"

Inside, that part of her whispered, *Yes.* Miklos' eyes were too dark, like the dark that got all over everything. He saw too much, knew too much.

"I don't want to talk about it," Abby said, and walked away. Benny called after her but she kept walking, head high, chin up. She joined another group of people, hanging politely on the outskirts. They were talking politics, four artsy pale liberals and one healthy, tanned Republican man who looked as if he owned the tuxedo he wore.

Out of the corner of her eye she saw Benny start after her, but Miklos put a hand on her shoulder and held her back. Benny turned, shoulders set in angry square lines, and strode off toward the bar in the corner of the room.

"You look hungry."

Abby focused in surprise on a red skewer of cheese cubes that appeared at eye level, turned slightly, and found the man who held it out. He looked like the kind of man who lived for a party, a little wild around the eyes. When she shook her head he bit off the cheddar cube on the top of the skewer and chewed enthusiastically.

"I know you," he mumbled. "Abby, right? We went to Cincinnati together."

He *did* look vaguely familiar, after all. She frowned, thinking about it, and said, "Piano?"

"Violin. Larry Colchester, remember? We built a snowman outside the studios one day."

She *did* remember, oh, God. Larry, the sole wild fling of her college days. Half an hour in the snow, making obscene snow sculptures, another ten hours inside by the fireplace with peppermint schnapps. He was the first stranger she'd ever gone to bed with.

Before John Lee.

"Sure, I remember," she said, fighting the sunburn heat of a blush. "How have you been?"

"Ah, okay, you know. Kicked around for a while, finally got a chair in the Denver Phil, doing all right. I'm down here with my wife, Yvette—you remember Yvette, right? Clarinet, probably a year after you."

Yvette was a squeaky, rather bitchy blonde who'd once tried to break Abby's reed on the way into an audition. Abby pasted a smile on and tried to look enthusiastic about the reunion as Larry looked around for his wife and waved her over.

Yvette had put on some weight in the last few

years, enough to make her low-cut dress seem desperate instead of sexy. She wore too much makeup and had already, from the way she clutched Larry's arm for support, had too many drinks too early.

"Abby," she cooed, sweet as cyanide honey. "I heard you were teaching in . . . where was it?"

"Midland."

"Oh, yes, Midland." Yvette let the silence drag on. "Well, isn't that nice. Larry's with the Denver Phil."

"Yes, I know, he told me." Abby cleared her throat. "How about you?"

"Oh, this and that." Yvette made a wide, sweeping gesture that almost clotheslined a diamond-sparkled symphony matron behind her. "You know. I'm holding out for one of the really big orchestras."

What she meant was that she hadn't won an audition since she'd left Cincinnati. Abby knew it was cheap to take any satisfaction from that, but that didn't necessarily stop her.

And then she noticed Larry watching her. *Oh, no*, she thought. There was that light in Larry's eyes, just like she remembered it. He was living some little fantasy here—maybe just the tension between his wife and a woman he'd slept with, maybe something more than that. Maybe he had something more exotic planned.

She looked around, spotted Benny's neon-green hair bow bobbing through the crowd, and said quickly, "Gosh, I'm sorry, I need to find my ride. Larry, it's been great seeing you again. Yvette, best of luck."

As she hurried away she heard Yvette say, too loudly, "Midland. Jesus, what a loser."

There were too many people, too many smiles, too many hands. She felt faint and sick as she pushed through the crowd, had to grab for support on the shoulder of an old gentleman with the hawk-sharp face of a conductor. He gave her a bristly stare from under caterpillar eyebrows.

Out. Something black bubbled up from just below her stomach. *Get out of here. Out!*

Her heels dragged in the thick hungry carpet and she passed the double doors, the music dying behind her, leaving only the stupid babble of a hundred different conversations. She passed the corpse-pale Renata Harhuis, who stopped her conversation to stare at her and say something cutting. Abby plunged down the stairs, ankles threatening to turn with every step, and stopped halfway down to breathe in deep, cool, unobstructed gasps.

Behind her, a man's voice called, "Pearl?"

She stopped, one hand on the cool wooden rail, and turned. Miklos stood at the top of the stairs near Renata. His face was tense and pale.

"I'm sorry but I felt you needed help. Don't you?"

Benny made a motley shadow at his shoulder. Abby swallowed her panic and forced her back straight, her voice steady.

"My name's not Pearl. It's Abby. And I don't need your help, any of you. Never have."

She turned away from the hurt on Benny's face and ran down the stairs in the foyer, dress swirling cool around her thighs. Outside, the dark pressed against the windows like one big mouth, waiting to eat. She gulped down panic and found a thick padded bench to sit down on, one hand over her mouth to cover the moans.

"He's not right," she whispered to herself, and balled her fist to pound it hard on her leg. "He's . . . not . . . right."

Then who am I? that part of her whispered.

Pearl. John Lee's mother's name is Pearl.

"No. No." Abby took a deep breath and put her hands down flat on her thighs, smoothed the black fabric of her dress. "I'm all right. I'm fine."

"Sure you are," said a voice from behind her. She twisted around to look behind her and found an older woman standing shadowed by the stairs, a thin cigarette held in her equally elegant fingers. She tapped ashes into a potted plant with bored abandon. "I always talk to myself when I'm doing just fine. Forgive me, I'm rude. Mrs. Georgette Caulfield."

"Abby Rhodes," she mumbled automatically—she didn't want to talk, but she couldn't seem to stop, either.

Mrs. Caulfield raised a plucked eyebrow. "My. You children of the sixties really didn't fare well, did you? I suppose you're one of those tiresome music people. They're all so dreadfully self-centered. Would you like a cigarette, dear?"

She held out a gold foil package. The cigarettes all looked thin and elegant, nicotine on a diet. Abby shook her head.

"God, not another health nut. This town is rotten with them. I suppose you eat tofu as well, whatever that is. Tell me, dear, what is it that you're assuring yourself isn't right?" Mrs. Caulfield took a drag and exhaled a gray stream into the air. "About a man, is it?"

"Not—not exactly. Yes, I'm a musician. What do you do, Mrs. Caulfield?"

"I spend money, dear. I have made a thriving career of contributing to causes I care absolutely nothing about. Oh, *do* tell me your problems. It'll liven up an otherwise dreary week. Or need I buy you a drink first? You don't look like a drunk, but then most of my friends don't."

"I don't think you'd understand my problems." Abby shoved her hairspray-stiff hair back from her face. "There's some people upstairs I don't want to talk to."

"Life is too short to talk to anyone you don't want to, dear. Rudeness is an important social skill. Do you want to leave?"

"I was going to catch a cab but . . ." Abby looked out at the dark pressing on the windows.

"Cabs." Mrs. Caulfield tapped ashes over a philodendron. "My God, child, not public transportation, surely things aren't as bad as all that."

"I think . . ." Something moved out in the dark—someone walking past, or a car cruising by without lights. "I think I may have information about a murder."

Mrs. Caulfield sat down on the bench beside her, facing the opposite direction. Her perfume settled like a fine mist of White Shoulders. Up close, the dove-gray silk dress looked hand-tailored, the beads individually sewn. Her earrings were rich clusters of diamonds and pearls. She very deliberately did not look at Abby.

"How very interesting. I've never met anyone involved with a murder." Mrs. Caulfield thought it over, tilting her perfectly groomed head to one side. "No, that's not quite true, there was that dreadful Parkinson boy, but that wasn't really a *murder*, that was quite sordid. I think all the best murders are intriguing, don't you? None of those messy crimes of passion. Yours wasn't a crime of passion, was it?"

"I don't know." Abby rubbed her hands together, remembered the numbing, tingling pain of snakebite. "I don't even know if it really happened."

"I'm hardly an expert, of course, but you really ought to be sure about these things before you start talking about them. Otherwise people will simply think you are insane."

"I'd like to be sure." Tears stung Abby's eyes, and she blinked them back out of terror for her mascara. "I don't know what to do about it."

"Start with a practical solution," Mrs. Caulfield said. "Go to a psychiatrist."

"What?"

"I've never met a problem that couldn't be solved by someone paid two hundred dollars an hour." She seemed perfectly serious. "Oh, I do understand, not everyone can afford the best. I suppose a hundred-and-fifty-dollar rate would do. The point is to feel the money flowing out of your pocket. It has such a healthy effect."

"I'm a musician, Mrs. Caulfield," Abby pointed

out. "I don't think I'll be able to afford that kind of solution."

"No?" The older woman unsnapped her beaded purse and pulled out a handful of business cards. "Where do you live, dear?"

"Midland."

"Well, well. You know, I have a cottage there in Midland. My late husband built it during the oil boom. I go there when I'm feeling sentimental." The cream-colored card she handed over said RICHARD D. URDIALES.

"You have a psychiatrist in Midland?"

"Midland, Dallas, Houston, New Orleans, Los Angeles, New York. And one out in Saint Thomas, if I'm feeling very low." Mrs. Caulfield stood up and crushed out her cigarette against the brass planter. "You're an interesting child, Abby. Thank you for an entertaining few minutes. God knows they are few and far between in this life. I'll call Richard and tell him to expect your call."

"But I can't—"

"I'll tell him to put it on my account." Mrs. Caulfield offered her a handshake in farewell. "Believe me, child, it certainly won't matter to me."

She strolled off, in no particular hurry, and gave orders to a uniformed chauffeur who stood near the entrance. He touched his cap and disappeared out into the dark. Mrs. Caulfield turned and proceeded up the stairs, her dress sweeping in an elegant beaded fan behind her.

Near the middle of the ascent, she turned and leaned slightly over the rail.

"Now, you will call him, won't you?"

"Yes, ma'am." Abby had no intention of doing it, but it seemed to be the only polite response. "Thank you."

Mrs. Caulfield had already dismissed her. Abby watched her until she disappeared into the crowd at the top of the stairs.

"Ma'am?" She turned to find the chauffeur standing behind her. He touched his cap and smiled. "I have the limousine outside. I'm to take you anywhere you want to go."

"The limousine?" Abby watched him for any sign that it might be a joke. "But—"

"Mrs. Caulfield's orders, ma'am." He gestured toward the doors. "It would be my pleasure."

If he was lying, he was a damn good liar. Abby cleared her throat and smoothed her dress down over her thighs.

"Sure," she said, and smiled. "I've never been in a limousine before."

He gave her a wide smile as he opened the door for her.

"Oh, I think you'll like it just fine, ma'am."

In the morning, Abby caught a cab to the airport— quite a come-down from the opulent purring luxury of Mrs. Caulfield's limousine, which had been the experience of a lifetime. She lounged in the boarding area, half asleep, and jerked back awake as the intercom blared out a message that ended in "... Gate Twenty-seven." She looked around and saw the other passengers standing up, gathering baggage,

shuffling into a rough semicircle around the closed
boarding doors. Obviously they had better hearing
than she did. She grabbed her bag and shuffled into
line, too, clutching her blue plastic boarding pass. It
looked like a wolfhound had chewed on it, but she
thought it said 17 on the top.

"Hey! Hey, wait!" Somebody in lime-green stretch
pants leaned over the railing and waved. "Damn,
Abby, wait! Please!"

Benny. She'd called the hotel, of course, but Abby
hadn't answered and had thrown away the phone
messages. Too late to duck out now. Abby sighed
and stepped out of place; somebody surged in to
claim it. She approached the rail where Benny
waited.

"Hi," Benny said. She looked bruised around the
eyes. Her smile looked weak and bruised, too.
"You okay?"

"Yeah." Abby looked at a point over Benny's
shoulder, a safe middle distance. "I'm fine. How was
the party?"

"Bummer. A total waste. Five more minutes and
you could have had a ride. Did you take a cab?"

"A limousine." Abby risked a look at her friend's
face. "You and Miklos looked cozy. I didn't think
you'd miss me."

"Of course we—" Benny stopped and blew her
cheeks out. "No offense, Abby, but you're acting like
a total shit. I actually got out of bed before ten to
see you. You could at least give me a shot here."

Behind her, the boarding doors banged open and

a flight attendant called for passes one through thirty. Abby held up her blue pass. Benny squinted.

"Hundred seventeen."

"Seventeen," Abby corrected. "See you."

She hesitated, though, drawn by that wounded look on Benny's face. After a second or two, she reached over the rail. Benny met her halfway, and for a few heartbeats the warmth and Benny's cinnamon perfume held her safe from the memories.

And then she had to pull away, and the cold settled in again. She turned away from the darkness in Benny's eyes and hurried to wave her boarding pass at the harassed flight attendant. Just before she entered the shadows of the carpeted tunnel she looked back, but the rail was empty.

She wasn't actually sure that Benny had even been there, except for the fading scent of cinnamon clinging to her jacket.

The flight seemed slow and bumpy, full of crying babies and grumbling businessmen. Abby sat at a window and stared out at pale gray mist while the gray-suited woman next to her cursed under her breath and punched keys on a laptop as if they'd personally offended her. She tried to think about John Lee but memory shifted and turned sepia, as unreal—or as real—as Pearl Jordan and the pain of the snakebite. Reality ended now at her skin. Maybe she hadn't woken up at all; maybe she was still lying in a rented hotel room, dreaming Abby's life.

Her eyelids slipped shut, sealing out the plane, the clouds, the dream life. Against the curtain of darkness she saw the house again, sepia in sunset. She walked up the cracked concrete steps and swung the screen door open with a sharp squeal of metal. All the lights blazed in the living room, a feathery glow over thin carpet and threadbare chairs. The glass-fronted bookcase was shadowed with dust, the few books toppled sideways . . .

. . . as they had been since they came and took Pearl's mother away. Daddy had taken most of the books out and burned them in the backyard the day after Mother left; she remembered watching from her bedroom window while the fire spun higher and higher into the hot noon sky, blowing charred words up to the sun. He'd stayed out there in the heat until the fire was ashes whipped by the wind. Later, in the night, he'd turned on the lights.

All the lights. And he'd never turned them out again. Every week he'd gone to town and bought five brand-new light bulbs, stacking them in yellow cardboard piles in the hall closet. She remembered waking in the middle of the night weeks later, hearing him screaming. She'd had to go open one of the boxes and take the cool smooth light bulb into the darkness, unscrew the one that had burned out even though it was hot enough to scorch her fingers, and screw in the new one until the light flooded out over his staring eyes and open mouth. In a few seconds he'd stopped screaming and it was like it had never happened at all, except for her blistered fingers and the broken light bulb on the floor, as well as the blood where her bare feet had stepped on the sharp invisible pieces of glass.

She'd never cried. Neither of them had ever cried,

ever. They'd just gone on changing the light bulbs. She'd been real careful to do it before the old ones burned out, after that.

She never asked him what Mother had done, because she knew he'd never tell her. But the other children told her, mean biting whispers in the schoolyard, taunting yells as she ran for the safety of home and the bright lights.

Killed

Killed her own

Killed her own baby drowned it in the bath killed it killed it

Mother, staring blankly at the wall as she sat on the old couch, sweaty hair curling damp on her forehead. *Go to bed, Pearl. Go to bed.* There'd been something so cold in her eyes that Pearl had run down the hall and jumped in her narrow hard bed, pulled the faded quilts over her head, and waited, waited. It seemed like hours until the screen door screamed and she heard Daddy say, *What in the world's got into you, Anna, you look like you seen a ghost,* and then nothing, nothing at all until his heavy footsteps went down the hall and the bathroom door creaked open and he'd made this sound, this quiet sound.

Next day they came to take Mother away and they'd buried Baby Timothy at the Eternal Grace Cemetery in Midland, all the way to Midland with that small white casket, the smell of dying lilies and Daddy sitting there staring out into the gray afternoon.

Two nights later he'd woken up screaming about the dark. He'd told her all about the worms and the beetles and the skin slipping off little Timmy's bones, then he'd turned all the lights on.

On the day he'd died, she'd gone around and turned them off, every single one, and sat on the couch in the shadows while the beetles whispered and the worms crawled and the dark ate. They'd made her go out to the funeral at Eternal Grace, where Daddy was buried next to Timmy and a grave with her mother's name on it. When she'd come back she'd broken every light bulb in the house and when people came calling she didn't let anybody in at all. After a while they stopped coming, except for the boy who delivered the groceries and the preacher who kept knocking on the screen door every Saturday, asking her if she had accepted Jesus as her personal savior.

For so many years, nobody had come at all.

The plane bounced Abby hard, a full-body slap, and she came awake clutching the plastic armrests, panicked beyond reason, while a sweetly smiling flight attendant asked her for the untouched Diet Coke she still had sitting on the tray table in front of her.

The mist of clouds was gone, and the sky was a cool china blue, the sun a bright curve just visible over the wing of the plane. The ground below was geometric, like quilt blocks, neat straight roads and square fields, some stubbornly green even this close to Christmas. The land had a dry red haze to it.

Home. Abby leaned her forehead against the cool plastic window and closed her eyes.

But whose home was it?

Sonata:
December 11, 1994

He was the one thing in the world that still felt real to her, the clean musky smell of him folding her close an instant before his arms did. She clung to him and turned her face into the crook of his neck, pressed her lips against the warm beard-rough skin of his throat. He put his mouth close to her ear and said her name, just her name, and that was enough.

To her horror, she heard herself ask, "What was your grandmother's name, John?"

He moved back a little, looking down at her face, dark eyes puzzled but indulgent.

"Pop quiz already?" he asked, and leaned in to kiss her. She was hungry enough to eat him alive but there it was, the question, strange enough to separate them again once the kiss was done. "Anna. Why?"

She forced the questions back and brought out a smile for him instead. He reached for her carry-on bag and shouldered it. Around them deplaning passengers drawled greetings to friends and family, as business travelers stalked toward the cab stand near the baggage claim, a suited and polished herd with identical leather briefcases.

"Just wondered," she said. "I realized that I had some friends named Jordan in Dallas, but I don't think they're any relation. Funny thing is, one of them was named Pearl Jordan."

"Yeah?" John Lee's hand slid naturally into hers, warming her chilled fingers. "You know, my first girlfriend had the same birthday as my mother. Life's full of strange stuff like that. So, breakfast, and you tell me all about those men you went dancing with in the big city."

His tone was teasing but there was something in the words that alerted her. He was watching her face carefully.

"I didn't dance with anybody," she said. "Jealous already?"

He thought about it with a rueful expression settling over his face. "Maybe. Guess I shouldn't be doing that?"

She punched him in the shoulder. "I didn't dance with anybody, John, and if I had it wouldn't matter. I missed you."

"Yeah, I got that impression on the phone last night."

The memory of it made her blush hotly, from forehead to toes. The memory, and the gentle sexy rasp of his voice, pitched low for her ears. No matter how real Pearl might seem, no matter how strange the memories, *this* was real, *he* was real. She could bear the rest of it, for this.

"Let's skip breakfast," she said. They began a slow walk toward the long snaking conveyor belts of baggage claim, the freedom of the parking lots beyond.

The flat chill of the wind surprised her as they passed through the electronic doors, though the whisper of dust across her face didn't. "It's gotten colder?"

"Yep. Weather says it'll probably snow again tomorrow, this time dump a bundle on us. No breakfast?"

They ventured out into the broad yellow crosswalk. A sun-rusted pickup truck rattled to a stop for them. Once they were in the parking lot John Lee nodded toward his car, parked two rows over. She tugged him to a stop.

"John . . ." She searched his face helplessly, waiting for words that didn't come. She wanted to tell him all of it, everything, but the hard cold pressure of Pearl inside stopped her. If it was Pearl, if it wasn't Miklos and Benny and LSD in her tea. John waited, eyes slowly warming to concern. "I'm too hungry for breakfast."

Even out here, in the cold wind, she felt the temperature between them suddenly shift upward, bodies acting on a shared thermostat. He stepped forward and cupped her face in one hand. She closed her eyes and leaned into the warmth.

"I'm starting to get a little hungry myself," he said, and his lips touched hers, soft at first and then strong, sensuous and skillful. The taste of his tongue in her mouth sent an electric shock through her nerves. She wound her fingers in his soft, curly hair and dimly wondered if anybody was watching them, thirty-year-old teenagers necking in the parking lot. She decided she really didn't give a damn.

What she did give a damn about was getting to the car.

The road was nearly deserted—not a lot of cars went to Fall Creek, for any reason, and even fewer went on Sunday mornings. John Lee drove moderately fast, listening to her talk about the party and Benny's mother; they both pretended that she didn't have her hand on his leg, gradually moving up until her fingers were gently massaging the bulge in his blue jeans. As she fit her hand over it he pulled in a deep breath.

"Sounds like you had a pretty good time," he said, voice gone deeper in his throat.

"I plan to keep it up, if you're willing."

John Lee glanced down at her hand, lips quirking in a grin. "Looks like I might be willing to give it a try."

She massaged him in a slow circle and slid her fingers up to open the top button on his jeans. His back straightened.

"Now, Abby . . ."

"Want me to stop?" She tugged gently at his zipper, easing it down a couple of slow clicks.

"Now, how the hell am I supposed to answer that? I'm just scared if that zipper comes down it ain't going back up real easily." He stopped talking as she finished unzipping.

"How far to the house?" she asked.

He had to think about it. "Twenty more minutes. Abby—"

"Let's pull over." She had her hand inside his

pants now. *Bad girl*, she thought absently. *You have become a very bad girl. When did this happen?*

"You sure?"

"If you don't pull over you're going to have to drive with one hell of a distraction," she said, and leaned over.

The car jerked to the right and crunched gravel as it slowed and stopped. She sat up, meeting his eyes. He turned the engine off.

"I haven't done this since I was sixteen," he said. "Not even sure I remember how."

"I think it'll come back to you," she murmured, and reached for the lever under his seat. He looked surprised as he slid backward from the wheel. "Trust me."

She had just peeled his underwear back when she heard an engine behind them. John Lee heard it at the same second and looked up at the rearview mirror. His expression blanked, as if he couldn't believe what he was seeing, and then he pulled his underwear up and fumbled with the zipper on his pants.

A cop in a khaki uniform tapped on the window. He had on a Stetson hat and mirrored aviator glasses, and there was something about the face but she couldn't place it in the fury of her embarrassment. John Lee slowly rolled down the window.

"What do you want, Terry?" John Lee asked, staring not at the cop but out at the road. She remembered him now, the grinning bastard from John Lee's house, impeccably pressed. He wasn't grinning now, but he looked satisfied.

"Step out of the car, sir," he said, so polite it was

unnatural. The rage that simmered in John Lee's eyes was frighteningly close to breaking out. Abby grabbed his hand in hers and squeezed hard, hard enough to make him look at her.

"It's okay," she said. He nodded as if he didn't really believe it and stepped out into the cold air.

Terry looked him up and down.

"You always ride around with your johnson hanging out, Mr. Jordan?" Terry asked evenly. John Lee, without replying, zipped his pants. "That might be a ticket for indecent exposure. Let me see your license."

"Oh, for God's sake, Terry—"

"Show me your license," Terry said. His lips parted in a smile, showing big square teeth. "Now, you don't want to make trouble for the little lady, do you?"

John Lee froze, one hand still on his zipper, watching Terry's reflective shades. After a few seconds he slowly reached in his back pocket and pulled out his wallet. Terry showed his teeth.

"Take it out of the plastic, sir."

John Lee held out the license. Terry took it without even tilting his head down to look at it.

"Proof of insurance, sir."

"Terry—"

"Now, sir."

John Lee's breath steamed white on the freezing wind. "It's in the car. Want me to get it?"

Terry's smile thinned to just his lips. He stepped back and bent to look through the car window; Abby couldn't see his eyes, but she felt them focus on her, hot as lasers. He straightened and walked around the car, slow grating steps on the gravel.

"Leave her alone," John Lee said, so quietly it was almost lost on the wind. Abby's door creaked open and Terry motioned to her.

"Out, ma'am." His sunglasses swiveled up sharply toward John Lee. "Sir, you stay right there. Don't move."

She slid out of the car and into the cold air; Terry was taller than she'd remembered. She focused on the first thing at eye level—his badge. Her face was a dim smudge on the spotless cheap metal.

"The insurance is in the glove compartment," John Lee said. "Don't do this, Terry."

"Turn around, ma'am," Terry said. "Hands on the car."

"What?" she blurted. His smile disappeared. "Okay, okay. Like this?"

She turned, pressed her palms flat on the roof of the car. On the other side, John Lee's eyes were narrow and dark and focused not on her but on Terry. He looked like he might come across the hood at any moment.

Terry's hands shoved her forward, hard against the car. He kicked her feet wider apart and suddenly, horribly, she remembered the dream that wasn't a dream, her face pressed to the dusty coarse upholstery, a man's cruel weight on her back.

Terry began to slowly, leisurely run his hands down her legs.

"Terry!" John Lee snapped. He slammed his hands down on the roof of the car. Abby shook her head mutely, rejecting something, either Terry's invasive hands or John Lee's anger, she wasn't sure which. "Goddammit, she's not part of this! You want to play your pathetic little games, play them with me!"

"Just doing my job," Terry said. His hands moved up to her waist, slid up her sides and curved in toward her breasts. "Sir. You want to register a complaint, you just do that tomorrow at the station."

"It's okay," Abby said breathlessly. "John, please, it's okay. Don't piss him off."

"He's going to fuck around with us until he gets tired. Right, Terry?" John Lee showed his teeth, but it was far from a smile. "Why don't you come over here and pat me down? You afraid?"

Terry stopped with his hands cupping Abby's breasts. "You wouldn't want me to find some concealed weapon on her, would you, now, John Lee? I really don't think you want that."

"Officer?" she said, keeping her voice as even as she could. "You take your hands off me right now and I won't file a civil suit against you tomorrow. How's that for a deal?"

To her surprise, he did take his hands away. And then he slammed her hard against the car, hard enough that she saw real fear in John Lee's eyes. John Lee started to move but something—maybe some expression from Terry, behind her—made him freeze and spread his hands wide.

"I don't think you want to smartmouth me, missy," he whispered, breath hot like a tongue in her ear. "See, out here it's just you and me and ol' John Lee, and nobody believes him if he says the sun comes up in the east. And no big-city teacher is gonna win any goddamn suit against me, not in this county. Are we clear?"

"Yes." She bit the word off so hard she tasted blood in her mouth. "Let me go. Now!"

He kept her pinned for another couple of seconds, just to let her know he could, and then he stepped away. Before she could catch her balance he was gone, walking back toward his cruiser as if he'd forgotten all about them.

"Oh." He pivoted on one foot, halfway inside his cruiser, and flipped a square of white into the center of the road. "Your license, sir. Ya'll drive safely."

As the cruiser gunned past them out to the highway, spitting pea gravel like hail, John Lee turned to watch him go.

"John?" Abby asked.

He closed his eyes and took a deep breath. "Someday soon, it's gonna be him or me." He went out into the road and picked up his license, dusted it off absentmindedly against his pants, staring at the receding taillights of Terry's cruiser.

He tossed his license onto the dashboard. Once they were both in the car, both buckled securely in, she reached over and took his hand in both of hers.

"Promise me something," she said. He looked over at her, a quick glance that told her more than his words could how much Terry scared him. "Promise me that you won't do anything stupid because of me. He's not going to hurt me, you know that. He can't afford to. All he can do is push you."

He put the car in gear and peeled out on the road,

spraying gravel the way Terry had. The heater
blasted too warm in her face, but their hands felt
cold as ice. After a few seconds his fingers squeezed
hers, and some of the ice began to melt.

"Don't you underestimate him," he said. "Don't
ever do that. And don't ever think he won't hurt
you, 'cause he will."

"Why?"

John Lee glanced at his speedometer and eased off
the accelerator as the speed limit sign flashed by,
rotted by shotgun pellets. "Terry's my brother."

They sat in the living room where they'd first
made love—it seemed like years ago, she thought, as
she hung on the drowsy edge of sleep. She was
curled up in the embrace of his arm as he combed
his fingers through her hair in slow, regular strokes.
She turned her face toward his chest and breathed
him in. He adjusted the soft magenta and blue Indian
blanket closer around her shoulders.

"His name's not Jordan," she murmured. "Saw it
on his uniform. Terry Bollinger."

"Yeah, that's right. I guess I should have said my
half-brother." She opened her eyes wide enough to
see his half-smile. The tension had gone out of him
again, but the shadow was still there. "His mother's
always said his daddy was some truck driver from
Oklahoma, but everybody knows it's bullshit. He's
Grady's kid, all right."

"Brothers," she murmured. He looked down at
her, smile gone. "But your mother never admitted
it, either?"

"My mother's just about as stubborn as you are.
She told me I was my own man, didn't matter
whether my father was George Washington or Custer
Grady, all that stopped the minute I was born." His
fingers stopped their slow progress through her hair.
"Might've seemed right to her, but it's never that
simple, is it?"

She wrapped herself tighter in his arms and said,
"No. Never."

This is the only place I am warm, she thought.

"When I was ten years old Terry kicked my ass
for the first time and started telling me about Custer
Grady. Some of it was true, a lot of it just meanness.
I went back and I asked my mother, straight out. She
told me to ask her again in a year. Well, old Terry
wasn't in the mood to wait, so he and I went 'round
and 'round, every day, every year. I never asked her
again, and she never brought it up." His fingers
glided warm over the soft skin of her temples. "Some
things it's better to just live with."

"Like Terry?" She felt his stomach muscles stiffen
against her cheek. The name had that effect on him,
like he'd braced himself for a sudden attack. "Sometimes it's easier to have an enemy than nobody at
all."

When she opened her eyes he was staring at her
face, eyes naked and vulnerable, and what looked
out of them was so wounded her heart skipped in
alarm. In the next second it was gone, replaced by
the sardonic smile.

"Better the devil you know," he said softly. "Your

hair looks like I combed it with a vacuum. You hungry yet?"

She purred deep in her throat. His grin brought out laugh wrinkles around his eyes.

"Hungry for lunch, lady. We don't have time for anything else."

"Are you absolutely—" And then it hit her what he meant, what she'd completely forgotten about, between the dreams and seeing him again and Terry's dark shadow over everything.

They were supposed to have lunch with Pearl Jordan. Or the woman who claimed to be Pearl Jordan. For a second she felt panic so extreme she thought she might faint, and then the cold, hard-edged practicality she'd come to think of as Pearl slid to the front. She didn't want to go—wanted, in fact, to tell him all the reasons she couldn't go—but she couldn't. She got up from the couch, folded the blanket with quick, mechanical gestures, and picked up her purse and discarded coat.

John Lee was still sitting where she'd left him, watching her. She ran a distracted hand through her hair.

"Ready?" she asked. He stood up and nodded. "Then we'd better get going."

It was only a short drive down the highway to her memories; she felt her skin tighten when she saw the houses silhouetted against the cool blue winter sky, empty fields covered with veils of drifting red dust. The Jordan house looked different in the daylight. They'd painted it, she realized, bright white paint and light blue trim around the windows. In the far distance, the wreck of Custer Grady's farmhouse was a leaning corpse of sun-grayed boards and the gaping wounds of windows.

"They should've burned that," she said. John Lee, turning onto the dirt road that led up to his mother's house, glanced at her in surprise and saw where she looked.

"Nobody dared." It never occurred to him to ask how she knew whose house it had been; he just assumed everyone knew. Maybe everyone in Fall Creek did.

She turned forward and watched the warm white house drift closer. Dots of color clustered around the base of the walls resolved into yellow and purple winter pansies. That hadn't changed. The pansies had always been there, but not so many, never so many. Cool white lace curtains in the windows like frozen snowflakes. A smiling, red-cheeked cardboard Santa in the wide front window, where she remembered only dust and the thick backs of sun-rotted drapes.

John Lee had gotten out of the car and opened her door before she'd even realized they'd stopped. She locked eyes with him and wondered if he saw the fear in her, the dread, the longing to know, once and for all, if she was crazy or not.

The steps had been repaired—no more crumbled concrete, no more chicken-wire webbing showing through on the sides. There was a welcome mat outside the door; it was printed with a cheery Dutch house and stylized tulips. She wiped her feet on it, feeling ever more distant. Not even the cold wind seemed real now.

The new screen door made a hissing sound as John Lee pulled it open. She closed her eyes for a second, fighting back the dreams, and opened her eyes as he turned the knob.

She passed into memory.

The dusty old couch was gone, hauled away with its tattered matching chairs. Carpet covered the cold wooden floor she remembered. The new sofa was delicate beige with pastel flowered pillows. She froze when she saw the bookcase, glass-fronted, now holding a full collection of hardcovers and paperbacks. The broken pane she remembered on the bottom had been replaced.

The room was too dark. She remembered the blazing, relentless glow of Daddy's naked light bulbs, casting harsh shadows. This room was dim and soothing and airy, too open for safety.

From the kitchen, a voice called, "John Lee? Honey?"

He must have answered her but Abby didn't hear, couldn't hear anything but the sound of that *voice*, older now, thinned with age, but she knew it in her guts like a stab wound knew the knife. She swayed and braced herself with both hands on the smooth rounded corner of her mother's bookcase—*no, not her mother's, why was she thinking*—and in some strange part of herself she was glad, *glad*, as if she'd been waiting to hear it all her life.

John Lee had turned to look at her. She managed to force her lips into a smile.

"I feel dizzy," she said, which was nothing but the truth. He must have read it in her face because his arm slipped around her waist to help her. She leaned into his warmth, needy as a child.

I can't be here, she thought. The words came crystal and hammered at her with the weight of fact. *I can't be here and know these things. I have to go.*

"I have to go," she said aloud. John Lee's protest was noise. She pulled away from him, looking toward the safety of the doorway, the world outside that could be just the same as she'd left it, if only she left *now*—

"Are you all right, dear?"

She turned toward the voice even though she knew it was the end of everything, the end of herself, the end of John Lee, because this thing *could not be happening.*

The old woman smiled at her in concern and said, "Abby?" The right side of her face was a network of pale scars. Her right eye was covered with a black satin patch. Her right arm was twisted and withered, and she had it in a clean white sling, strapped close to her body.

Her left eye was the same warm, welcoming brown as John Lee's.

"Hello," Abby said in a pale whisper. The woman frowned in concern. She reached out to steady her but Abby flinched away into John Lee's close embrace. He guided her over to the new, clean sofa—wrong, it should feel coarse and lumpy and have the bitter taste of tears and dust—and said something about cold water. His hand covered her forehead with warmth but it wasn't real, nothing was real except that face, aged so many years.

Memory waited until she closed her eyes and then she fell into the dark, a cold hand around her ankle, and the face loomed out of the shadows, broken and ruined and bloody. All the wounds. So many wounds.

Abby opened her eyes and said, "I'm fine. Really. Just some water."

John Lee's mother hurried off to the kitchen, quick steps with a peculiar limp-shuffle rhythm. John Lee stayed where he was. His fingers traced light, soothing lines across Abby's forehead.

"Abby, I'm calling that doctor of yours," he said. She reached up to grab his wrist. "Damn, woman, don't argue with me, you're gray as a ghost. Just stay there."

"I'll be all right," she said, and poured all of her intensity, her desperation, into the words. "Please, John, don't. Go help your mother. I'll be just fine."

He drew back, frowning.

"One more spell and I'm driving you to the emergency room myself."

"Deal."

He watched her for another few seconds and finally, reluctantly, went to help his mother when she called his name. In the cold absence of him, she closed her eyes and breathed in the smell.

Home.

She was home again.

Nobody was going to take it away from her.

The lunch was baked turkey and cornbread dressing, smooth giblet gravy, sweet whole-cranberry sauce. Mrs. Jordan was a pie maker. She set out a coconut meringue, the top dusted delicate brown, and a refrigerated cocoa pie with thin shaved chocolate curls nested in whipped cream. Abby turned her dessert fork over and over in her fingers. She remembered the ornate flowered pattern, the old, heavy feel of it. This had been her mother's silver, obsessively polished and hoarded for special occasions. Daddy had sold most of it off, one piece at a time, to pay for Mama's treatments.

The plates were old, too, bone china turned delicate ivory with age, the winding rose pattern faded. Her dessert plate had a chip on the edge. She rubbed it with a thoughtful finger.

"Abby, honey, would you like some pie?"

She looked up into that ruined, age-softened face and wanted to leap up and stab her mother's fork into the deceptive, hypocritical smile. Instead, she said "Yes, please, the coconut looks great," and held out her plate for a slice.

The food tasted like dust on her tongue but she smiled and ate. The woman filled up her own plate with chocolate pie.

"John Lee tells me you're quite a musician," she said. "I used to love music, but I never was any good at it myself. How long have you been playing?"

"Since I was about twelve years old. Excuse me, do you have any more coffee?"

"Oh, lands, yes. Just one minute, I'll get it." Pearl pushed her chair back and started to rise. John Lee, mouth full of pie, shook his head and got up for her. Once he was turned away, Abby let her smile drop.

"I know," she said. Pearl looked up, a vague concern on her scarred face. "I know what you did."

The smile burned to ash. Pearl's skin turned a sudden dirty gray, and there was something terrible in her eyes, like death staring out. *That* was what she remembered, that death-face, coming out of the dark. In a flash it was gone, replaced by a brave, nearly convincing smile. Why did the woman have to look so *old*, so *vulnerable*?

"Why, honey, I don't know what you—"

"Let's go see. Why don't we go see." Abby shoved her chair back and stood up. The kitchen hadn't changed much, except for gleaming new appliances and a clean white floor; the door at the far end hadn't changed at all. The crystal doorknob glimmered like a diamond where the weak winter sunlight struck it.

"Abby?" John Lee turned away from the coffeepot, staring, a Pyrex beaker in his hand. "What're you talking about?"

She came around the table and pushed by him. As she reached for the doorknob, she heard Pearl's uncertain shuffling step behind her.

"Honey, if you're not well, why don't you lie down? There's nothing down there but—"

"But what?" Abby put her hand on the crystal. It was blood-warm, smooth as skin where her fingers touched it. "Did you tell him all about it? Is he protecting you?"

"Damn it, that's enough." John Lee left the coffee on the counter and came to rest his hands protectively on his mother's shoulders. "What the hell are you talking about?"

She opened the door. Cool, dark air breathed out, crawled over her skin.

"Pearl Jordan," she said, and stared into the woman's one good eye. "Isn't that right? I'm talking about Pearl Jordan."

The old woman fell back against John Lee, clutching at his hands. Her face twisted into a shape of pain.

"She's still down there, isn't she?" Abby demanded, and let go of the doorknob to take a step toward the old woman. John Lee held out his hand to stop her but she ignored it, intent on the ashen terror in the woman's face. "Rotting in the root cellar, isn't that right? Dead and rotting, and all this time you've been living her life—"

"I didn't," the woman whispered. "I don't know what you're talking about. Please—"

"Please? That's what *she* said, please, please don't kill me!" That *face*. It wasn't fair that she'd survived, that she'd had a son, that she'd lived so many good years that had rightfully belonged to someone else. Abby reached out in a white-hot fury, willing to kick, to punch, anything to get the truth out of her, but John Lee came between them. He grabbed her and slammed her back against the root cellar door. The crystal doorknob dug into her spine. She tore at his hands, leaving long scratches on his arms, but he held her there until she went limp.

He looked so scared. So scared of her. For a second she saw herself in his eyes and was terrified, too.

Pearl gave a low moan of pain and sagged against the kitchen counter. John Lee let her go and spun away to help his mother to a chair, to brush her thin silver hair back from her face. Abby fumbled at her back for the doorknob.

"Abby!" he shouted. She turned away from him into the dark, down the stairs, quick steps that turned slow and ceremonial on the fifth one. She paused and closed her eyes against the memory.

The smells were all the same—damp earth, that faint, never-ending taint of decay. She took the rest of the steps with her eyes shut, the feeling of falling only barely averted. She felt a ghost-hand close cold around her ankle. When she'd reached the flat dirt floor she fell to her knees and pressed both hands against the damp cool earth. For an instant she imagined the dirt moved and she felt the scrape of bony fingers along her palms, and then John Lee said from the top of the stairs, "Abby?"

She sat unmoving, staring into the darkness. The room was so quiet but it wasn't dead, not at all. The fury trapped in it seethed under her hands like twisting worms.

His weight made the steps creak. He flicked a switch and flooded the small room with bright light. On the shelves his mother kept canned goods with cheery bright labels, boxes neatly labeled and stacked. The floor was clean and even.

She looked up to where he stood, one hand still on the light switch. His eyes were wide and dark, looking for explanations, for a reason to forgive.

"Your mother isn't Pearl Jordan," she said. "Ask her. Ask her who she is."

He shifted his weight as if he thought about coming down to her, but he stayed where he was, watching her. The distance seemed more than a few wooden steps.

"I think you'd better come on home now."

"Ask her!" she screamed. The sound of her voice ran around the walls like a trapped, wounded animal. "Ask her who she buried down here! She's not Pearl Jordan, she never was, she's lying to you, she's been lying all along! You have to listen to me! You have to believe!"

He came down the steps carefully, one at a time, never taking his eyes off her. He held out one hand to her, half invitation, half warning. She showed her teeth to him, but it wasn't a smile. There was no smiling in this place.

"Come on," he said. He eased forward, gesturing her up. "Now, Abby, come on out of here. Right now."

She looked at the hand, the tense, wary face behind it.

"I need you to believe me, John. I need that."

He touched her cheek cautiously. When she didn't flinch away, his fingers closed around her arm and pulled her to her feet.

"I'm taking you home," he said. She closed her eyes and felt the fury seethe around her like invisible wind.

"I am home."

They'd driven thirty minutes, in silence, before he said, "I never should have taken you there."

"That's true." She turned her face away toward

the gloomy afternoon outside the passenger window. "I might never have known the truth."

He slammed his hand against the steering wheel. "Truth? What goddamn truth? You think my mother—who never did any harm to anybody in the whole goddamn world—*killed* somebody?"

"Not somebody," Abby said. "Pearl Jordan. The real Pearl Jordan. The one who had a mother who went insane and drowned her little boy and was committed to an asylum. The one whose father never turned off the lights. That Pearl."

He was quiet for so long that she thought she might have convinced him. When she looked she saw tears in his eyes, bright in a glimmer of sunshine.

"I'm not crazy, John," she said. "Please. I'm not crazy. She *did* kill her. She *did* take her place."

"When?"

She hesitated, trying to remember, but it had come in such confusing, out-of-sequence blocks. "Before you were born, I think. Pearl was living alone in the house and this—this *woman*—hid in the cellar and killed her with a shovel when she came down the stairs. I saw it, John. God, I don't want it to be true, I swear I don't, but it is."

He scrubbed at his face with his hand, wiping away the tears. When he didn't answer, she turned back to the road, the thin yellow ribbon of the highway divider unspooling on it. From time to time the ribbon wiggled, as if the painter had twitched.

"Will you help me?" she asked. The tires hummed and whined on rutted truck tracks in the road. "All I'm asking for is the truth, I swear. Justice."

"You going to get justice out of ruining a seventy-year-old woman?" he said. "Christ Almighty, you need help. More help than I can give you."

"You think I'm crazy?"

"What the hell am I supposed to think?" He slowed for the turn that would take them into Midland. Five minutes to her apartment. "You listen to me, Abby. You leave my mother alone. You go to her house again, try to make trouble, I'll call the police, I swear I will."

She smiled out at the clouds. "You going to call Terry into this? You really want to do that?"

He reached out and put his hand on her knee, not a friendly grasp but one designed to get her attention. She looked at him and saw his face stony with determination.

"I'll do whatever you make me do to keep my mother safe, Abby. I don't want to hurt you but I'm not going to let you come in and do this, I can't. You put me in the middle, you know which way I've got to fall."

On *Mom's* side, of course. Why believe anyone else's story? No reason he should.

Unless Abby could prove it to him, of course. But she had no doubt at all, looking at the barely suppressed anger in his eyes, that he meant what he said. If she came near the woman who called herself Pearl Jordan, he'd have to try to stop her.

She couldn't stay angry, not away from the house, away from *her.* The anger boiled away into grief thick as oil in her stomach. She watched the day float past, cold and bright, and tried to remember the perfection of that first morning, the vision of him turning in the shower, the taste of his skin.

"You're home," he said, and stepped on the brakes. She blinked and realized they were in the apartment parking lot, surrounded by old pickups and new sedans. A bundled-up neighbor unloaded groceries farther down the row. She dropped a big plastic bottle of soda and chased it as it bounced and rolled down the slight hill toward the sidewalk. "Abby? You never asked about Carlton."

She heard the name with a jolt like a slap—gone two days, and she'd never even thought to ask about her dog. John Lee had promised to feed him but couldn't keep him, of course, not in that house of his loaded down with breakable glass. "Isn't he okay?"

"He's fine. I just figured you might ask." He got out and popped the trunk on the car to retrieve her bag. She stepped out to the ground and took a deep breath of ice-cold air; it tasted of sharp burning mesquite and the not-quite-metallic tang of snow. She dug in her purse for her keys and heard him coming up the walk behind her.

As she slotted the key in the lock she heard Carlton start to bark and the last of her—Pearl's—anger bled away into affection. She opened the door and stepped in, ready for Carlton to leap on her and lick her face.

Instead Carlton barked, loud, angry, snapping sounds. His claws clicked as he scrambled backward, watching her.

"What's wrong?" John Lee asked, and eased in behind her. "Hey, boy. Hey there."

"Two days and he forgets who I am. I never said he was really . . ." She held out her arms toward the dog, smiling, and his lips pulled back, showing strong, sharp teeth. She'd never heard him growl that way before, a cold, stomach-deep grinding sound.

And then he lunged at her.

She screamed and tipped backward, head slamming into the door. The impact with the floor seemed strangely soft, the cool wood against her cheek fluffy as a down mattress. John Lee's legs moved in front of her. He had hold of Carlton's collar, holding him back, and all of a sudden Carlton wasn't the dog-demon anymore, he was whining in confusion and straining at John's hold on him. He gave a short, yipping bark of alarm and squirmed to get free.

"Abby?" It took her a second to realize John was saying her name. She got her hands under her and pushed up from the floor; the world tilted strangely and she felt the door at her back. Sitting up. "How's your head?"

"Fine," she said. Her ears felt stuffed with cotton. "Just a little dazed, that's all. What the hell was that?"

John Lee sat down, too, holding Carlton's collar. Carlton, now calm, sank down to his haunches and started panting, long pink tongue lolling.

"Maybe he didn't recognize you," John Lee said, and scratched Carlton's head. The dog closed his eyes and whined in happiness. "Look at that. Good dog."

Abby leaned forward and made it to her hands and knees, felt the first twinges of pain along the back of her scalp. She crawled over to where John Lee sat and sank down next to him, leaning into his warmth.

"You can let him go," she said.

"Sure?" When she nodded, John Lee let the dog go. Carlton climbed into her lap and licked her face, pausing to stare at her mournfully now and then. She scratched his neck and he sprawled possessively over her lap, head propped on her thigh.

"Sweet boy," she said, and kissed the top of his head. His big chocolate eyes rolled up to watch her. "You didn't mean it, did you? Don't scare me like that."

She felt John Lee's arm settle around her back.

"Good advice," he said, and kissed the back of her neck. "Don't you scare me again like you did today, lady. Don't you do that. Listen—I think you ought to see somebody professional about this thing."

"No," she said. Flat and calm.

"Abby—"

"I said no, I mean it. I told you how I feel about doctors." She shrugged off his arm and turned to face him.

It was obvious from the look in his eyes he didn't want to fight, but he didn't back off. "I don't give a good goddamn how you feel about it, you almost *hurt my mother*. You're looking to hurt yourself, too, sooner or later, and I'm not about to stand by and watch that happen. Now, maybe he can help you, maybe he can't, but either way, honey, you're going to go, I swear that."

She felt anger rise like filth bubbling from a ruptured sewer, a black wave that made her look him directly in the eye and say, "Make me."

He hesitated. She saw the doubt in his face, the pain, and then he shook his head and stood up.

Carlton growled softly, then trailed into a whine. He pulled away from Abby's patting hand and trotted limping down the hallway, head down, tail still.

"It ain't a fight, Abby," John Lee said. "And you won't win. You want to be crazy and stupid, you go ahead, but I'm not going to be there to pick up the pieces."

He turned away. As she watched the door close, she called out, "I'll talk to you later!"

He didn't answer.

Solo:
December 13, 1994

Dr. Richard Urdiales had a big-city look to his offices. Abby sat quietly, hands folded, in a comfortable wing chair and listened to the soothing tick of the large grandfather clock in the corner. The other chairs were all empty, though they *felt* full, somehow, full of watchers. The receptionist—the wood nameplate on the desk said her name was Carolyn—was being very careful not to stare. She'd probably had a lot of practice at ignoring patients. Considering the thick expensive money-green carpet, the original artwork on the walls, Dr. Urdiales would have to have a large client load. A loaded client load.

Abby fidgeted, not for the first time, with the thought of getting up and leaving. Carolyn looked up at her and gave her a friendly, professional smile.

"Would you like something to drink?" she asked. She had a professional voice, as well. Smooth and too cultured to have come out of local Midland society. She was a smallish woman but well-dressed, with a pleasantly round face and glossy black hair that fell smoothly back from her face and just reached

her shoulders. "We have hot tea with honey and
lemon, or coffee, or soft drinks."

Hot tea reminded her of Miklos. Abby shook her
head and looked over at the magazines fanned on
the shiny coffee table. *Vanity Fair. Cosmopolitan. Ladies
Home Journal.* She pulled a new, glossy issue of *People*
from the arrangement and tried to concentrate on the
lives and disasters of movie stars.

The room had a faint, pleasant scent of cinnamon
and the more seductive tint of Carolyn's perfume.
It was cool, but not unpleasantly so. Abby shivered
anyway, just on general principle, and wished de-
voutly that she hadn't promised John Lee this,
wished she could think of something, anything to
pull her away.

Carolyn's telephone hummed musically for attention. She murmured a greeting into it, made respon-
sive noises, and wrote something on a pad on her
desk. She replaced the receiver in the cradle and continued making notes. Without looking up she said,
"Abby?"

Maybe somebody had called with a reprieve. Abby
clutched her magazine so hard it crinkled. "Yes?"

"You can go in now. Right through that door."
Carolyn pointed with her gold pen toward the entrance. Abby swallowed, nodded, and put her magazine back in its proper place in the arrangement
before standing up. Her feet didn't want to move but
they did, shuffling through the expensive, springy
carpet. Her hand went out to turn the doorknob. The
door squeaked just slightly as it swung open, and a
blast of warmer air washed over her. More cinna-

mon, stronger this time, and the biting, fresh smell of men's cologne.

On the other side of the money-green carpet, Dr. Urdiales stood with his back to her, watering a large green English ivy. He set the silver water pitcher aside and turned toward her. His smile was the first thing she noticed—wide, unforced, full of even white teeth. His skin was the golden brown most people paid tanning salons to achieve, and his age showed in fine tight lines around his eyes and feathery gray in his dark hair.

"Miss Rhodes?" At her nod, he made a vague, circular gesture toward the area around his desk. "Please, have a seat."

She took the chair closest to the desk, a pale blue wing chair identical to the one in the reception area. There were three other chairs available—a straight-backed wooden one at a safe middle distance, an iron-and-velvet creation that looked more like art than comfort, and a leather one that had a vaguely masculine air.

"Was it a test?" She looked directly at Urdiales as he came around the desk. He paused a second, then took his seat.

"What?"

"Which chair I took?"

His smile this time was more cautious. He sat back and tilted his head to one side.

"Should I call you Miss Rhodes or Abby?"

"Abby's fine." She shifted in her seat and focused on his desk rather than the too-bright shine of his eyes. There were only three items on the shiny, spotless wood: a blank yellow legal pad, a silver pen and pencil set, and a thick square block of turquoise that might have been a paperweight, if there had been any papers to weight down. The silky wood grain rippled like a pond in the gray afternoon light.

"Abby it is. Abby, I find it useful sometimes to videotape sessions for later reference. Would that be acceptable to you?"

She shrugged, eyes fixed on the turquoise. He opened a drawer and took out a remote control and pointed it at the wall to his left. A VCR started up with a muted, soothing hum. She glanced around for the camera but didn't see one.

"Now, you understand that this is simply a preliminary interview. We will not necessarily have a full session today—I think it is much more important to become familiar with one another first." At her nod, he said, "Tell me something about yourself, Abby."

There was no point in asking *what*, she knew that immediately. "I'm a musician, I live here in Midland, I teach private lessons through the high school."

"Were you born here?"

"No, I . . . my family lives in Dallas. I went to school in Lubbock, then in Cincinnati. I moved here for my job."

"Anything else you think is important for me to know?"

"No—I—no." She fidgeted uncomfortably away from his stare and focused on the turquoise paperweight.

"I understand you've been feeling some extreme anxiety. Could you tell me how that started?"

The turquoise gleamed too bright for the real world. She looked away, to the dark cherrywood walls. He had a raw of framed diplomas, all with official-looking seals and signatures. One was from the University of Southern California, another from the University of Texas.

"Can you hypnotize me?" she asked. In the silence she heard his chair creak as it adjusted.

"I have a number of techniques available, but I only use them when I feel they are warranted." Dr. Urdiales had lost his smile completely now, and without it his face looked older and more severe. He laid both hands on the desktop in front of him and toyed with the silver pen. "Why do you suppose you need that particular kind of treatment?"

She realized that she was still holding her purse balanced in her lap, wondered what he thought about that. She picked it up and dumped it on the floor without looking where it landed.

"Because I think I had a previous life, somebody murdered me, and my murderer is still alive and using my old name."

After the first widening of his eyes—so small she could barely see it—his face took on a carefully non-committal expression she imagined they taught in psychology school. He put the pen down crosswise on the pad and folded his hands together. A wedding ring winked gold in the pale sunshine.

"How did this previous life come to you?"

"Slowly. It started—it started when I met John Lee—John Lee Jordan. He's my—he's a friend." The word *boyfriend* seemed ludicrous at her age.

Urdiales noticed her hesitation, of course. "It's not necessary to be polite here, Abby. You can say exactly what you mean."

"I mean—I mean that I'm sleeping with him."

"How do you feel about him?"

"I just said I'm sleeping with him," she snapped. He gave her a sad smile.

"Many people have sex with people they care nothing at all about, or whom they actually despise. How do you feel about John Lee?"

She looked down at her clasped hands. It was getting chilly in the office—but even as she thought it, a heater clicked on and blew warmth over the back of her neck.

"I think I'm in love with him," she said. It ached at the back of her throat like unshed tears. "But that's impossible, the way things are."

"And how are things?"

Here, in the quiet womb of Urdiales' office, there was no sense of time except the regular breaths she took. She felt some of the tension ease out of her back, as if the chair had absorbed it. "Terrible." And she told him, told him all of it, the visions, the memories, the visit to John Lee's mother. Her own violent impulses. At the end of it he was sitting quite still, watching her with those warm intelligent eyes but quite expressionless.

After a few seconds of silence she asked, "Am I crazy?"

He gave her that smile again and said, "Clearly, you are distressed by what you're experiencing, and that distress is changing your life—a real problem, a real effect. There is nothing crazy in that."

"I want to be hypnotized," she asked. "Wouldn't that help? I might remember more about Pearl Jordan. I might find something that could help me."

He cocked his head. "Help you what, Abby?"

"Help me prove that woman murdered Pearl Jordan."

"Is that so important, after all these years? You tell me she is an old woman. Is it so important that you destroy her last few years of life?"

Coldness rose up from her stomach like bile; it settled behind her eyes and took control of her mouth, and she said, "Yes. An eye for an eye, that's the Bible's way. I believe in that. She killed, and she's got to be punished for it no matter how long it takes, how many years. She did more than kill, she *stole*. She stole my *life*."

"Am I speaking to Pearl Jordan?" he asked politely.

"Pearl Jordan is dead."

"Is she? I noticed your accent changed, Abby. And your language. This would seem to me more than a series of dreams and memories." He reached for his pen and made a note on the legal pad. "I'd like you to come back to see me. Is Thursday at four p.m. acceptable to you?"

"What about the hypnosis?" she asked.

He met her eyes. "I must warn you that I place little credence in theories of past lives. I will not reject the possibility out of hand, but neither do I accept it as the only possible explanation." He smiled and rose to his feet. "I suppose the answer to your question is, we'll see. I hope that is sufficient."

She stood up, too, remembered her purse, and bent to retrieve it. When she straightened, Dr. Urdiales had come around the desk and passed her on the way to the door.

"Carolyn will make the appointment with you."

"How does the billing work?" she asked.

"Mrs. Caulfield gave me to understand that she would be billed for your sessions. Is that not correct?"

"No. I should pay you."

Dr. Urdiales faced her and said, "Can you?" Heat climbed into her face. "I believe it is important for you to work out your problem, Abby. We can work out an alternative billing arrangement later. Is that acceptable?"

They paused together at the door, and he extended a hand to her. It felt startlingly warm, the skin soft and well cared for. A second's pressure and he let her go. The door swept open ahead of her.

"Carolyn will give you the private voicemail number as well as my beeper number. If you feel you need to talk to me, use those numbers aggressively."

She passed through into the chilly confines of Carolyn's domain, then looked back. He was still watching her.

"Dr. Urdiales?" she asked. "Any words of advice?"

"Stay away from her."

There was no question who he meant.

Hernandez Transmission finally released her car, for a ransom of three hundred sixty-two dollars. She wrote the check with her fingers crossed and handed over her drivers' license when the underfed mechanic wanted to see it. He wrote down every number he could find on the card—license number, identification number, birth date. She was surprised he didn't write down her driving restrictions code, too. When he was satisfied he handed back the license and gave her the car keys.

"Where is it?" she asked. He shrugged and gestured vaguely to the north. She picked her way around piles of gritty used cans and grimy boxes to the door in that direction. Outside, ice-cold wind greeted her and combed her hair back from her face with chilly fingers.

Her car, a 1984 sun-faded Toyota, waited patiently in a row of equally aged and faded cars. She got in, breathed dust and mold, and started it up. The car roared like a new lion. The employees of Hernandez were lousy housekeepers but great mechanics.

She drove home with a feeling of contentment that surprised her—Urdiales had calmed her, a little, and having a working car took a lot of pressure off, too. At least she had the illusion of being able to run away from her problems. In celebration, she swung by the grocery store and picked up peanut butter and jelly, bread, milk, and other vital essentials of life.

Carlton greeted her at the door, happy and panting. All was right with the world.

As she opened the refrigerator to put the milk away, the phone rang. She finished what she was doing, deliberately lazy, and let the answering machine pick it up.

"Abby, if you're there, pick up, it's Harris. Abby!"

There was an orchestra tuning up in the background. She frowned and grabbed the phone off the kitchen wall.

"I'm here." Yes, it was an orchestra, all right, the screech of violins tuning clearly evident. A trumpet blared, too close to the phone. "Where the hell are you?"

"I'm where you're supposed to be."

She whirled to stare at the calendar taped to the refrigerator. On December 13, she'd neatly written REHEARSAL CIV AUD 6 P.

"Oh, Christ," she breathed. "Ten minutes."

"He's already here, you'd better move your ass."

"Tell them I'm in the bathroom. Jesus!" She hung up and darted for the bedroom, grabbed her instruments and counted quickly to ten to be sure she hadn't forgotten anything. She ran to the door, paused, ran back to the bedroom for the music she'd left lying on the dresser. Carlton barked, enjoying the excitement, and she had just enough time to pat his head before she slammed the door and locked it in the same motion.

No cops, which was damned lucky; her newly revived car roared all the way to the Civic Auditorium. When she slammed to a stop in the parking lot the clock read 6:07. She choked and grabbed everything in one untidy armload and fled inside, to the darkness.

Too late. The tuning had taken on an air of purpose, the pure unwavering tone of the oboe, the strings falling in to echo. She took the quick way backstage and assembled all three instruments in the darkness behind the curtains, quick, efficient twists of her wrists. The clarinets were seated in the center of the orchestra; she'd have to make it past at least five chairs and stands to get to her spot. Luckily, the conductor was turned away, talking to a stage manager. She took a deep breath and hurried, dodging violin bows. As she dropped into her chair next to Harris the conductor turned and gave them all a blank, unfocused stare. It quickly narrowed to drill into her alone.

Abby pretended not to notice and concentrated on adjusting the reed on her B-flat, holding her breath to keep from panting from fear. *I have always been here*, she thought. *I'm not late. I'm never late.*

"You, where have you been?" the conductor demanded. She couldn't remember his name, Jonathan something, but she remembered the affected British accent, the shrill, stressed voice. He claimed to have directed the London Symphony Orchestra, which left the obvious question of why the hell he was taking jobs in Midland, Texas. She continued adjusting her reed and, after a second, looked shocked and touched her chest. *Who, me?*

"Sir?" she asked.

He tightened his thin lips and lifted his chin. "I do not tolerate lateness. I can always find another clarinetist. They are quite literally a dime a dozen. Are we clear?"

"Clear," she said. He stared a moment longer, then dismissed her and turned to deliver a hiding to a late-coming second violinist. "God, I forgot what an asshole he was." The last was said under her breath, directed to Harris, who'd sat very still and quiet through the exchange. He leaned forward and flashed her a grin.

"Yeah, he's a charmer. I hear he's wearing out his welcome with the Symphony Guild faster than old Harry Pine."

Harry, a hard-drinking, foul-mouthed old bastard, had lasted for four concerts before mysteriously vanishing from town. Gossip had it that he'd been caught with his pants down with the wife of a local politician, but nobody knew for sure, and pictures hadn't circulated. Abby would have asked for details, but Crusty Butt was tapping the stand for attention.

"Since the violins are so woefully in need of the practice, we'll start with the Wagner," he announced. Abby sighed and flipped through her folder to locate the dog-eared sheet music. Naturally, since she'd broken laws to get here, he'd start with something for which she had to count eighty-four measures of rest before her entrance. She settled herself more comfortably and listened to the violins hack their way through the first forty measures.

"Again."

It was going to be a long evening, she saw that already. She reset her mental measure counter to zero, and back to zero again. The violins practiced twelve measures, over and over.

The woodwinds were getting restless. The brass section looked like they'd gone to sleep. She stared at the dots of sixteenth notes on the music until they spun into a tiny black whirlpool, sucking her down to the accompaniment of distant unhappy violins.

"Hey!" A sharp pain in her side as Harris nudged her. She blinked and looked up just as the conductor motioned with his baton to bring them into the music.

She'd missed the entrance. She fumbled her clarinet and came in late, making up for it with round, full tones, precisely in time with Harris's.

The conductor cut them off with a slice of his baton and pointed its thin white tip at her. She watched him warily.

"You," he snapped, "will bloody well pay attention. Measure ninety, everyone."

She concentrated on coming in precisely right, playing every note correctly, aligning herself with the almost inaudible heartbeat of the music and blending into the shifting sounds and textures. In measure 198 she had a short solo in tandem with the oboe. She skated into it with perfect confidence.

The oboe was late and out of tune. She stopped when the conductor cut them off, waiting for him to jump the oboe's boxcar, but he continued to stare directly at her.

"You were late," he said. In the stillness, she heard the oboe player breathe a sigh of relief. "Again. Play the entrance."

She felt a sting of resentment and terror but she obediently put the instrument to her lips and played the entrance, got two notes into it before the baton sliced like a razor.

"Late! Again."

She did it again. He let her get four notes in before cutting her off. By now she felt light-headed, aware that she wasn't coming in late but that for some reason she'd become his particular punching bag for the evening. His handsome, hateful face pinked with swelling rage.

"Again!" he shouted, brought her in and cut her off three seconds later. "We will do this until you get it right. Again!"

She put her instrument down and stared at him. He waved his baton at her. Everyone was staring, eyes crawling over her like slugs. Strangely, she wasn't afraid.

"I don't think so," she said. "Sir."

The pink in his cheeks turned bright red. He threw his baton down on the stand with a clatter.

"*What* did you say? You *won't*? Do you think I'm asking your *opinion*, you brainless little twit? Play the entrance or get out!"

She froze for a second, then opened her folder and put the music back inside.

"Don't bother to take the music, you won't be coming back!" he screamed. "Out! Get out!"

She stood, instruments balanced in her arms, and said, "Go to hell."

As she turned to make her way past the dumbfounded, amazed violinists, something hit her in the back, a pinpoint of pain in her right shoulder. A gasp went up from the orchestra. She turned back to see his baton rolling on the floor at her feet.

The concertmaster stood slowly, holding his violin

by the neck as if he might choke it, and said, "I think that's quite enough, sir."

He pushed his chair back and stalked offstage. The second- and third-chair violinists hesitated and then hurried to follow, and then the entire section rose en masse, whispering nervously. All around the orchestra, people got up and made their way out. The conductor watched, openmouthed, as they left him standing alone on the podium.

Harris grabbed her elbow and dragged her back into the darkness behind the curtains.

"Hold still," he said, and leaned over and planted a warm, wet kiss on her mouth. She flinched backward and wiped her lips with the back of her hand. "Goddamn, you're something! What are you, nuts?"

"I wasn't late on the entrance," she said flatly. "And he's a complete fuckhead."

"Fuckhead or not, you'd better go lick the concertmaster's shoes because if he hadn't backed you up you'd be riding the musical rail out of town, if you get my drift. And you still may be facing the little old ladies' brigade." He squeezed her shoulder, too hard. "Too bad we don't have a union here."

"We couldn't afford one. I guess I'd better get it out of here before he beats me up in the parking lot." She found her instrument case and started tearing down the clarinets, slotting the pieces in their soft velvet cradles. "Thanks for reminding me to show up."

Harris grinned. "Yeah, like it mattered. Peace."

She split her fingers in his direction and made her way over to the concertmaster, Stephenson, who was holding court near the soda machines. He accepted her thanks gracefully, promised her he'd stick by her, and even appointed a burly cello player to walk her out to her car.

Another educational evening of fine arts.

At home, after accepting Carlton's happy greeting, she stored the instruments and sat cross-legged on her rumpled bed, staring off into space. After a while, she reached over and rescued a large artist's sketch pad from the floor. She opened it to the first page.

She'd sketched two crude likenesses of John Lee's mother, scars and all—one as she looked now, faded and softened, and one as she had looked in the cellar, strong and bony and battered. On the next page she'd sketched John Lee. She lingered over that one, tracing the rough pencil lines with her fingers. The next page—the last one filled in—had a floor plan of the Jordan house.

She reached for a pencil, chewed on the eraser for a few seconds, and drew in a small square in Pearl Jordan's bedroom. In neat tiny letters, she labeled it *window*.

Now that she had her car back, she could go for a little drive.

She passed the pale dirt road to John Lee's workshop with a sense of longing that was almost like the pull of a magnet; she hadn't seen him in two days, and her body was starved for his comfort. She continued on, keeping her eyes firmly on the road as she passed the Jordan house, and drove on into unknown darkness, until weak lights on the horizon indicated some kind of town. The billboard on the right side of the road—half-eaten by sun and age—had a fresh-faced white family looking hopefully into the setting sun. The caption said FALL CREEK: A GOOD PLACE TO BE. Some wit had marked out BE and substituted LEAVE in uneven thick letters underneath. Somebody else had painted GEV + JEAN '82, which was a pretty good indication of how long it took for the town to fix things. Even after the sign, there was nothing to indicate Fall Creek really *was* a town—a run-down gas station with round-shouldered pumps, the name whited out and plywood over the windows, followed by more desert road, and then suddenly a brightly lit 7-Eleven, parking lot empty, with a darkened video rental store next door. Abby slowed the car as the highway turned to a street and a sign informed her the speed limit was thirty miles per hour.

If downtown Midland was seedy, downtown Fall Creek was devastated—empty stores with shoe-polished FOR LEASE signs, broken windows, a very few stores that looked, if not prosperous, breathing. Among those was Josie's Restaurant, a long expanse of dusty windows. Abby pulled her car into an angled space in front of it and sat staring at it, pulling in deep breaths of cold air that tasted metallic as blood.

Not Josie's Restaurant, not all those years ago—it had been the Fall Creek Diner then—but the Formica tables looked the same, the serving counter, the peeling wallpaper. She remembered eating there once, shoving food in her mouth as quickly as possible, aware of everyone staring at her like a freak in a sideshow. It was after Daddy's funeral, that was it. It had been the last time she'd come to town.

Someone with her, she remembered now, sitting on the other side of the sparkled Formica, eating a thick steak and potatoes. Just a shadow, a suggestion of a voice.

She flinched out of the past and looked at the sign in the window. CLOSED. The diner closed at six p.m. The only thing that seemed to be open in the darkness was the gaudy glow of the 7-Eleven and, at the far end of the street, a Dairy Queen.

There used to be a dress shop down there, on the left where the windows were broken. Hilda's? Helga's? She remembered her mother grimly trying on dress after dress one hot Saturday afternoon, perspiration shining on her face.

There were lights in one other place, at the very end of the street. Abby pulled out and drove in that direction.

A police cruiser was parked in the angled spaces in front of the door that said FALL CREEK POLICE DEPT., and through the windows she saw a tired-looking fat woman in a khaki uniform behind a microphone, and in a chair opposite her another cop, a man, wearing a ten-gallon white straw cowboy hat. He had his feet propped up on the desk, revealing point-toed boots. Abby quickly turned her head and made a right turn into the Dairy Queen for a cold drink. The teenager who took her money looked monumentally bored with the entire event, but the Dr Pepper was good, thick and sweet.

Better not to take any chances with Terry if she

could help it. Abby made a left out of the Dairy Queen back through town again, past the billboard and into the dark.

The Jordan house had its lights on. She pulled over to the side of the road and watched it for a while, the warm inviting glow of it, and felt sick with tension. *Go home*, part of her advised. *Call Dr. Urdiales.*

But she'd never learn anything that way, never know. She wasn't going to hurt anyone, after all. All she wanted was a little information.

She left the car on the side of the road with its emergency flashers on and darted across to the other side. Even with the flashlight she kept pointed low and ahead of her feet, it seemed like a long walk in the cold with only the whine of the wind in her ears to keep her company; the night had a bite of snow, and the clouds looked pregnant. It seemed so empty out here, so dark. She thought she caught a whisper of voices, but when she turned her head it was gone. Her heart thudded faster and so did her feet, and when the flashlight caught the pale white glow of the house itself she shut it off and continued slowly and carefully, feeling her way with sweeps of her hands in front.

A television was playing inside the house, the jolly theme music of a Christmas special. Abby put both hands flat against the cold smooth wood of the house and eased up until she was even with the windowsill. Through the pale lace curtains she saw the living room, empty but brightly lit.

She slid around the corner to another lighted window, this one at the kitchen. She glanced in and quickly dropped, because the old woman was standing just a few feet away, stirring something in a pot on the stove. Around back, then, to the darkened windows. Both had screens on them. She took her car keys out of her pocket and pried carefully at one, freezing whenever it made a squeak, and the screen popped out with a rattle that nearly made her scream. She held on to it, breathing quickly, but no lights came on, no voices called. She eased the screen to the ground and propped it against the wall. The window wasn't latched. She slid it up, one careful inch at a time.

An alarm went off, lights flaring, sirens honking. Abby squawked in surprise and lost her balance, fell on her back in the dirt while the halogen lights drilled into her head. *Of course*, she thought stupidly. *Of course she'd have an alarm.*

And then she scrambled up and ran headlong into the darkness, stumbling over invisible obstacles, arms flailing. In the distance, the emergency flashers on her car blinked out a message: *Hurry, hurry, hurry.* The woman would call John Lee, of course. John Lee would make it in five minutes, maybe less. Maybe she'd call the police, too. The prospect of being at Officer Terry's mercy was terrifying. Abby fumbled the flashlight out of her coat pocket and flicked it on to light her way as she ran, while behind her the alarms continued to shriek.

She stumbled across the highway and collapsed against the door of her car for a second, chest aching with fear. Her hands were shaking so much she could hardly get the key in the lock to open the door.

Headlights burned down the road that led from
John Lee's workshop. She froze, watching them, and
jammed the key in the ignition.

It cranked stubbornly. She screamed in frustration
and slapped the steering wheel, tried it again.

The engine roared. She released the brake and
floored it, heading for Midland and safety, and behind her headlights made a turn from John Lee's
road to the highway. Would he follow her?

No. He turned off at his mother's house—making
sure she was all right. Abby swallowed an almost
chewable lump of fear and willed her muscles to
relax, heard tendons creak in her hands as she
succeeded.

He didn't need to follow her, of course. He'd know
who it was, or he'd have a pretty damn good idea.
She'd been wearing gloves, so there wouldn't be any
fingerprints, but John Lee wouldn't need a finger-
print to connect her to it.

Christ, what had she been thinking? It had seemed
like the right thing to do, the only thing to do, but
what good would it be if she got arrested? Who'd
believe her? No, she was going to have to be smarter
about this. More careful.

She needed information.

More than that, she needed allies.

As she blasted past the last billboard at the edge
of Fall Creek, blue and red lights popped and
swirled. She gasped and hit the brakes hard enough
to make her balding tires slip, but it wouldn't do any
good; he had her, had her good. She looked down
at her speedometer. Sixty-five miles an hour—okay

on a Dallas freeway, not okay outside a small town. The patrol car pulled in behind her. The chances of her ancient Toyota outrunning the cruiser were so laughable they weren't even worth considering. She pulled over to the gravel shoulder and hissed to a stop, swallowing convulsively, over and over. The Dr Pepper she'd bought at the Dairy Queen bumped her hand when she reached down for her purse, and she grabbed it and took a big sip to quiet her lurching stomach.

Behind her, the police car was a black, menacing shadow, painted red and blue in alternating sweeps. She fumbled her wallet open and pulled out her driver's license, remembered with a sinking heart that she'd need her proof of liability insurance, too. She began combing through the folded scraps of paper stuffed in with the few dollars.

A brilliant flashlight beam blinded her, and the cop knocked loudly on her window. She rolled it down and held out her license before he'd said a word, squinting to see him.

"Ma'am," he said. She didn't know him, was overwhelmingly relieved. His name tag said his name was WILSON. "Going a little fast there."

"Yes. Yes, I'm sorry, Officer. I lost track—"

"This your current address?"

"Yes." She hesitated. "Uh, no. I mean, I moved."

"You know you're required to update your license when you move?" He clipped the license to a board and began writing.

"Yes, sir. I'm sorry."

"Okay, you make sure you do that next week. I'll need to see your insurance."

"Yes—" She looked back down at her wallet and pulled out papers, one after another, dumping them on the passenger seat. Old grocery receipts, gas receipts, receipts with no explanation at all—

"Ben." Another voice, from outside the car. Officer Wilson looked up and around. "C'mere a minute."

Wilson gave her a warning look and disappeared from the window. She kept her head down, diligently searching, fingers sweaty and trembling. What a completely stupid fuckup this had been, beginning to end. And now to have lost her insurance card on top of everything—

No, wait, there it was. She snagged it and unfolded it, breathed a sigh of relief. The flashlight reappeared in her window and she turned toward it, holding up the paper.

"I found it . . ." Her voice died. It wasn't Officer Wilson.

It was Terry Bollinger. He smiled at her and took the proof of insurance from her numbed fingers.

"Well, if it ain't the nice schoolteacher," he said, and looked down at his clipboard. "Speeding. That's a real pisser."

"I want to talk to Officer Wilson," she said.

Terry maintained his smile. "Oh, I'll just bet you do. Trouble is, he's busy calling dispatch right now. Why? You got something against me, Miss Teacher?"

She stared at him and slowly lowered her hand to her lap. He concentrated on the clipboard, checking

things off, writing descriptions. He handed it back
to her.

"Sign this."

"What's the ticket for?"

"You want to argue with me?" He raised his eyebrows. "Out of the car."

"But—"

"Get out of the car, ma'am, *now*." Terry opened the
door. She unlocked her seat belt—thank God she'd
remembered that, at least—and stepped out.

At the cruiser, Officer Wilson straightened to
watch. "Trouble?" he called.

Terry shrugged. "Naw, not really. Gonna give this
lady a sobriety test, that's all."

"I'm not drunk," she said, looking up at his face.
The flickering bubble lights made him by turns cold
and blazing. "You know I'm not. Why are you
doing this?"

"I smelled alcohol on your breath."

There was no arguing with him, not really. She
walked the line for him, stood on one foot, touched
her nose. She could tell it amused him to see her
perform like a trained seal, and he made her go
through the entire process, including the field breath-
alyzer, which of course registered negative. At the
end of it, even Officer Wilson was bored. Terry gave
her a ticket for ten miles over the speed limit.

Behind them, headlights came from Fall Creek. A
car slowed—maroon sedan, late model. She saw the
shadow of John Lee's face as he turned toward them,
but he kept driving, and she was glad. Bad as things
were, they'd have only gotten immeasurably worse

if he'd stopped. Terry would have had a whole new play toy.

As he was handing her license and insurance card back, he leaned in close and said, "I ought to give you a ticket for public indecency, too."

She looked down at herself, at the loose blue jeans, the sweatshirt, the tennis shoes. Up into his face, where his eyes had taken on a bright, glassy shine.

"Why?"

"It ever occur to you that when you call a man on his cellular phone people can intercept it? I got a police scanner at home. There I was, minding my own business, and I hear you telling John Lee to come in your mouth. Now, is that fitting talk for a lady that teaches kids?"

The shock burned down her spine, all the way to her feet. Her mind went furiously blank, and a horrible feeling of violation blossomed in her stomach. She couldn't look away from the magnetic pull of his eyes, his full lips smiling at her.

"I got the whole thing on tape. It's pretty steamy. I been listening to it, on and off, when I'm feeling lonely. You got a real nice telephone voice, Miss Rhodes."

Blood rushed into her cheeks, hot enough to boil. She fought to keep her voice even.

"Are we done here?"

"Here"—he nodded—"I expect so. You want to talk about that tape, you give me a call, ma'am."

He dug a card out of his pocket and handed it to her. She let it flutter into the darkness of the floor. He touched the brim of his hat, an ironic salute, and switched the flashlight off. She was trapped in a darkness so thick it threatened to drown her, blinking furiously to clear the ghostly dots from her eyes. by the time she'd managed it he was gone, and the cruiser was pulling out, flashers dying away, and heading back the way it had come.

She rested her forehead against the soothing cool plastic of the steering wheel. She knew what it was in Terry's eyes now, though she hadn't been able to recognize it in the shock of the moment.

She'd turned him on.

Accelerando:
December 14, 1994

She'd expected John Lee to be waiting for her at her apartment, but she'd been wrong—just Carlton, glad to see her as always, mostly because she needed to take him out to deposit fertilizer. She did it with a newfound wariness, watching shadows, flinching at sudden movements. She wasn't honestly sure who it was she was scared of, John Lee or Terry.

She slept fitfully, listening for noises and interpreting every creak and doggy shuffle as an intruder. *Karma in action*, she thought as she lay alone in the dark, staring at the spackling overhead. What was it Benny had said? Secret messages in the ceiling? Maybe this one said, *Act like a complete asshole*.

She threw her arms over her face and gave in to the misery, let it drag tears up out of the hurt in her stomach. Carlton climbed up on the bed and flopped down next to her, whining unhappily, licking the back of her neck to comfort her. She turned and threw her arms around him, petting his head, until she felt better. She sat up and looked at the clock—four-thirty in the morning. For some people, the workday was starting.

She got up and made hot tea with honey from a squeezable plastic bear and lemon concentrate from a plastic lemon, and sat on the couch staring at the blank TV screen. Damn, she wished Maria were back, but then Maria was never back, not really; when she was in town, which was seldom, she was shopping or dating or visiting, and the only time she ever spent in the apartment was conducted mostly in her bedroom. Usually that was a fine arrangement, but not now. Now she needed somebody to talk to.

She looked over at the phone and thought about calling John Lee, but it was a stupid idea, instantly dismissable. Impossible to have anything to say to him right now.

She finished her tea and stretched out on the couch to stare up at the ceiling. More spackling. She tried to figure out the messages, finally turned on her side and growled at Carlton, who was sitting patiently watching her. He growled back.

The door vibrated under a strong series of knocks. Abby sat up, staring, as Carlton launched into ferocious barking at smoke-alarm levels. She grabbed his collar and held him back, looked through the peephole.

John Lee. Oh, God.

She took a deep breath and swung the door open. Carlton immediately fell silent and licked his chops, received a quick rough rub on the head as John Lee came inside. Abby shut the door and locked it without ever looking directly at him.

"I know it's early," John Lee said. His voice sounded fuzzy and difficult. She glanced at him and saw the wet shine of his eyes, the loose set of his lips. "I been drinking."

"I see that," she said. "Come in and sit down."

He made it to the couch and flopped, head bouncing against the cushions as if it had come loose from his spine. He sighed and closed his eyes.

"You didn't drive here, did you?"

"Taxi," he said. "My first time. Wasn't much fun."

She sat down cautiously on the other end of the sofa, knees drawn up under her. He looked so tired, so vulnerable.

"Why're you doing this?" he asked, voice soft and indistinct. His eyes struggled open. "You enjoy scaring her, Abby? That it?"

"No." She looked down, away from the obvious misery on his face. "I didn't think she'd ever know I was there. I just wanted . . . I wanted to look around."

"And what if she did find you? What if she came in on you in some dark room? She's an old woman, Abby, she's just an old, tired woman who's been through hell in her lifetime, and she don't need you bringing any more."

"John—"

"She never told me how it happened but I read the police reports, Terry showed 'em to me. Custer Grady knew they was coming for him so he came over to hide out, and when she wouldn't help him he beat the shit out of her, beat her so bad he broke her arm in four places and shattered her knee and cut up her face with a broken bottle. And then he left her there to bleed to death." His breath came in uneven, hitching sobs. He sat up and leaned forward, hands covering his face. "I expect that's when he raped her, too, but I don't know that."

Such a huge burden for a little boy, the monster-father, the disfigured, disabled mother, a town turned against them both. Abby inched closer to him and touched his tensed back with the flat of her hand.

"Don't you do it to her again," he said, and took his hands away to show her the tears in his eyes. "Abby, I know you, I know you're a good woman. Please, let her be."

She touched his cheek, wiped away a tear, kissed his soft damp lips. He tasted smoky and dark, like whiskey.

"I have to know," she said, and rested her forehead against the beard-rough skin of his cheek.

His arm went around her and pulled her into his embrace and they stayed that way for long slow minutes, two hurting people aching for the warmth. She felt that she could have stayed there forever, safe in his arms, but then he let her go.

"You seeing that doctor?" he asked. She nodded but the chill had settled in between them and she retreated to her own end of the couch.

"All right." He tried to stand up, failed, tried again, body loose as an unstrung puppet's. "I don't guess I'll be back for a while, until you get things straight."

He tried again to get up and collapsed back to the soft cushions, eyes flickering shut. She sighed and grabbed his legs to stretch him out full length.

"Go to sleep," she said, and grabbed a discarded afghan to drape over him. He had already taken her advice by the time she'd finished tucking the afghan around him; she took the opportunity to smooth his hair back, to take one last look at the lines of his face. She kissed the spot he liked, right under his ear, and put her hand to her mouth to hold in the tears as she walked back to her dark, empty bedroom.

John Lee said softly, muzzily, "Please don't hurt her, Abby. Please."

She stopped where she was, tears sliding cold down her face, and waited for him to say something else, anything, but instead she heard a light, muffled snore. In spite of herself, she felt a smile twist at her lips.

"I'll try not to," she said.

He was gone before she woke up, but he'd left a note on the couch. She sank down on the cushions and pulled the afghan over her lap before unfolding the paper. She smiled at the sight of his neat, rounded handwriting. His teachers would have been proud.

I don't know when I'll see you again, it said. *Be careful and don't do anything stupid.*

I love you.

She read the note over and over until her eyes blurred with tears, then she carefully folded it and pressed it to her forehead. After a while, when she felt able, she got up and took it to her bedroom and put it in the drawer next to her satin bra and panties.

And then took Terry's business card out of her

purse, where she'd stuffed it the night before. Terry had handwritten a number on the bottom—square block numbers, readable but strangely childish. She settled herself on the couch with the afghan wrapped around her—an echo of John Lee's embrace—and set the phone on the cushion next to her. It took her three tries to dial the number correctly.

Terry sounded rusty, clogged with sleep; she was viciously happy about it.

"What do you want for the tape?" she asked. There was a long silence, indistinct background noise that might have been his throat clearing, the sheets rustling, a gun loading, anything.

"Miss Rhodes?"

"Are you blackmailing a long list of people?"

He coughed, an explosive wet sound so close she imagined spit hitting her ear and had to pull the phone away to swipe at it.

"Well, now, I wouldn't exactly call it blackmail," he said. He was back on track again, smooth and cool. "Blackmail's against the law."

"So's harassment. And I'm pretty damned sure feeling me up like that the other day was illegal, too."

"I'll bet you took some of those law classes in college, right? In between philosophy and art appreciation and all them other things they don't teach in the public school system out here in the dust. Tell me something, Miss Lawyer, they teach you the Latin word for blow job in college?"

"Fellatio," she said. "Want me to spell it?"

He laughed. It took her by surprise, the laugh; she

hadn't expected to hear genuine amusement in it. "Hell, no, I'll take your word for it. What the hell are you doing with John Lee?"

"None of your business."

"Oh, it is my business," he said softly. "You just don't know what kind of a beehive you've stuck your hand in. Ol' John Lee, there, he's a couple cards short of a full house, and his mama ain't no better. One of these days he's gonna turn around and wham!, you'll be wishing you'd made a few more friends 'round here. Or a few less."

It occurred to her, unwillingly, that she really didn't know anything about Terry except what John Lee had told her. Or, for that matter, anything about John Lee from an outside source. She said, "Why should I believe anything you have to say about it? You're the one who's acting crazy."

He gave it a full fifteen seconds of silence before he answered. "Yeah, I suppose it'd look like that, all right. You ever hear of a girl named Marlene Hargist?"

"No."

"Look it up in the Midland papers, if you want. August 1986."

"Why?"

"You look it up, then you ask me why."

She sensed from his tone that he was about to hang up. "Wait! Terry—what about the tape?"

"Think I'll hang on to it for a while," he said, and she could almost hear the smile. "I wasn't lying. You got a real nice telephone voice."

She hung up before he could and sat staring at the phone. As she picked it up to move it back to the coffee table, it rang, vibrating in her hands like a living thing. She dropped it in surprise, fumbled the receiver up from the floor, and said, "Hello?"

"Caller ID," Terry said. "Ain't technology wonderful?"

On Thursday she went to the library and was talked through the microfiche procedures by a helpful librarian. It wasn't hard to find the article on Marlene Hargist; it took up half of page one of the paper on August 16, 1986.

FALL CREEK HONOR STUDENT MISSING.

Marlene had disappeared from behind the counter of the same 7-Eleven Abby had noticed on her way through Fall Creek; she'd been working the graveyard shift. The article was full of grief and pain from family and friends. Her mother pleaded for Marlene's safe return.

Her eyes were drawn to a paragraph near the bottom: Hargist, 21, *recently became engaged to Officer Terry Bollinger of the Fall Creek Police Department. They plan to be married in September after her graduation from the University of Texas at Austin.* There was a grainy black-and-white photograph of Sheriff Hayes laying a comforting hand on a seated Terry Bollinger's shoulder. Terry's face was eerily blank.

August 19's headline was LOCAL MAN QUESTIONED IN DISAPPEARANCE. *Terry*, she thought immediately, but it wasn't Terry. In the accompanying photo, Terry held the elbow of the suspect as he guided him past cameras. The suspect's hands were up to shield his face. She skipped down to the caption:

Local glassmaker John Lee Jordan is escorted to questioning by Officer Terry Bollinger, fiancé of the victim.

"Oh, no," she whispered, and sat back in her chair. The warmth of the research room clung to her like sweat.

She advanced pages to August 20. Nothing but a rehash of previous events. August 21:

JORDAN CLEARED BY POLICE IN HARGIST DISAPPEARANCE.

They'd caught John Lee looking up in the flash of the photograph, eyes blank, face tensed. Terry Bollinger was nowhere in the picture. Instead, John Lee was being guided down the steps by a portly, awkward-looking man who must have been a lawyer. He had one hand out to fend off the photographers.

We don't have any evidence to hold him. That was a quote from Sheriff Hayes, and it had all the warmth of a pit bull's growl. Terry Bollinger had made no comment at all.

The story hung around for a few more days, getting shorter and shorter column space, and finally dropped off altogether by September. She couldn't find any mention of an arrest, and none at all of Marlene Hargist being found, dead or alive.

That night, she dialed Terry's number at eight o'clock. When he answered, she said, "Did you ever find her?"

"You ever think about saying 'hello' or something friendly?" he asked. "She's dead. Marlene's been dead since the night she disappeared, I know it. And I know John Lee did it."

"Why?"

"He'd always had a hunger for Marlene, but she

never would go near him. He used to hang around the store when she was working, stare at her. She told me it made her nervous but I told her she was just being crazy, he wasn't going to hurt her, not with me around." He cleared his throat. "Yeah, I know he did it. And with the least little opportunity, I think he'll do it again."

"It's been almost ten years. If she was dead, wouldn't you have found a body by now?"

"Out here?" Terry snorted. "Miles and miles of unmarked graves out here, teacher. America's dumping ground."

"Even if that's true, what makes John Lee part of it?"

"Bad fruit of a rotten tree, my mother always said. Custer Grady's kid. I guess you know about old Custer."

She took a deep breath and said, "I know he's your father, too."

The response was immediate—laughter. Genuine, derisive laughter. "Don't have to ask who the hell told you that. Hell, lady, my daddy's a truck driver from Tulsa named Jake Fry. I even got a picture of him. John Lee's been pretending that little lie for so long I guess he believes it now. He tell you about his daddy?"

"Enough."

"Oh, I doubt that. Big news, back in the fifties. They dug up four graves on his farmland, probably could've dug up a few more if they'd looked harder. I think they were scared to look. Custer was a mean, snake-cold son of a bitch, and John Lee's the spitting image of him, 'cept for the eyes. Grady's got eyes so blue they're like water—closer you get, the less color they have. He ain't any daddy of mine, all you have to do is look at me to know that. I wouldn't be any kind of a cop if my daddy was a killer." Terry paused. In the background, she heard a cop show on television, sirens screaming, guns blazing. *A lot of protest for something you believe in, Terry. Or is that why you became a cop? To prove Custer couldn't be your father?* "You want that tape back?"

"Yes," she said immediately.

"Stop seeing John Lee."

"You're kidding."

"Hell I am. You stop seeing him, I'll send you your tape." He sighed gustily. "I'm trying to save your life, stupid. John Lee ain't no kind of catch, believe me."

"Forget it," she snapped.

"Then I hope you're ready to explain to that tight-assed principal of yours why you're moonlighting on phone sex. Or maybe I'll just send a copy to all the parents of the kids you teach. Which one you prefer?"

She closed her eyes, felt the stairs under her feet, the dizzy fall into darkness. If what she remembered was true, she and John Lee were doomed, anyway. If it wasn't true, she was crazy and they were doomed.

The promise didn't mean anything, one way or another.

"One thing," she said. Her voice didn't seem to be her own; it was cold, hard, and certain. "You help me get into Pearl Jordan's house. I need to look for something."

"You're just one surprise after another," he said. "Come to think of it, you were tearing out of Fall Creek awful quick the other night. Wouldn't have been you that set off that alarm at her house, would it?"

Caught, she said nothing. After a second or two his chuckle throbbed through the phone. "Don't make me have to arrest you, Abby. That'd be a damn shame."

She hung up. She didn't mean to; it was a sudden convulsion of muscles. The phone slammed down hard, and she was left gaping at it in surprise. She expected it to ring back but he'd made his point. Vividly.

If she gave Terry what he wanted, he'd help her.

He hated John Lee too much to pass up the opportunity.

That night at her appointment, Dr. Urdiales said, "Why?"

She blinked and focused on his attentive, polite expression. He was wearing a well-tailored cream-colored shirt and a blue and green impressionistic tie with the rich gleam of silk. His office had a gentle scent of pine today, in honor of the approaching holidays. The reception area—still meat-locker cold—had discreet, nondenominational decorations. Carolyn was wearing a festive red sweater with green trim.

Outside, snow fell, thick as cotton balls. Snow ought to make noise, she thought. The silence of it was frightening.

"What do you mean?" she asked. Dr. Urdiales

steepled his well-manicured fingers together and rested his chin on top of them. They'd abandoned his desk and sat now in a cozy conversational area, just two people talking, friends, only of course he was getting paid. He *was* good at it, though. From time to time, when he smiled or made some offhand comment, it felt like she really knew him, trusted him. If she wasn't careful, she might actually learn to need him. "Why do I want to prove Pearl Jordan is a murderer? Because she shouldn't get away with breaking the law."

"When you drive, Abby, do you exceed the speed limit?"

"Sometimes," she said, watching him cautiously. "Everybody does."

"And do you feel a compelling need to expose that abuse of the law?"

"This is *murder*, it's not a traffic violation! It was cold-blooded murder!"

"And you're sure that what you remember is correct, absolutely correct. There is no doubt in your mind."

She took too long to say "No," and knew he'd put his finger on it. "I need proof."

"What sort of proof?"

"A body—what else do you prove a murder with?" She looked down at her clasped hands. "I told you, I want to be hypnotized so I can remember everything."

After a second or two of silence he said, "All right."

She was startled enough to look up and meet his

eyes, and then couldn't look away. He had a quiet, pensive expression. Concerned.

"First you must make me a promise, Abby. You must promise that you will not speak to John Lee, his mother, or Terry until you see me again."

"That's a week away."

He continued to watch her. "Do you feel a need to act sooner than that?"

She nodded.

"I will ask Carolyn to make you an appointment early next week. Is that acceptable?"

She nodded again and swallowed a suffocating mouthful of fear. In the far corner of the office, the grandfather clock chimed the half hour, the end of their session, but Dr. Urdiales did not move to show her out.

"You *will* call me if you feel you need to talk?"

"Yes." She raised her chin, met his eyes directly, and said, "I'd feel better if I thought you believed a word I said."

"I do believe you. I believe in your distress and your conviction. As for the rest, I will keep an open mind and give you the opportunity to explore the possibilities. Is that acceptable to you?" When she nodded, he sat back and said, apparently offhandedly, "It seems to me that your friend Benny would be supportive of you. It's odd that you're so intent on shutting her out."

"I have my reasons." She reached down to grab her purse. "Time's up."

Smiling faintly, he said, "I believe that was my

line. All right. Please check with Carolyn about an appointment before next Friday."

Carolyn consulted a leather-bound appointment calendar and marked Abby in for Tuesday at four-thirty. There were no appointments after her.

"That's unusual," Carolyn remarked as she wrote out an appointment reminder card for Abby to keep. "Tuesday night's his evening with his family. He doesn't usually let anything keep him here after five."

"He has a family?" she asked, startled. "He doesn't have any pictures of them in his office."

"No," Carolyn agreed, and looked as if she regretted bringing it up. "He had a problem some years ago with a patient who—who became obsessive about the photographs of his wife and children. It turned out badly."

"For Dr. Urdiales?"

"For the patient."

"What happened?" Abby asked.

Carolyn shook her head; her tiny silver bell earrings tinkled. "See you Tuesday." She pressed the appointment card into Abby's hand and gave her a professional good-bye smile. "Happy holidays."

That night she had another symphony rehearsal, which she arrived for twenty minutes early. Harris seemed surprised to find her there, but he didn't say anything; she noticed that everybody avoided eye contact with her as they took their seats, except for the concertmaster, who nodded to her briskly. Not

quite a leper, then. More like somebody with an unpleasant social disease.

The conductor, what's-his-name, breezed onstage,
took the podium, and pointed at the principal oboe,
who complied with a straight, steady note. The
strings joined in atonal waves that splintered into
harmonics and arpeggios as soon as they'd gotten a
vague notion of the tuning. Abby adjusted her reed
and studied the conductor. He was most definitely
not studying her.

He signaled for silence and got another tuning note
from the oboe. Abby joined the other woodwinds
and brass in matching it, wiggling the joints of her
clarinet in and out in microscopic increments to get
the perfect match.

When they were done, the conductor flipped pages
in his score and said, "We'll begin where we left off
last time. Measure 198."

Jesus Christ, what a single-minded jerk. She braced
herself, took a deep breath, and came in when he
brought the baton down, heard the oboe join in a
fraction of a second late, saw the unholy flash of glee
in his eyes. He cut them off, put the baton down,
looked at Abby for a moment, and then said, "I sin-
cerely apologize. You are not incompetent."

She waited for the other shoe to drop. He turned
his stare away from her and focused it on the oboe
player. "*You*, however, are unforgivable."

The oboe player went chalk-white and sat back in
her chair. Abby knew just how she felt but she
couldn't help but be grateful that it was somebody

else's turn. She slowly sat back in her chair until her back touched cold, comfortless plastic.

After ten minutes the oboe player burst into tears. The conductor threw his hands up theatrically—*look what I have to work with*—and started them in measure 205.

They stopped often to give the strings remedial practice time. She fell into a kind of musical trance, counting measures, listening to strings, counting measures. Harris's elbow in her ribs caught her by surprise, and when she glared at him, he grinned and nodded toward the conductor.

The conductor was concentrating hard on the strings. She frowned and shrugged. Harris sighed and pointed carefully past the conductor, out into the auditorium.

John Lee was sitting alone in the middle of the empty seats, barely a shadow in the dim wash of light from the stage. She forgot all about counting measures, wished she was close enough to see his eyes, his smile. God, she'd missed him. Her whole body ached with relief from tension she hadn't even known was there.

Harris elbowed her again, warning her of an approaching entrance. She picked up the thread of the music and played the melody as if her heart were breaking, soft and sad and passionate. The conductor's eyes flashed toward her, a bare second of surprise, a grudging touch of acceptance, and then he found a viola player to savage.

The concertmaster suggested a break. The conductor checked his watch and shrugged. Abby stood up and shaded her eyes to look for John Lee.

He let was gone. Her lips parted in disbelief, and she grabbed Harris's shoulder as he got up to edge his way out.

"Where is he?" she demanded. Harris lifted his hands helplessly. "Damn."

She pushed past chatting flute players and into the long concrete hallway that led back toward the dressing rooms and bathrooms. Empty, though there'd be a crowd following her. She passed the dressing room where she'd warmed up that afternoon of her concert—God, it seemed so long ago now—and paused. The door was closed. She reached out and flattened her palm on the wood, pushed tentatively. It creaked open.

John Lee was sitting on the makeup counter, long legs dangling, looking down at his plain battered cowboy boots. He didn't look up as she came in but she felt the shifting of his attention.

"Guess I'm not as strong as I thought I was," he said. "I had to see you, Abby. How're you doing?"

She dragged a dented folding chair over and sat down, not too close, not too far. Her legs felt weak. She thought she might have a fever.

"I'm okay," she said. "Did you finish the stained-glass window?"

He had a fresh cut on the back of his hand and a burn the size of a quarter. He rubbed at the spot idly.

"Maybe." He cleared his throat and looked up at her; his eyes were heartbreaking. "I'd like your opinion on it. How about I take you out for a bite and show you what I've got done?''

"John—''

"Please.''

She'd promised Dr. Urdiales, hadn't she? But then she'd already broken that promise, just by sitting so close to him, exchanging those few words. And she couldn't hurt him, not again. Not now.

"We should be done in another hour and a half,'' she said. "Can you wait?''

He nodded, looking down again. She stood up and walked to where he sat, waiting.

She stepped in between his legs and wasn't quite sure who moved faster, him or her, only that their lips met with bruising force, starving, and the taste of him made her heart dissolve. He didn't let her go even when she pulled back for air, his eyes enormous and lazy with pleasure, his mouth close enough to brush hers.

"How long's your break?'' he whispered. His breath stroked her cheek a second before his lips did. She leaned into him and felt his hips tighten against hers.

"Not that long,'' she remembered to say. His tongue traced a hot, wet line over the tender ridge of her ear. "Oh, my God.''

His hands retreated from her back and came around to slide warm over her breasts. His thumbs traced the firming buds of her nipples and before she could think to protest he'd opened two buttons on her shirt and his hands were on her skin, hot and firm, and then his lips, hot and soft.

"John . . ." She pulled herself out of the haze and tugged at his hair, gently. "John, I have to go back. I have to."

He let go of her and she backed away, feeling for the support of another counter behind her. Her breasts tingled as if sunburned and her hands shook when she tried to button her shirt. John Lee stepped in and helped her. His fingers traced the V of her exposed neck when he was done, and he bent to kiss her once more, a slow slide of lips and tongue.

"Hour and a half," she said breathlessly. "I swear."

She wondered if it showed in her face when she hurried back to her chair, wondered if Harris smelled it on her; when he looked over at her she snapped "What?" and got a longer look in return.

"I was going to ask if you wanted to go for a drink after this. Bernie and Jen are going." Bernie was a trumpet player, Jen a French horn player. "Jeez, don't bite my head off or anything. Did you find that guy?"

"Yes." She turned away from him and rustled music busily. She played five or six difficult measures, backed up and played them again. Harris opened his music and played them with her, adding a subtly muscular strength to the tone. They continued to play, diverging into harmony where the parts led them, for the remaining minute or so before everyone else got settled.

As the conductor stepped on the podium, Harris said, with a sly smile, "Wait'll I tell the ladies at school about that hickey on your neck."

*   *   *

They had dinner, drove to John Lee's house, made love in the wrought-iron bed, and lay quietly, body to body, sealed with sweat and kisses. Later, in the two o'clock stillness, John Lee took her out to the workshop, turned on the lights, and showed her the window.

The sun was still there, a glowing blaze of orange, but he'd added rays falling from it onto the face of the woman who knelt on green grass and held up her arms to the warmth. Her eyes were closed, her mouth smiling. She had brown hair that fell back from her face in simple waves, tinted red where the sun touched it.

It was utterly breathtaking.

He looked at the window, not at her, as he asked, "What do you think?"

"Oh, my God, what can I say? It's magnificent. It's . . ." The beauty he'd created made her ache inside, made her aware of the black cancer of fear and hated she'd brought into his life. "It's the most beautiful thing I've ever seen," she said, and then she couldn't stop it, the tears kept coming like a flood, pouring out of a wound she hadn't even felt. She sank down on the floor, cradled by soft sawdust, and John Lee sat down with her, holding her close. When she got her breath under control again she whispered, "I'm so sorry. I'm so sorry for what I'm doing to you."

And for what she was going to do to him.

Rallentando:
December 20, 1994

Somewhat surprisingly, Carolyn the Wonder Receptionist was not at her desk when Abby arrived for her appointment. Instead, a woman in her early sixties was sitting in Abby's usual armchair perch, hands neatly folded in her lap. She looked thin and nervous, and her eyes had a glitter of panic.

Abby returned the quick, furtive smile and got a magazine from the table. She took a seat on the other side of the room.

"Are you new?" the woman asked. Abby looked up and shook her head. "Oh, I thought I knew all of Richard's patients. I thought you were probably new. Well, I'm Evvy."

She looked familiar—not startlingly so, but enough that it made Abby feel uneasy looking at her.

"Abby," she said. "Nice to meet you."

"Well, that's funny, isn't it? Evvy and Abby. Our names are so much alike. Twinsies." Evvy let out a brittle, annoying laugh. "Would you like some coffee? I can get you some coffee."

"I'm fine, thanks." Abby went back to her magazine, hoping to use it as a magic shield of indifference, but Evvy kept talking.

"Well, it *is* a little late in the day for coffee, that's true. I think he has soft drinks in there, too. Would you like something else?"

"No, nothing." Abby glanced toward Dr. Urdiales' closed door, wondered if she should knock, if Evvy was actually just an overinspired hostess or a psychotic killer.

Maybe she should retire to the bathroom for a while.

As she picked up her purse, the office door opened and Carolyn came out. She smiled at Abby, caught sight of Evvy, and the smile froze solid.

"I'm here for my appointment," Evvy said quickly. Carolyn went to her desk and consulted the leather-bound appointment book.

"I'm afraid there's been some mistake," Carolyn said gently. "Your appointment isn't until tomorrow, ma'am. You'll need to come back then."

"But I came all this way!" Evvy protested. Abby got up, indecisive; Carolyn's eyes flicked toward her.

"You can go on in, Abby, the doctor is ready."

"Well, I'll just *wait*!" Evvy said, and crossed her arms. Carolyn faced her squarely, plainly ready to do battle.

Abby escaped into the inner sanctum and let the door swing shut.

Dr. Urdiales was sitting behind his desk, making some notes. She took her accustomed chair at his welcoming gesture; he tilted his leather chair back with a creak, crossed his arms, and said, "Trouble outside?"

"Someone named Evvy who's got the wrong day."

"Ah." Did she imagine it, or did his face go just a shade paler? "Carolyn will straighten it all out, I'm sure. Are you ready?"

She took a deep breath and said, "Yes, I think I am."

"We can have a regular session, if you have something you'd rather talk about."

"No," she said flatly. "I want to be hypnotized."

"Then we'll follow certain ground rules. I reserve the right to end the session at any time, is that understood? And I will only take you as deep as I feel you are ready to go. Agreed?"

She nodded and filled her lungs with a deep breath. He hadn't changed scents this week—the pine was still there, and the smooth bite of his cologne. It reminded her of John Lee's smell, his touch. It reminded her, with unexpected pain, what Christmas was going to be like without him.

"When do we start?" she asked. Dr. Urdiales came out from behind his desk, dragged a chair close to hers, and put a small spindly-legged occasional table between them. On its smooth cherrywood top, he set what looked like a compact disc with hologram triangles on its surface. He gave it a flick of his fingers, and the disc shimmered into rainbow lights as it spun.

"Now," he said. "Watch the disk, Abby."

Rainbows. The dark closing in around her, hungry.

"Listen to my voice."

She tried to tell him to stop.

* * *

Somebody was saying a name she didn't recognize, so she ignored it and watched the wind sweep sheets of red dust toward the horizon. She shaded her eyes with one hand and stared out while behind her the noise went on and on, a terrible barking sound. She absently told it to hush. The wind's hot hand trailed over her cheek and blew her hair free of its pins.

A pickup truck appeared on the horizon, trailing dust like a comet.

"He's coming," she said. "He's coming back."

"Who is it?" She didn't recognize the voice of the questioner but it didn't matter, nothing mattered but the heat and the dust and the truck coming over the horizon toward her.

"Him." There was only one *him*. "He's coming."

"How do you feel about it?"

She smiled. "Real good."

The pickup squealed to a stop in the dusty yard. She stood where she was and watched as he got out of the truck. Custer was wearing his Sunday-go-to-meeting clothes, black trousers, a black jacket, a plain white shirt only a little yellowed around the collar. He'd even put on a tie.

"Got me a real good deal on the watch and rings," he told her. "Bought you a bag of sugar, that was what you wanted."

She nodded and reached out to him. He put the sugar in her hands, a big thick bag of it, but then the seams busted open and the sugar poured out, white and fine, and she couldn't hold on to it and he laughed and laughed, right up until she threw the bag at him and got sugar all over his good clothes and he dragged her back in the house—

"Where are you?"

"On the couch." Her voice sounded smeary and deep and strange. He held her face down in the dusty cushions. *Teach you, missy, teach you good.*

"What is he doing on the couch?"

It hurt, it hurt so bad, she begged him to stop, voice choked with dust and tears, but he didn't stop, and he didn't say a word, never a word.

In the distance that noise went on, an animal crying.

When he was gone she lay on the couch alone in the oppressive heat, dress twisted up around her waist, and when she licked her lips she tasted sugar and sweat. The pickup rattled like a cough and sputtered away.

And the noise went on and on and on, until she grabbed her head with both hands and screamed for it to stop, stop, stop.

"What does the noise sound like?"

"Dog," she muttered, and battered her fists against her skull. "Dog barking. Dog."

"Is it your dog?"

"Dead."

"Your dog is dead?"

She remembered the mound of dirt in the back, Daddy shoveling and stamping it flat.

"Everything's dead now."

She sat up and smoothed her dress down over her legs, tugging the rough faded cotton into place. Her underpants were filthy. She washed them out in the tiled bathroom in lukewarm water, scrubbed with soap until her hands turned red.

The telephone rang, one short, two long, her party line code. She left the panties to dry on the side of the sink and hurried to the kitchen where the black, heavy phone sat. She held the receiver to her ear.

"Who's talking to you?"

It was Dora Jean Garrison. *Terrible, just terrible. Sheriff Parker's out there now.*

"What's Dora Jean telling you about?"

Found the body. Found the body.

She let the telephone slide out of her fingers and thump back on the cradle, cutting off Dora Jean's buzz in midword.

She went to the door at the end of the kitchen.

Darkness.

"Abby?"

She looked up suddenly, surprised at the creak in her muscles, and saw Dr. Urdiales sitting tensely on the edge of the armchair across from her. He relaxed and leaned back but she'd seen the anxiety on his face and wondered what the hell had happened.

"Yes?" The room was dark and quiet, only the reassuring tick of the grandfather clock to mark time. She glanced over and saw the gleam of the gold clock face.

Six forty-five.

"How do you feel?" he asked.

"Fine." Now that she thought about it, better than fine. Relaxed. She smiled and said, "Very good. But that was a lot longer than I thought we were going to be—we started at four-thirty, right?"

"Closer to five, I should think, but yes, it was a long session. I didn't want to stop you." He was looking at her very strangely. "What do you remember?"

That was a good question, and she wasn't sure she had an answer. She shut her eyes and saw a flash of red sunset, a face, tasted sugar.

"I'm not sure."

He looked as if he intended to ask another question but shook his head and stood up instead. She stood, too, hearing a creaking protest from knees locked too long in the same position.

"I need to review the videotape before we discuss the session, Abby, if that's all right with you. May I make an appointment with you for later this week?"

He opened the office door and stood politely aside while she walked out to the empty reception area. He slid into Carolyn's chair and inspected the appointment book, tapping the paper with a sleek Mont Blanc pen.

"Do you believe me now?" she asked him as he wrote her in on Thursday. The pen froze for a second. He finished what he was doing, sat back in the chair, and met her eyes. "Or do you just think I'm crazy?"

"Do you want my honest assessment?" At her nod, he crossed his arms over his chest and said, "I think it is very likely that what you interpret as having occurred in a past life may be repressed and heavily fictionalized memories."

She stared at him for a long time, then reached out for the appointment card he held out.

"In short," he said, "I believe you. And I think it is more important than ever for you to stay away from the Jordans and Fall Creek."

She dialed Terry's number one-handed as she stared out at the sunset. When he answered, she said, "I want to talk to Custer Grady."

After a long pause, he said, "I want to bump hips with Cindy Crawford. What's your point?"

"You can get me in to see him. You're a cop."

"I ain't seen you do anything for me yet," he said. She let the blinds snap closed and sat down on the couch, pulled her legs up underneath her. On the other side of the room a sitcom played without sound. Carlton lay watching it, head on his paws, doggy eyes lazy with boredom.

"What exactly do you want me to do?"

"Stay away from him." His voice went deeper, raspier. "You want a good fuck, you could sure do better than that little half-fag."

"Do you want me to tell you all about it, Terry, is that what you want? You want to hear about me and John Lee in that big iron bed, is that it? Why is that? It's not because you're jerking off to the sound of *my* voice, is it? More likely John Lee's."

"Shut up!" She'd finally gotten under his skin. She heard the rage shimmering right out of the telephone receiver. "You don't know what the hell you're talking about."

"Then tell me."

Silence. His breathing was rough. In the background she heard a shadow of laughter that matched the silent pratfall of the sitcom on her television.

"Will you take me to see Grady?" she pressed.

"You making some kind of an offer here?" he asked, the edge still in his voice. She swallowed a throat full of ache.

"Maybe. Will you take me to see Grady?"

The silence was very long. The sitcom gave way to a bright, chirpy commercial.

"You better not dance around with me," he breathed. "I mean it, now. You want to see Custer Grady, I'll take you to see him, but I'm gonna want something in return."

"Oh, I know," she said. "I know."

"Day after tomorrow. I'll hook it up. You be ready at eight A.M. sharp, I'll pick you up." He didn't give her time to say anything. The irritated click of the phone chewed at her ear until she hung up.

Carlton turned his head to look at her. She smiled at him with trembling lips and said, "Good dog, Carly. You're a very good dog."

He whined and put his head back down.

The Christmas season was always light, as far as lessons went—kids got lazy, got sick, or got excused. After all, there was always next year.

Her one shining exception was Delilah Kimble. Del never missed a lesson, unless she was so sick her parents refused to let her out of bed. She never blew off the lesson. She *practiced*.

And, most importantly, she had the fire. Abby

closed her eyes and listened as Del blazed her way
through the opening, deceptively simple phrases of
the Debussy *Clarinet Concerto*—a little too loud, a little too rough, but those were things that time would
smooth out. Del had an almost uncanny feel for tex-
ture. The notes she played had a clear beginning,
middle, and end, and she never played throwaways.
Not bad at all for a seventeen-year-old. Del no longer
worried about getting into the Texas All-State Band—
hell, she'd done that in her sophomore year. She was
now worried about what *chair* she was in the All-
State Band, and whether she'd end up as one of the
eight All-State Orchestra clarinetists or only as a
dreaded alternate.

Abby wished all her kids had such problems. As
Del finished the first section, she intervened and had
her play a couple of rough spots again, for confidence. Del's pale, angular face tightened with concentration, but there wasn't any fear in her. She
didn't dread performance; she lived for it.

The tougher the material, the better.

"Miz Rhodes?" Del asked when she'd reached a
breathing spot. Abby blinked and looked over at her.
Del dropped her eyes. "Do you think I can—can really do this? I mean, for a living, later?"

Abby regarded her very seriously, the slender,
fragile-looking hands, the tensed body. "It's tough.
It's very, very tough, I'm not going to lie to you
about that. Performing is the most competitive thing
you could do with your life. Every audition, you'll
go head to head with three hundred other players
just as good as you are, and maybe better, and half

the time it'll come down to politics and favors as to who gets a seat. You'll have to deal with arrogant jerks, and that's not even mentioning the conductors."

Del's fingers worked the keys of her instrument, a fluid, graceful dance, and she shook her head. "My mom says I should go to college and get a real job. You know, something secure. She says music's no good."

"That's true." Abby let it lie there, cold and brutal, until Delilah looked up at her. "It's not good at all for making money. You'll never have a big house and nice car and money in the bank. If you do it, you do it for the love of it. That's all."

"Should I go for it? Do you think I should?"

Abby hesitated, then reached out and patted the girl on one bony shoulder. "Play. Play as much as you want. You've got a shot, Del, I'm not lying to you. If you keep working, keep practicing, you're going to be good enough. The question is, do you have enough desire? Because that's what you must have to go the distance."

"You didn't," Del said, and put her hand to her mouth in horror that she'd blurted it out.

Abby grinned. "Yeah, you might end up like me."

Del blushed and said, "I think that'd be just fine, ma'am."

Abby hugged the warmth close for a few seconds, staring at the kid, and then said, "Buttering me up isn't going to get you out of playing this again, you know. Start here."

She sat and listened to Del's beautiful music for one uncritical moment, and wondered how in the world the girl would ever get out of Midland, Texas, with a drunk for a father and a hardworking, lower-middle-class mother who wanted to keep her child safe. Maybe she could make it, though. Enough talent, enough sheer dumb stubbornness, and she might just make it somewhere.

A tap on the door interrupted both Del's playing and Abby's thoughts. Harris stuck his head in and said, "See you a minute?"

Abby nodded and eased past the metal stand to join him out in the hall. He closed the door, looked at his shoes, and said, "We've got to tell her some bad news."

"What kind?" Abby frowned. He heaved a sigh and looked around the band hall with its jumble of plastic chairs and matte black metal stands, its busy emptiness.

"Her dad crashed his car head-on into a concrete abutment out on I-20. He's on life support but it doesn't look good. Her mother's coming to pick her up."

They both knew what it meant—huge medical bills, emotional trauma, no money for Del's college and even less to indulge anything as unnecessary as music. Abby bit her lip against a surge of tears and said, "I'll tell her."

"No, that's my job," Harris said. He had a frown grooved between his eyebrows and rubbed at it in distraction. "Damn it, why her? Of all the kids I've ever taught, she's the one I'd pick to make it. Now this."

Abby took a deep breath and shook her head. She

stood to one side as Harris opened the practice room door, and waited while his voice, hushed and quiet, delivered the news.

Del was too bewildered to cry. When Abby looked in she saw Harris sitting uncomfortably next to her as Delilah methodically broke down her instrument and put it away, swabbing each section carefully. Her hands were shaking but her face looked rigid and blank.

"Your mom will be here in just a little while," Harris said. She nodded and stowed the swab in its plastic bag, folded it carefully, and put it in the proper slot. "Can I get you something? A Coke?"

"Thank you, sir, I'm all right." Del looked up at him, then past him to focus on Abby's face. Her brown eyes were so desperately empty. "I'm sorry, ma'am. Maybe we can have a makeup lesson."

Abby bit her lip and turned away as tears bloomed in her eyes.

Morning dawned dull and cheerless. She woke and stared up at the darkened ceiling and tried to remember what it was she was waking up for—no lessons today—no school—

Terry. Terry was taking her to see Custer Grady, and he'd be ready to go at eight.

She showered and dressed in plain, sturdy, warm clothes, and waited at the window as a few mournful-looking neighbors wandered out to their cars and drove away. At 7:58, a pickup truck made the turn into her apartments and pulled to a stop beside her own car.

He honked.

She locked the door behind her and hurried across the yard toward him—and even though she was on her way, he laid on the horn again. She saw curtains and blinds twitch as neighbors peered out. She opened the passenger door and climbed inside without looking directly at him, slammed the door, and belted herself in strict compliance to state law.

"Morning," Terry said. She shot a quick glance in his direction. He looked different without the uniform, less imposing. He wasn't looking at her, either. "Coffee in the thermos if you want it."

He put the truck in reverse and put his arm across the back of the seat, close enough that it brushed her hair and felt warm across her neck. She kept facing forward and watched her apartment recede in the headlights.

After Terry had turned the truck onto highway blacktop, she twisted the top off of the thermos and breathed in the earthy smell of fresh, hot coffee. He handed her a small Styrofoam cup—clean; she checked—and watched her pour. She blew on the steaming surface and watched the road.

"Might as well get comfortable," Terry said. "Mind pouring one of those for me?"

She silently found another cup and poured. When she passed it over he handled it with smooth confidence, never taking his eyes off the road, sipped and pulled a face.

"Damn, I never did learn to make decent coffee. Should have made you bring it."

She decided the bait was too obvious, shook her

head, and turned to stare out at the dim, hazy countryside. The sun was fighting to get up but the clouds weighted it down. They wouldn't be passing through Fall Creek, which was a mercy; she didn't think she could stand the guilt of driving past John Lee's house just now.

"What do you want to talk to Custer about?" he asked. Radio stations gabbled and hissed as he began dialing for choices.

"John Lee."

"Hell, might as well turn around right now. He can't tell you anything about him." Terry settled on a station playing old country favorites, slide guitar and nasal-voiced cowboys. "You want to know about John Lee you just ask; I'll tell you everything you need to know."

"No offense, Terry, but I don't think you could exactly call yourself unbiased. You guys have hated each other for so long you don't really even see each other anymore, just a target. Even the insults have gotten old."

Terry nodded. "Until you came along." He seemed strangely pleased. "Never knew he was vulnerable like that. He always had a steel stomach and an iron ass, but when I had you spread-eagled on the car, damn, the look in his eyes. I think he might've shot me if he'd had that damn shotgun of his."

"And you're happy about that?"

Terry shrugged, yawned to show wide white teeth. He slurped coffee. He smiled crookedly at her when he saw she was staring.

"Tell me why you're with him," he said. She immediately looked away, out the window. "And don't you tell me he's a good fuck or I'll smack you one."

He was half joking, but only half. She said nothing, staring out at West Texas, thinking how dry it was, how unforgiving. Maybe that was what had made Terry so bitter. The view.

"Fuck you, then," Terry muttered, and turned up the radio.

She fell into a light, uneasy doze and woke up when the truck lurched to a stop. Terry opened his door and got out while she was still blinking away sleep, and she caught sight of the rank of square sun-faded pumps out of the driver's-side window. Terry saw her watching, opened the door, and said, "You're paying for the gas."

She nodded and dug in her purse for her wallet. Once she'd found it she stared stupidly at it, convinced for a second that it wasn't hers, because hers was brown leather, wasn't it? But the moment faded and she opened the blue zippered wallet and checked her cash supply. She handed Terry a twenty. He took it without comment and walked toward the leathery old man behind the counter. She couldn't help noticing that Terry's jeans fit well—not as well as John Lee's, maybe, because Terry had more of a linebacker's build and thick, muscular legs. She caught herself staring and slumped back against the seat. The sun visor was down, revealing what a car salesman would have called a vanity mirror. She looked at her pale skin, the dark circles under her eyes, the unruly mess of her hair, and thought vanity was probably the wrong word.

"What are you doing?" she asked herself. Mirror-lips asked the same question. "What do you want?"

She shook her head and flipped up the sun visor, cutting off the questions. Terry came back and climbed in the cab and turned the engine over.

"How much farther is it?" she asked. She started to unscrew the top of the thermos.

"We're here."

Coffee sloshed, barely in the cup as she flinched.

"Huntsville?" she blurted. "But—"

"Huntsville's a goddamn ten-hour drive. Do you think I'm insane? I never said I was taking you to Huntsville, and anyway, you didn't say you wanted to go to Huntsville." Terry was enjoying her freak-out. He'd put on his aviator glasses, his cop face with them. "You said you wanted to talk to Custer Grady. Custer left the prison weeks ago, and he left the town proper yesterday."

"Where are we?" She licked hot drops of coffee off the back of her hand and tried not to think about the cold sinking sensation in her stomach.

"Big Spring. Custer Grady's coming in on the ten-thirty bus from San Angelo." His smile faded, leaving something cold and bleak behind. "Man's been in prison for thirty years, no telling how talkative he's going to be. But I figure he'll still have an eye for the ladies."

She gave him a long look and said, "You're using me."

"What makes you say that?"

Big Spring was not, in fact, very big, and it didn't take long to get to the tired-looking concrete bunker of the bus station. Abby drank the last of her coffee as Terry pulled the truck up to the curb. He checked his watch and said, "Ought to be pulling in any minute now. I'll give you fifteen minutes, that enough time?"

She nodded. She had absolutely no idea whether it was or not, whether she'd even get a word out of him, but she was too nervous to bargain. She stepped down out of the cab and slammed the door.

The pickup glided away around the corner. She hugged her coat close against a blast of winter air and opened the glass door.

The Big Spring bus station had an art-deco theme, as if the architects and builders had gotten together and said, *This time it's not going to look like a bus station.* It still looked like a bus station, but an upscale one. Cool blue and green neon gleamed behind glass brick walls, and the floors were painfully clean. A TV set murmured in the corner, tuned to a faded-looking western.

No matter how neat they kept the bus station, there was no getting around the passengers. Some of them—a surprising percentage, really—had neat, well-kept clothes and some concept of personal hygiene. Some had a wild-eyed, fragrant look, and clutched their battered suitcases or plastic bags close.

She sat in one of the hard plastic chairs and watched the sweep of the second hand on the clock. Fifteen minutes, he'd said. It seemed like a long time.

Three sweeps of the second hand later, air brakes

farted outside in the garage and red digital letters on a long black screen on the wall said 10:30 FROM SAN ANGELO NOW ARRIV . . . followed by, BOARDING 11:00 TO ABILENE. Some of the people in the lobby stirred and gathered their bags. Some, like Abby, just sat.

Outside the glass doors she saw people getting off the bus. They looked like the same people from the waiting room, only fatter, shorter, taller, younger, older. An older man got off the bus clutching a plain brown bag. Was that him? What if she couldn't recognize him? Did that mean it was all bullshit?

Another older man came down the steps, looked around, and opened his arms to a young girl about twelve, then her parents. The reunion held up the line for a couple of minutes. Abby stood up and came closer, one hand braced on the cool pebbled glass of the wall.

A young, fat, tired woman disembarked with two screaming boys in tow. One of them threw his Mickey Mouse suitcase down on the ground and kicked it. She patiently picked it up and put it back in his hand.

A shadow hesitated at the top of the bus steps, then took a step into the light.

Abby's knees went weak and there weren't any handholds on the glass, nothing to support her at all. She leaned hard against its coolness, pressed her cheek to it.

Custer Grady looked around, blue eyes cold and pale in a face several shades lighter than she remembered. Age hadn't softened him, it had preserved him, turned leather to wood, turned ice to crystal.

His shoulders were lower now, more rounded, and he looked smaller. His hands were gnarled and bumpy. She remembered, in the instant of darkness when she blinked, how his hands had felt on her, rough as sandstone.

He came down the rest of the steps and pushed open the glass door to the waiting room. She couldn't move, couldn't get out of his way, waited for the recognition to dawn in his eyes like an oil fire.

He stepped around her and headed for the bathroom. Once the door had swung shut behind him she made her way to the nearest chair and sank into it, breathless and shaken. *He hadn't known her.* Why would he? Why had she expected he would?

Three more sweeps of the clock's second hand before he came out of the bathroom. He went to the lunch counter built in an art-deco sweep in the far corner and ordered something hot; she saw the steam misting from the cup. He crossed to the chairs and sat down, legs out, crossed at the ankles.

There was a strange little half-smile on his face.

I should wait, she thought. *Terry will be here soon. I could just wait right here.*

It was an empty suggestion, and she knew it. Before she'd even finished thinking it she was getting up, feet gone numb, legs weak. The distance to him seemed huge and expanded by miles when he glanced in her direction. The touch of those eyes brought an unexpected thrill. She'd thought she'd be scared.

Before she could think what else to do she was

standing next to him, looking down as he looked up, and saying, "Mr. Grady? Custer Grady?"

God, she knew that smile, slick as oil. "Been a long time since a pretty lady talked to me. Sit down, honey. You looking for me? You a reporter?"

"Reporter?" she repeated as she took a seat next to him, balanced on the hard plastic edge. "No. Why?"

"I expected they'd be all over the place by now." He looked annoyed, almost pouting. "Me being a big star and all."

"Star?" She was starting to sound like a parrot. She took a deep breath and tried again. "You just got out of prison, didn't you?"

"Hey, are you Loretta?" He sat up straighter, eyes gone bright.

"No."

His smile clabbered. "Thought you might be Loretta. Sweet young thing, been sending me letters for years. All those women sending letters, I figured one of them would make the trip."

Ladies' man, Terry had said derisively in the truck. Custer still thought he was God's gift to women, Lord, hadn't he always? Silly old bastard, sixty if he was a day and he thought a herd of screaming girls would be welcoming him home. Abby blew out her breath in frustration and shook her head.

"If you ain't a reporter and you never wrote me letters, how come you're here?" Grady asked. She didn't like the sharp, assessing look he had, didn't like the strong, hard hands, either, but at least they were staying in his lap. "You ain't a Bible-thumper, are you? I got enough of that up-country."

"I want to ask you about Pearl," she said. He blinked, slowly. Around them conversation seemed to fade out, the bustle of boarding passengers, the hum of reunions, all that was gone and it was only the two of them, close as lovers.

"Pearl who?" He knew, though. She saw it in his oily smile, his febrile eyes.

"Pearl Jordan."

He picked at a thick callus on his thumb. "My old place was next door to the Jordan place, but I never had no doings with them. Crazy, you know. Whole house full of them, crazy as bedbugs. Say, you ought to buy me some breakfast if you're going to jaw at me."

"I know you knew her." Abby swallowed, swallowed again. Her mouth felt dry and gritty. "She was your lover."

Custer Grady gave a high-pitched, hee-hawing laugh that turned heads and made her stomach lurch. His eyes remained cold and fixed on her face.

"Listen to you, missy, listen to you. My *lover*, makes me sound like some rich man in a fancy house. Pearl Jordan was a light-stepping slut, what she was." He studied her closely and showed stained, crooked teeth in a grin. "That bother you, me talking that way? You a churchgoing gal?"

"I think Pearl Jordan died in her house before you went to prison and I think you know something about that."

Once she'd said it she felt dizzy and sick, the weight of his stare on her heavy as hands. He said, "You think I killed her?"

"No. I think you know who did."

He shook his head, looking away from her at the wall clock. "Missy, I got me a bus to catch soon and I've heard all your damn fool nonsense I care to. Pearl Jordan was alive and kicking, last I heard about it. If she's dead, I got me the tightest damn alibi in the lot. And that's all I know about that."

"Sugar," she said. "You brought her a bag of sugar after you'd sold some watches and rings. It broke open when you gave it to her and spilled."

She'd succeeded in surprising him but that wasn't much cause for satisfaction; his head snaked around and he said softly, "She tell you that, did she? She tell you what I gave her that sugar for?"

"So she wouldn't tell when you raped her on her couch," she snapped. He reached out and grabbed her wrist and the feel of it was just like she remembered, hard as bone.

"She never had any complaints of me."

"Let go."

"Pearl was a slut and she liked it rough."

"Let go!" She heard her voice rise as she jerked against his grip. He was hard as an iron bar. The memories of Pearl swarmed over her, choking as dust, and there was no place to go to get free of them, nowhere to run now because he was *here*, and the memories were *right*.

It was all real. Really real.

"You better let her go, hoss," said a new voice, shockingly intrusive in their private universe. Abby looked up and saw Terry Bollinger standing over them, silvered aviator glasses reflecting her strained, pale face. Grady's hold on her wrist tightened. "I ain't joking."

"Didn't think you were." Grady considered Terry with a sour expression. "Boy."

Terry's lips thinned and curled upward, but it wasn't a smile. "Let's take a walk."

"I don't walk so well, son, I'm getting up in years." Grady's tone slid into a trembly whine—and cranked louder, to gain attention, Abby was sure. "You just go on and leave me alone now. Leave me alone."

Terry bent down, close enough that Abby flinched back, and with his mouth no more than an inch from Grady's ear he said, "You get your ass out of that chair and take a walk or it's gonna be a real long ride back to Huntsville, and you'll be real glad when you get there."

Grady let go of her hand. She winced and pulled it into her lap, working her wrist in circles to shake off the feel of his touch.

"I ain't lived this long by going off with hard boys like you," Grady said. "You want to take me outside you're gonna have to drag me kicking and screaming. I ain't saying you can't do it, big old boy like you, but it ain't gonna look too good dragging a helpless old man like me out in the cold."

"You think I won't?" Terry asked pleasantly. Grady shook his head. "Just so we understand each other. You catching the noon bus to Midland?"

Grady sat silently, watching him. Terry reached out and brushed lint from Grady's ill-fitting brown suit.

"Change of plans," he said. "See, you ain't going

to Midland. You're going to cash in that ticket and buy one for anyplace but West Texas, 'cause I got a little message for you from Sheriff Al Hayes in Fall Creek.''

"Then I suppose you better deliver it," Grady said. "Boy."

From where she sat, Abby could feel the contempt searing the air between them, bitter as cyanide. Terry leaned forward and put one hand on Grady's shoulder. His knuckles went white with pressure. Grady's lips thinned.

"I ever see you in Fall Creek in my lifetime," Terry said softly, "it'll be the end of yours. Did you get that message, you murderous son of a bitch?"

Grady nodded, frowned, and said, "Do I know you?"

Terry let go of him and stepped back, turned his mirrored sunglasses toward Abby. "Time's up. Let's go."

"I do, don't I? You must be Evvy Doderman's kid, ain't that right? You got her face, you poor bastard." Grady's lips split open in a dry, bony grin. "Probably got my eyes, though, don't you?"

Abby froze in the act of rising. Terry said, still softly, "Not yet," and put a hand under her arm. There was no difference between his touch and Custer Grady's, no difference at all.

She pulled away, planted her feet, and stepped back as he reached for her again. He frowned and motioned her to come on.

"I'm not going with you, either," she said. "I don't

think you're ready to drag me kicking and screaming, either.''

Terry blew his cheeks round with exasperation,
stuffed his hands in his pockets, and shrugged.

"How the hell are you planning on getting back
to Midland? Hitching?''

She felt the smile that came to her lips, but she
didn't mean it. She said, "Hell, Terry, I'm in a bus
station. Figure it out.''

Sotto Voce:
December 22, 1994

"Today," Dr. Urdiales said as he set his hologram disc on the table between them, "I'd like to explore what you remember about the cellar."

Abby's breath caught, and she found herself looking away, toward the soothing, expensive art on his walls and the satin-smooth wood desk. Anywhere but into those calm eyes.

"If you don't feel comfortable about doing that, you can tell me," he said, and leaned back. The leather chair creaked and sighed around him. He'd gotten a new haircut, a little shorter in the back than before. It made his face seem longer and thinner, his eyes larger. She wondered what he was like out of the soft womb of the office—on a tennis court, maybe. He had the lean, sinewy look of a tennis player.

"I think maybe it's too soon," she said.

"Why?"

"Because it's . . ." She shook her head. "Maybe I don't really want to know anymore."

"Are you afraid you might be wrong?" he asked gently.

"I'm afraid I might not be."

"I will not force you to do anything you don't wish to do, of course, but sometimes it's necessary to face your fears to learn from them." Suddenly, disarmingly, he gave her an impish smile. "And, I confess, I am intrigued to hear your story. Indulge me."

She glanced at the clock—4:45 p.m. Surely, if she thought hard enough, she could come up with a reason to leave. Rehearsal. Illness. Death.

She heard herself say "All right," and the disc spun, and the colors dragged her down to the dark.

"Where are you?" The voice came from somewhere behind her, above her, soft as shadow.

"Kitchen." She pressed her hands on the peeling yellowed counter, stared down at the rusted hole of the drain in the sink. Dishes stacked untidily to the side, a smell of rotten meat heavy in the air. Outside the kitchen window the day blazed hot as hellfire. Her thin cotton dress clung to her back and wrinkled damp around her thighs. She swiped at her forehead with her forearm.

"Where are you going?"

The kitchen moved around her. Her hand touched blood-warm crystal and twisted the cellar doorknob.

"Why are you going to the cellar?"

She opened the door. The cooler air crawled over her skin. One step down, away from the dim refuge of the light.

"What do you see?"

"Dark." She'd broken the only bulb after Daddy

died. She hesitated on the stairs and closed her eyes, listening.

Hoarse, ragged breathing in the dark. A surge of rage caught her by surprise, a feeling so strong she wanted to grab hold of that thing down there and rip it apart while it screamed.

"Something down there," she said. "Got to get it out."

"What is it?"

She took another step into the dark. Wooden steps creaked under her weight. She reached out for balance and cold metal shifted under her fingers—the heavy blade of a shovel, gritty with dirt. She eased the shovel down from the hook and held it in both hands like a baseball bat.

Another step down.

"Come out," she said. "You come on out and I won't hurt you."

But she knew she would hurt it, would strike at it in a blind red fury until it stopped its breathing and moaning and moving. She took one more step into the dark.

Something cold closed around her ankle and jerked.

Her face appeared out of a storm of snow as Dr. Urdiales hit PLAY on the remote control. Abby leaned closer to the television, feeling sick and disoriented at the sight of her own face so . . . lifeless. It didn't look like her at all, did it? Was she really that pale, that plain?

On the screen, Dr. Urdiales' voice recorded the

time and date of the session, even though the cam-
corder had flashed the information at the bottom of
the screen. The video remained focused on her lifeless face, her staring eyes.

"Pearl?" he asked.

And her face changed. The eyes narrowed, the face
tensed, her shoulders hunched protectively. Abby
winced at the feral look in her own eyes.

"Go back to the last day, Pearl," his voice said.
"Where are you?"

"Kitchen," Pearl said shortly. Her face froze on the
screen, chopped apart by lines of static as Dr. Urdiales hit PAUSE.

"You see the change in your body language?" he
asked, and watched as she nodded. "Do you remember any of this?"

She thought she did—flashes, quick impressions.
She stared at her frozen, suspicious face and swallowed hard.

"I remember going down the steps—taking the
shovel off the wall. I think I fell."

She couldn't tell him about the drowning flood of
emotions—the despair, the fear, the rage. She didn't
have the words.

"And then?" he asked. She glanced up at the soft
gold face of the grandfather clock. "Don't worry
about the time, Abby. What do you remember then?"

"Darkness."

"That's all?"

"That's all there is," she said, but felt something
hard under the words, like concrete. Was that true,

or Pearl protecting herself? How could she be sure if Pearl was real?

Dr. Urdiales sat back and crossed his arms. She couldn't tell what he was thinking, if he was thinking anything at all. She waited, hands nervously tapping a fingering pattern on her knees.

"Have you spoken to John Lee since we last talked?"

"No," she said immediately. "No, I haven't."

He smiled warmly. "And would you like to tell me who it is you *did* talk to? Was it Mrs. Jordan or Terry Bollinger?"

"Terry," she said, and looked away. "I went with him to talk to Custer Grady. He just got out of prison."

Dr. Urdiales leaned forward and touched her hands lightly, just enough to drag her gaze back to him.

"How did it feel to see him?"

"Frightening," she whispered. "Familiar. Exciting. I *knew* him."

"Did you?"

"I . . . felt that I did. I thought he recognized me, too."

His expression didn't change from its usual mixture of concern and interest, but she thought she knew what he was thinking, and it scared her. She flinched away from it and groped on the floor for the soft leather of her purse. When she'd found it she pulled it into her lap like a shield.

"I know I've asked you this before, but I want you to think about the answer, please. Is it possible that you might be wrong about all this? About Pearl, about the cellar?''

If she said yes, she'd reassure him that she wasn't going crazy, that he wasn't watching her disintegrate before his eyes. If she said yes, he'd give her more room.

If she said yes, she'd be lying. Without question, lying.

"I suppose I could be wrong," she said.

Lying was better.

A truck followed her home from Dr. Urdiales' office. She drove slowly, careful of the ice-slick roads, and kept a nervous eye on the steady glare of headlights behind her. She didn't go home, not directly, and after four turns the truck peeled away and left her alone in the cold December night.

She pulled into her apartments and parked, her mind only half on the process of retrieving her belongings and separating keys to find the right one for the deadbolt. As she slipped it into the lock she heard the scrape of footsteps behind her and cold slid down her throat and puddled in her stomach, squeezed her lungs hard as she gasped and turned to face what was coming.

The lights behind him cast him into a dark outline in a cowboy hat. For a thrilled fraction of a second she thought it was John Lee before she remembered he didn't drive a truck.

Terry did.

Terry stepped forward into the light, blue eyes narrowed and teeth showing in a grin.

"Not too careful, are you?" he asked. She tried to catch her breath to tell him off, but he nodded toward the keys in her hand. "Let's talk inside."

"I don't have to talk to you. Get the hell away from me." She turned back to the door and fit the key in the lock with trembling fingers. The cold made it difficult to turn. She shouldered the door open and faced him again.

He hadn't moved except to cross his arms across his chest.

"You cut me off pretty fast, Miss Abby. I sure do want to know what Custer Grady said to you."

"Fuck off, Terry." She tried to slam the door in his face but he was fast, very fast, and caught it with the palm of one hand. She pushed harder, but it was like pushing against a block of wood. "I'll scream!"

"Goddamn, you watch too much TV. Go ahead if it'll make you feel better; you know damn well I'm not gonna hurt you. I just want to know what Grady told you."

She let go of the door. He wasn't fast enough to stop the door from crashing back against the wall, and Carlton came charging out of the bedroom, snarling and barking. Abby caught his collar and held on to him with difficulty as he scrabbled for purchase on the wood floor, jaws parted and lips drawn back. He was so strong he dragged her forward almost within biting range before she braced her foot against the wall.

Terry didn't retreat, but his hand had moved close to his coat.

"I'll shoot that fucking thing if I have to," he said.

Looking at his eyes—god, blue eyes, the same shade
as Custer Grady's—she had no doubt he meant it.
She hauled on Carlton's collar and dragged him back
to the bedroom, shoved him in and slammed the
door a second before his weight hit it.

Terry had quietly shut the front door behind him,
and waited in the living room, at home on the couch,
feet on the coffee table. He had the remote in his
hand as he flipped channels.

"You need cable," he said, and tossed her the control. Behind them, Carlton kept up a furious assault
of barking and door-banging. "Make this easy on us
both. The faster you talk, the faster you see my ass
out that door."

Most people had to work to get under her skin;
everything Terry said seemed to inject itself directly
into muscle. She felt her spine stiffen. "I hope you're
comfortable. Can I get you something? Coffee? Tea?
Gosh, I'm sorry I don't have any wine."

He had perfected Custer Grady's blank stare, and
if he noticed her humor it didn't crack his face. His
stare was hard enough to drill diamonds.

And he waited. Damned if she was going to let
him panic her. She stripped off her coat and hung it
up in the closet, went into the kitchen and filled the
kettle with water, then set it on to boil. She turned
on the radio and played it loud, humming along with
Aerosmith even though she didn't really care for the
song, because it helped her ignore the man sitting on
her couch, waiting.

And the phone rang. She turned down the volume
on the radio, grabbed the phone off the wall, and

said, "Hello." Even before she heard his voice she knew who it was, who it had to be.

"Hi. Are you busy?" John Lee's voice had the power to tilt the world; she reached out for the counter to pull it back. Now that she heard him she felt the loss of him like an open wound.

She turned her back on Terry's stare, fought to keep her voice steady as she said, "I'm afraid so. Can I call you back in a little while?"

He sounded so far away, so fragile. "Sure, if you want. I'm on the car phone."

From the living room, Terry said loudly, "Hey, honey, what're you doing in there?" She whipped around to glare at him in panic and instinctively tucked the phone closer to her neck.

"What?" John Lee asked. "Sorry, what'd you say?"

"Nothing. It's the TV. Listen, I've got to get going, but I'll call you back, okay?" How to tell him that she cared, that she hadn't forgotten him? She hesitated, indecisive, and felt heat at her back an instant before she heard Terry's voice near her ear.

"Tell him I said hello."

She hit the disconnect button fast—fast enough?— and stepped forward out of Terry's warmth before she turned on him. He was smiling, blue eyes mild with pleasure.

"You son of a bitch."

"Couldn't resist. You think he heard me?"

"You want to know what Grady said to me? Nothing! Grady thought I was a goddamn jailhouse groupie, does that help you? He's just like you, like

father like son, so get the hell out of my house right
now or I'll call some *real* cops!"

Behind her, the kettle rose to a scream. She reached
out to turn it off but Terry's hand got to hers first
and grabbed, crushingly hard.

"You better get something straight," he said. He
was close enough that his warm breath felt like a
touch on her cheek. "I'm not fucking playing with
you, Abby. Your boyfriend killed Marlene and I'm
gonna see him pay for it, one way or another, and
you had better get the hell out of the way 'cause
there ain't no neutral territory, not here. You had a
nice little chat with Custer Grady and I can't help
but think about Custer killing those women in the
fifties and his son killing Marlene. You have a talk
about that, did you?"

"No," she said, breathing hard. "I asked him about
Pearl Jordan."

"Jesus Christ." His grip on her loosened enough
that she pulled free and turned off the burner. The
kettle died to a moan, then to silence. "Now, why
would you want to do that? Pearl Jordan never done
anything illegal in her life I know about, except having a son like John Lee."

He sounded almost defensive. She remembered the
sweet, vulnerable smile on Pearl's scarred face. She
might seem that way, to anyone who hadn't been in
that blood-soaked basement, seen the damaged face
twisted up with hate.

"If you're going to try to tell me Pearl killed Marlene—" he began derisively.

"No. But I think maybe she knows something.

Something about Custer Grady and maybe about Marlene's death, too." She forced a smile. "Maybe I should ask Pearl about Marlene. Maybe nobody ever did that."

For a long moment he just looked at her. She became aware of the small kitchen, the blank wall behind her, the kettle full of boiling water on the stove between them. There was some of that awareness in his eyes, too.

In the bedroom, Carlton stopped barking. He whined, thumped against the door, and went silent.

"If you like," he said. "Go right ahead."

She turned away and opened a cabinet and took down a mug, lifted a second and raised her eyebrows at him. He hesitated and nodded.

An ironic smile flashed over his lips when she took hold of the teakettle. She poured two cups and watched the white steam breathe.

"Hot tea okay?"

"Fine." He leaned an elbow on the stove and watched as she hunted down teabags. She set out a honey jar and went to the refrigerator for lemon. "You know something? Something about Marlene?"

She let the tea bags stew. They bled brown strips into the hot water. She squeezed them with a spoon and stirred. The crushed wet hulks went into the trash. When she turned back to the tea Terry was stirring honey into his mug, thick golden spirals. Without looking at her, he said, "Well?"

She reached past him for her mug and drank it without flavoring, hot enough to leave a warning tingle on the roof of her mouth. She missed the strong clean taste of Miklos' tea back in Dallas. Hers tasted dry and musty.

"I need to get into Pearl's house."

He put the mug down on the counter with a wet thump. "What do you mean?"

"All we have to do is get inside—"

"Whoa." When she opened her mouth to reply, he held out a hand to stop her. Big hands, she remembered. Capable hands. She closed her mouth. "Stop right there. I ain't going down that road with you. I'm an officer of the law."

"When it suits you." She sipped tea and looked longingly at the honey jar by his side. "All I'm saying is that we pick a time when we know she's not home—"

"She's always home."

"—and we disable the alarm. I'm sure you know how to do that—"

"Listen, Abby—"

"—and we *look*, we just take a *look*! Isn't that what you want? To prove she's guilty?"

She stopped, breathing hard, and saw that he was frowning. He said, "She?"

She turned away to pick up a dishrag and wipe at the tea he'd spilled on the counter.

"I thought you said you weren't gonna tell me Pearl Jordan killed Marlene."

"I'm not," she said. The dishrag was stiff and unabsorbent. The tea ran stubbornly away. "I think she killed somebody else."

He could have called her a fool, could have laughed. Instead, he asked, "Who?"

A reasonable question. *Me* didn't seem to be a very reasonable answer.

"I think the woman living in that house isn't the real Pearl Jordan. I think she killed Pearl and buried the body in the cellar and took her place."

"Oh, and none of us noticed that. She may be a stay-at-home but she ain't exactly a hermit, either. Plenty of people know her."

"Now," Abby said, and swiped the rag over the tea until it softened. "How many people knew her before Custer Grady beat her so badly she almost died?"

Dead silence. She finished wiping up the mess, picked up the mug, and handed it to him. His fingers wrapped around it but he didn't seem to notice its weight; he was still frowning, shaking his head.

"That was back in . . . what? In '58? Something like that. Hell, I guess just about everybody knew her back then. Small town, nothing to do."

"Fact is, Pearl Jordan's mother ended up in a mental institution and her father was just about as crazy. Pearl never went out of the house after her mother was committed until her father died, and then only to go to the funeral. She never let anybody inside, either. All of a sudden she ends up beaten badly enough to have her face reconstructed. Everybody knows her then, don't they?" She watched his face as he nodded. "But maybe *that* one, the one that was beaten, that wasn't Pearl Jordan at all. Pearl Jordan was already dead in the cellar."

He thought about it a full minute before he asked,

reasonably enough, "Then who is she if she's not Pearl Jordan?"

"I don't know," Abby said, and saw the flash in his eyes as he dismissed the whole idea. "No, wait, just because I don't know doesn't mean it's not true!"

"Where'd you get this story, out of some damn detective magazine? You buy it off some bum at the bus station?" His eyes narrowed. "Custer Grady tell you that fairy tale?"

I saw it in a vision.

"Yes," she said. "Custer Grady told me."

"Then it's total goddamn bullshit. Custer Grady was full of stories when they put him away, the crazier the better. He told the judge that the cotton plants used to come up out of the ground and talk to him. He told his lawyer that the Nazis killed those people and framed him." He swiped his hand in the air, wiping the whole idea away. "You oughta get some professional help for that gullibility problem."

"I am. You know it. You followed me from Dr. Urdiales' office, didn't you?"

He seemed surprised that she'd noticed. "I saw you there last week when I came to pick up my mother."

"Your mother?" She thought, absurdly, of the elegant receptionist, her professional smile.

"Evvy Bollinger."

I'm Evvy, she'd cooed in the waiting room, honey-sweet. She'd never said her last name but then strangers didn't, did they, when they met in a psychologist's waiting room? Something had rung a bell but it had been a distant ringing, far as the horizon.

COPPER MOON 265

She'd thought it had been a Pearl-memory. Instead it had been the shape of Evvy's face, the mouth, because those showed plainly on Terry's face, carved heavier.

He was still watching her. Waiting for something. "What?" she demanded. He leaned against the kitchen counter and let his eyelids slip half closed.

"You want your tape back?"

The words stuck somewhere down around her heart in a painful lump. She cleared her throat and nodded. He had that lazy, predatory look again. She remembered his hands sliding hot up her legs while John Lee watched, helpless.

"Say please," he said. She clenched her teeth hard enough to make her jaw muscles ache, relaxed them, and smiled.

"Please."

He moved a step closer. She put her hand on the teakettle, still half full; it made a protesting whisper and breathed steam. She saw Terry's eyes flick to it.

He leaned forward, face so close to hers he filled the world, and said, "Custer Grady ain't my goddamn father, Abby. Don't you ever say he is again."

Her hand flinched around the handle of the teakettle but then he was gone, stepping away. Her lungs hurt as if he'd sucked all the air from the room.

He opened the front door and walked out, leaving it swinging open behind him. She let go of the kettle with an effort and went to push the door shut. He was walking down the sidewalk, careful of the thin, slippery coating of ice. His down parka made him look even broader in the shoulders than he really was.

As he got in his pickup she caught sight of a car parked in the row behind, lights off but motor running, exhaust rising like a ghost-trail into the cold. She couldn't see it clearly, couldn't see if anybody was sitting in the driver's seat, but she knew the car.

"Oh, God," she whispered.

John Lee had just seen Terry leave her apartment.

The next morning dawned with an odd sense of normality—Christmas was coming, she had things to do, presents to buy, had to clean the house and get everything straightened up before Maria came back from her latest trip and threw a fit over the state of the floors. Carlton was a big, fluffy dog, and he left guilty, hairy evidence everywhere he went. She set about vacuuming the living room, kicking furniture out of her way when she could and ignoring it when she couldn't. Carlton hid in the bedroom near the bed, ready to dive for even more cover if she brought the roaring metal monster near him. She filled up one bag with disgusting-looking crap and started a new one for the second half of the room.

She hadn't had the courage to call back John Lee. What could she have said? If that *had* been him in the parking lot—and she knew in her heart that it was—there was really nothing to say. On the other hand, she felt she had made inroads toward getting Terry's help. He didn't believe her story, but he wanted to hurt John Lee, and she'd offered him a golden opportunity to do it through Pearl Jordan.

All she had to do was wait.

She hummed as she cut green foil paper and wrapped a thick sweater for her father. She'd hunted for days for something for her brother but he was difficult to buy for, very picky about his clothes and anything he liked. He didn't like gadgets. She might be able to find him an interesting tie, but that was about it.

Benny. She felt so mixed about Benny at the moment that she'd put off buying her gift for last. Usually Benny was the bright light at the end of the tunnel, a joy to shop for because all she had to do was look for the coolest, most outrageous thing she could find, match it with the tackiest thing she could find, and Benny would drool like a Saint Bernard. But right now Benny was mixed up with the dark place in her head, with Pearl and blood and the taste of Miklos' honey tea. Nothing seemed very funny about it.

God, she wanted all of this over with, finished. She wrapped her father's present grimly now, matching ribbon and choosing a flat bow that wouldn't crush too much in mailing. She wrapped it in brown paper and parcel tape and wrote his address on it.

Carlton whined from the corner. He was looking out the window at falling snow.

"Yeah, I know, baby, you need a walk. Give me a minute." She dumped all the wrapping accessories into the box and set the package on the table, went back to gather up boots and gloves and coat and hat. She bundled herself up and found the leash; Carlton immediately went into ecstatic leaps and turns, bouncing up and down like a furry rubber ball. She grabbed his collar and hooked him up, then opened the door onto winter.

The air felt breakable with cold, sharp on her exposed face but sweet on her tongue. She tasted a snowflake, caught another on the wool of her glove, and watched the lace dissolve into damp glitter. The sidewalk was padded with snow and scarred with two or three sets of footprints, going in the direction of the parking lot. She hauled Carlton—and was hauled by him—off to the softer snow that covered the grass. He scrambled awkwardly around a leafless powdered tree, led her in a complete circle around the base, and lifted his leg. His cheerful yellow stain was the only color in the world besides her blue coat. He sniffed the result and went on to the next spot, a patch of apartment wall that looked identical to everything around it. She passed the time by counting the number of apartments that had smoke coming out of their chimneys and estimating the number of mesquite trees being cut.

Carlton made three more stops before running out of ammunition and informing her he'd like to go home. She detoured him to the parking lot to test the pavement—slippery, but acceptable. She'd driven in worse. There was still time to shop for her brother's tie and finally find something for Benny.

And, she decided, something for John Lee. She could take it over, as a peace offering. Explain about Terry, somehow. Fix things.

She had no idea how to do that, but one thing at a time. First, a present.

* * *

John Lee had a visitor.

Abby sat parked in the dim afternoon on a field of white, her heater blasting lukewarm dry air hard enough to ruffle her hair. His glass shop sign fluttered in the wind, and swirls of snow blurred the outline of the front door. John Lee's car was parked in front, newly swept clean, and the falling snow landed on his hood and melted immediately. He'd driven far enough to get his engine good and hot.

She saw him pass in front of the kitchen window again, where the bright lights were on. He had on a checked blue flannel shirt and his mouth moved as he talked to whoever it was in the room with him. He turned toward the stove and stood there. Making dinner, she thought. She remembered their first dinner with a pang, could almost taste the hamburgers and the honey beer and the wild dark flavor of his kisses.

It had to be a friend, she thought. An old friend, surely. Someone he hadn't seen in years, had come in for the holidays, maybe an old school buddy in town visiting relatives.

She had to know.

Outside of the car the wind was harsh and it whispered cold snowflakes into her ear; she pulled her ski hat farther down and hunched her shoulders and shuffled through the ankle-deep snow.

John Lee moved away from the window and left a blank view. She pressed against the wall and edged carefully around to peek inside. She got a slice of the kitchen and the workshop brilliantly glittering beyond. Shifting her position, she saw John Lee's elbows moving as he served something from a skillet to a plate.

Another shift and she saw him smiling. She took a deep breath and prepared to shift another half step to see his guest, but then she saw the hand reaching out a spoon to ladle potatoes, and it wasn't necessary to see her, wasn't necessary at all.

The nails were long and painted in screaming pink and neon orange stripes. The hand was strong and sturdy, the fingers long. The wrist jangled with about fifty different bracelets.

She didn't have to see the hair or the face or the clothes to recognize Benny. Her best friend was having dinner in John Lee's kitchen, laughing like an old buddy, drawing that brilliant smile out of him. Maybe later he'd step up to her, slide those warm hands up her sides . . .

Abby found herself sitting in the snow, her face cold where the tears were drying on her cheeks. On the snow in front of her a picture painted itself, warm yellow light and John Lee's flickering shadow, a flash of movement that might have been Benny reaching for the salt or for John Lee. She remembered John Lee's interested stare that day at her recital—staring not at her, but at Benny. She'd thought it was just shock, but it hadn't been, had it? Had he called her up in Dallas and invited her down? Had she called him? *Are you and Abby having troubles? Well, why don't you tell me all about it. Let me kiss it and make it better.*

Oh, God. Goddamn them. *Just like all the rest of them, all the rest of those women making eyes and flirting*

*with every man they seen, trying to take Custer away
from me—*

No. Abby pushed it away with all her strength, but
it wouldn't go away, not this time. She was too
strong, too angry. Hurricane Pearl.

*You just going to let them do that to you? You going
to let them lie to you and cheat on you and laugh behind
your back?*

It isn't like that. Benny isn't like that.

*The hell she ain't. She's turning the knife right now.
Look. Go on and look.*

She couldn't look. She felt sick but she swallowed
it, swallowed hard and climbed up out of the snow,
didn't care how much noise she made now or
whether or not they saw her. Her jeans felt heavy
and waterlogged, clinging wet to her legs. She
trudged back to the car and started it up with a roar.

John Lee peered out the window. She flipped on
her lights, on high, and saw him squint in surprise.

Then she turned and spun snow in the air as she
drove away. When she hit the main road and her
tires slipped, his package tipped to the floor in a
cascade of gold-flecked foil and silver angel bows. It
slid into the darkness under the passenger seat of
the car.

She left it there, along with the empty soda cans
and discarded fast-food bags and other rotten
dreams.

Fortissimo:
December 24, 1994

The next day, Fall Creek had a celebrity in town. It wasn't hard to figure out where he was—all she had to do was follow the gawkers.

Custer Grady was holding court in a peeling green leatherette booth at Josie's Restaurant, sipping Coke from a pebbled yellow plastic glass. The remains of his dinner drowned in a swamp of off-color gravy. His immediate audience was two teenage boys wearing identical blank looks of adoration. The other gawkers ate their waffles and omelets and tried to look like they weren't hanging on Custer Grady's every word.

It was a pathetic scene. Abby thought, from where she stood looking in the smudged front window, that Grady was having the time of his life.

A faded-looking waitress was hovering near the coffeepot and watching the door—waiting for someone, Abby thought. Maybe the Fall Creek Police Department was on the way. Maybe Terry was strapping on his six-gun to make Fall Creek safe from seventy-year-old ex-cons.

When she pushed open the door she heard Grady

saying, ". . . taught him a lesson, boys, I can tell you—" just before the cowbell clapped tin hands over her head and the talking stopped. Chairs scooted. Dim smudges of shadowed faces turned, but by some perverse trick of the light Custer Grady was perfectly clear in a patch of watery sunlight, blue eyes gleaming as he studied her.

"If it ain't the pretty missy from Big Spring. Them girls, they just can't leave me alone." He grinned for the benefit of the two boys at the table, but his eyes were steady and focused. "Pull up a squat, honey."

"I want to talk to you."

He leaned back and dropped his fork with a clatter, crossed his arms across his chest, and tipped his head to one side. Something about the position reminded her strongly of Terry, then—frighteningly, with a prickling along the back of her neck—John Lee.

"Ain't nothing stopping you," he said. "Go on, if you've a mind. Always nice to talk to a pretty one."

She flicked a look toward the teenagers; the taller boy leaned forward, lips parted to show a metal gleam of braces. His 4-H jacket was coming apart at the shoulder seams, at least two sizes too small. His friend, Mutt to his Jeff, looked like he might smother in the oversized Dallas Cowboys parka draped around him. His eyes were huge behind smudged thick eyeglasses.

"Ben. Zach." Grady snapped his fingers like they were dogs and, sure enough, the boys snapped to attention. "Git."

The tall one—Ben, she realized; the yellow

stitching of his name on his jacket was fraying so that it said only BE—scrambled up immediately, blushed a furious red, and slumped toward the door. Zach hesitated, coat dragging at him as if it had tackled him.

"Nice to meet you, ma'am," he said, all in a lisping rush, and hurried away as Ben stiff-armed the door and alarmed the cowbell again. Abby turned her gaze back to Grady and saw him staring after the boys.

"Pearl Jordan," he said flatly as he watched them cross the snowy street outside. "Ain't that right?"

"That's right."

"Lazy good-for-nothing crazy woman, that's what she was. Never did nothing nor meant nothing in this world. Her and her whole family." He looked down at his silverware, picked up his fork, and felt the tines for sharpness.

"Was," Abby said.

He looked up and smiled. "Pardon?"

"Was. You said she was. Not she is."

"Oh." He shrugged. "I figured she was dead, after all this time."

No, he hadn't; she saw the perverse glitter in his eyes. Terry had warned her, Grady had made a career out of lying, claiming one thing and another. And he dearly loved controlling women.

"The story is that you beat her nearly to death the day they arrested you for murder," she said. Behind her somebody's fork clattered loudly on a plate. Somebody else coughed and scraped a chair across the floor. "What do you say?"

"Why the hell should I have anything to say to you, *missy*?" He leaned his chair back on two legs, raised his voice, and said, "Jayleen! Get me a slice of that good old pumpkin pie you got on the counter, there. One for my friend, here, too."

The waitress sullenly pulled the pie out from the display and attacked it with a knife. She squirted whipped cream on top and slapped plates down on the table after shoving aside Grady's congealing platter of gravy. Her hand rested briefly on Abby's shoulder, and the long red fingernails reminded her, painfully, of Benny. Of John Lee.

"Coffee?" the waitress asked, in the tone she probably reserved for long-haired hippies and circus freaks. After a second too long, she added, "Ma'am?"

"No." All at once Abby felt tired and claustrophobic, sickened by the stares and the dry hot air and people always *watching* and *judging* and God, hadn't she asked for it, coming here? She was sick at the sight of Custer Grady, sick at heart for all the stupid people in this stupid town who would rather have a monster for a celebrity than no celebrity at all. "I don't want any pie."

Jayleen looked down uncomprehendingly at the plate in Abby's hand and frowned as if it were a misbehaving pet. "Fresh this morning," she said huffily. "Nothing wrong with it."

"Then you eat it," Abby said, and shoved it hard against Jayleen's soft middle so that Jayleen, in simple self-defense, had to take it. Whipped cream gave Jayleen's Santa apron a mustache. She backed away, glaring, and looked around the restaurant for support. Satisfied she had a consensus on her side, she said "Well, I *never*," and retreated back to the coffee-pot. She pasted on a too-wide smile and made a circuit of the room filling cups from her Pyrex beaker and pointedly ignoring Abby.

"Forgot about that," Grady said nonsensically, and chewed a thick cud of pumpkin pie. "Pearl had a hell of a temper, too. Hotter than a two-dollar whore at a Baptist convention. Wouldn't a thought it, looking at her. She weren't much to look at, even in her younger days."

"Did you beat her up? The day you were arrested?" When he didn't answer, Abby shrugged and reached down to pick up her purse. "Whatever. I just thought you'd want to get the story straight."

Grady said, too casually, "You some kind of reporter?"

It was her turn to smile and wait. He licked white foam from his fork, took a sip of coffee, ate another mouthful of pie. Then he said, "Pretty girl came to see me few years back, said she could sell my story and make me some money. You gonna make me some money?"

"Maybe."

"Have to do better than just a maybe."

"Maybe's all you get until I hear the story."

He threw his head back and brayed like a mule, showing molars brown as chocolates with black sticky cavity middles. She caught a whiff of his breath and nearly gagged.

"That's just what the other one said," he wheezed. "Well, well. Don't suppose you'd like to go off someplace private for a little conversation, just the two of us?"

He pumped his eyebrows up and down, in case she'd missed the innuendo. She swallowed a hard lump of disgust and shook her head.

Grady leaned forward. She hesitated but didn't see any way around it; she leaned forward, too, and entered the swampy atmosphere of his bad breath.

"Never hit her the day I was taken in," he said. Most of the exaggerated Texas drawl had dropped out of his voice, leaving it clipped and rough. "Never even saw her. Went by her house but she weren't there."

He was holding something back, waiting; she saw it lurking in the hard smile, the harder eyes.

"Somebody was," she guessed. "Who?"

"You're a damn sight cleverer than them yahoos went poking around my farm back in the fifties, ain't you? You think I'm gonna tell you?"

"I don't think you have a reason not to tell me."

He wasn't frightening, not the way she remembered him from Pearl's point of view. Not physically threatening. It was all control now, manipulation, games. That didn't mean that the games couldn't be dangerous, of course. She still wouldn't want to be alone with him, even for a moment.

He clearly thought she did.

"Miss High-and-Mighty Evalyn Doderman," he said, and leaned back. She grabbed a grateful breath of fresh air. "She was there. Told me Pearl had gone out. Gone out! In a pig's eye. Pearl never did go out past her own fence, scared to death of everything and everyone."

Evvy Doderman. Pearl-memories bobbed to the surface, too many to push away—Evvy the sweater girl, Evvy the popular, Evvy the beautiful. Pearl had hated her perfectly, despairingly, emptily. Evvy had never been in the house. Not while Pearl was alive.

"What did Evvy say?" she asked.

Grady laced his hands behind his head and grinned. "We was too busy to talk much, missy. Me and Evvy, we were real good friends. Had us a fine old time right there on Pearl's daddy's couch."

Whether she wanted to or not. Everything had been half true, after all—Terry *was* Custer Grady's son, child of rape just like John Lee. That was why Evvy Bollinger spent her afternoons in Dr. Urdiales' office in Midland, quietly desperate. That was why she kept up the obsessive fiction about Terry's truck-driver father.

Pearl hadn't lied to John Lee, at least. And both of the boys knew, didn't they? Terry knew. It showed in his rage, his fear, his terrorizing of John Lee.

She felt ill again, the world a crushing weight on her chest. She pushed back her chair and stood up, glad her knees held her. Everyone stared.

"Ain't much of a story yet," Grady said as she turned away. "Gets better."

She looked around the diner, the rapt faces, Jayleen's hard, triumphant smile.

"Why don't you tell them?" she shot back, and yanked the zipper up on her coat as she started for the door.

Outside the window, a car nosed into the snow and parked. Gold emblems flashed on the doors as two men got out. They wore thick blue parkas, gray slacks, and gray felt Stetsons. The taller one had on silvered aviator glasses.

Abby stopped halfway, trapped between Grady and the approaching disaster, watching as Terry held the door open for an older man who had to be Sheriff Hayes. Hayes made a show of brushing snow off his coat, stamping his feet, blowing on his chapped hands.

She didn't know why she found it such a surprise that Sheriff Hayes was black. Difficult to imagine Terry working for—having *respect* for—a black man, she supposed. And she certainly hadn't expected such a round, friendly-looking face on a man who'd sent Terry to terrorize an old man.

"Whoo-ee, I'm froze up like an ice cube. Jayleen, honey, how about a couple of cups of that fine coffee?" Hayes had an apple face, shiny and cheerful. His eyes were quick and, Abby thought, frighteningly aware. He favored her with a smile as sweet as a streetcorner Santa's. "Hey, there, Miss Rhodes, how are you? You looking forward to Christmas?"

She nodded in shock, less surprised that he knew her name than that he knew her on sight. He turned and greeted a couple more people by name, nodded hellos to three or four more, and sat down at one of the rickety tables near where Abby stood.

Terry waited by the door, leaning against the wall, head tilted down so his hat hid his face. She couldn't leave without passing him, close enough to touch.

That alone held her where she was, waiting while Sheriff Hayes was served his coffee, asked for cream and sugar. While he stirred his cup, staring down at it, he said blandly, "Can't say it's nice to see you again, Custer."

"Now, hold on, Sheriff. I'm a reformed man!" Grady said, and leaned back in the booth. Plastic creaked like old wood. "Been nearly forty years since you saw me, don't you think a man can change?"

"Jayleen, let me have a slice of that apple pie, there, if you please. And some of that whipped cream. Grady, I expect any man can change except you. You're a lying, murdering, black-hearted son of a bitch." The sheriff lifted his gaze from the coffee and smiled, but it wasn't the jolly Santa smile from before. "Fall Creek's turned into a nice little town while you been gone, and it's full of nice folks. I don't think those nice folks want you back, Grady."

Grady slouched his shoulders and looked down in his lap and said, "Don't want no trouble with the law, Al, you know that."

The words were right but everything else was wrong, a parody of a submissive ex-con, a nasty grin half hidden on his lips. Abby pulled in a deep breath and looked over at Terry; the rim of his hat raised just enough that she felt him looking at her, too.

It did not reassure her.

"I expect you've got a bus ticket through to Midland," Sheriff Hayes was saying. "Dallas would be even better. Maybe El Paso."

Grady said, still looking down at his plate, "This here's my home, Sheriff. These here's my people."

There was just the slightest little lean on the word *my*. Every other person in the diner was white.

"Any of you good people ever rob, rape, and murder strangers for pocket money?" Sheriff Hayes' eyes did a lazy circle of the diner. Nobody moved, least of all Abby. "You, Mrs. Morrow? You ever bury some poor soul out in your field? Carl? You ever beat some skinny teenage girl to death?"

Mrs. Morrow and a tall, skinny kid Abby assumed was Carl developed a consuming interest in breakfast. Forks flashed. Carl finished first, by a swallow, and hauled out a fistful of bills that he left on the table. He mumbled an apology and brushed by Terry on the way out. Terry tipped his hat and smiled. Abby didn't much like the way he was smiling. It was that lazy, I've-got-a-secret smile.

"Maybe you oughta keep an eye on that Carl, Sheriff," Grady said. "Young fella like that, could be up to all kinds of things. Old man like me, I ain't no trouble."

Sheriff Hayes wiped his mouth, put his fork down, and got up. He put a hand on Grady's shoulder. It looked like just a friendly touch but Abby saw the look that came over Grady's face. Murderous. Frightening.

Hayes bent over and put his lips close to Grady's ear. Whispered.

Grady came out of the chair as if Hayes had stuck his tongue in his ear, and the chair went clattering across the floor. Somebody—it might have been Jayleen—yelped. Everyone jumped.

Sheriff Hayes faced Grady at a distance of no more

than a couple of feet. Grady still held his fork in one white-knuckled, wrinkled, trembling hand.

"I ain't takin' no shit from a nigger who wiped toilets when I was a man of property around here!" Grady's right hand jerked forward a little. Hayes held his ground. Terry had changed position so quietly that Abby was only aware of him when he was standing next to her. For a change, she didn't mind his closeness, as long as she could put him between her and Custer Grady.

Hayes said softly, "I think you better calm down, Grady, 'less you want a real short vacation out here in the world. Terry, why don't you take Mr. Grady someplace where he can cool off."

Grady looked past Hayes. For a heart-stopping second his eyes paused on Abby and she saw the hate that burned at his core, the kind of hate that had no reason or fear or caution. Then it was gone, sucked back down inside, and he held up his hands and let the fork drop to the floor.

"No offense, Sheriff. No offense meant," he said.

Hayes nodded. "Take my advice," he replied. "Take the bus. I don't want to see you around here spoiling my Christmas. Jayleen, thanks for the pie. Folks, sorry to disturb your breakfast. You go right on and eat."

He put his hat back on, nodded to Terry, and walked away, out the doors of the diner. Terry stayed where he was, next to her shoulder.

"Got something to show you," he said, as if Grady were not still standing there, staring at them. She shook her head. "Come on."

His hand closed around her arm, hard as a vise. She had to walk or be dragged.

The tin cowbell sounded alarm behind them as they stepped out into the cold wind. Snow brushed her face. She squinted up at the sky and saw more gray fleece clouds blowing in from the north.

"You want to let me go now?" she said.

Terry held on. "Not just yet. What the hell you think you're doing, screwing around with him? We got enough trouble around here without you bringing it in from the city. You get in your car and pedal right back where you came from." He gave her arm an extra squeeze and let it go. She clenched her fist to work the blood back through.

"What about Pearl Jordan's house?" she asked. He gave her a long, level look. Cold burned a red line around his nose, drew clown-spots high on his cheeks.

"Tomorrow night," he said. "She'll be out to church for Christmas services. We go in at six, get out no later than seven, whatever we find. Understand?"

"Where do I meet you?" She had trouble keeping her voice level; she wanted to gasp for breath even though the cold burned like water in her lungs. "Here in town?"

"Hell, no." He looked around quickly at the police car idling at the curb. Inside, the blocky shape of Sheriff Hayes' hat changed directions to look toward them. "I'll find you."

"And I get the tape back? After?"

He walked away and got in the car without answering her. She shoved her hands in her pockets and watched them pull away, exhaust spinning up like a banner into the air and shredding in the breeze.

Inside the diner, Custer Grady waved at her and blew her a kiss. She shuddered.

She pulled over to the side of the road where she'd parked before, got out, and looked at the gray outline of Pearl Jordan's house. The wind carried a faint smell of mesquite smoke toward her. There'd be a fire inside, in that fireplace Daddy had always kept boarded up. He'd had a fear of birds flying down the chimney. She remembered lying awake at night listening for the whisper of wings, the pecking of a beak like the tap of fingernails.

She wanted to know the woman's name, more than anything else. Wanted to scream it at her and see the shock, the fear, spread like disease. She couldn't call her *Pearl* anymore.

She was Pearl's murderer. Pearl had been dead in the cellar when Custer Grady had come to see her and found Evvy Doderman instead. Hadn't mattered to him which woman he bent over the couch.

In a way, Pearl would have been relieved.

"Evvy," she said aloud. Her voice sounded fragile as glass on the cold air. "Evvy was there. Evvy knows."

More than that. Evvy Doderman Bollinger knew Pearl Jordan was dead. She had to know.

Abby stared at the house for a few more seconds, then got back in the car. As she did she saw a car coming, slowing to make a left turn down the Jordan road. Maroon car, late model.

John Lee's face, first blank, then surprised.

In the passenger seat, Benny Wright, black and white hair slithering over her shoulders as she turned to look, purple sunglasses vivid even through the distance. Her mouth was moving but it stopped and the shock of recognition came over her, too, rippling like thrown water.

Benny's passenger window motored down. Abby stared at her pale, painted face.

"Abby?" Benny's voice came distant and high-pitched through Abby's still-closed window. "Hey, Ab, ah, surprise. Hey, roll the window down, okay?"

She sat, staring.

Benny fumbled off her sunglasses and leaned half-way out the window. "I was worried," she said. "Abby—"

John Lee got out of the car. He came around it in three long steps and yanked at Abby's driver's-side door, cursed softly when he found it locked. His face was as pale as Benny's but the lines of his face were angry and stiff.

"Get out," he said. She shook her head. He bounced his hand loudly on the roof of the car. "Get out, Abby! Goddamn you, you talk to me!"

"You're scaring her, John." The sound of John's name on Benny's lips jolted like an electric shock. "Hey, cut it out, okay? Let me talk to her. Please."

He'd never doubted he was Custer Grady's son. He'd stared in the mirror and seen it in his own eyes, the capacity for rage, the preying instinct. She remembered the look on his face when he'd told her about it. He was so afraid to be his father.

He'd never looked more like him.

"I have nothing to say to you," Abby said. If he couldn't hear her, he could read her lips. "Leave me alone."

"So you can stalk my mother some more?" He yanked at her door again, furiously enough that she felt the car rattle under her. "Your dog ever really get lost, Abby? Or did you arrange that, drop the poor bastard off knowing he'd head for the first house he saw? Pretty goddamn convenient, him coming back here again. You *used* me, didn't you? You *used* me to get to her."

Benny. When Abby looked past him she saw her friend flinch. Benny must have told him about the memories coming back in Dallas, about the visions of murder. After all, Benny never wasted an opportunity for a good fuck, did she? If Abby was too screwed up to enjoy it, why not scoop up the leftovers?

Abby gunned her engine and pulled out onto the road, blind with rage, heard John Lee scream "No!" a second before her tires skidded, before she heard the truck horn blare, looked up, and saw the huge red cab of a semi coming at her. The driver wore a blue baseball cap that said LLOYD'S FEED & SEED and he needed a shave. He looked very young, very frightened.

The semi's brakes made a hiss like a snake when they locked and the trailer began to twist sideways in front of her, an oncoming white blur that filled her windshield like a snowstorm. If she'd had time, she would have looked back at John Lee, at Benny.

At Pearl Jordan's house.

The impact threw her forward into the steering wheel and for a second everything was weightless, like space flight, her purse suspended in mid-air, a pen caught in midtumble, a bright glitter of glass like a colorless kaleidoscope.

A splatter of red on the dashboard. The car was still moving, turning on the ice, dancing with the semi like a child on her father's toes. Daddy had danced with her like that once, she remembered. She'd been little and Mother had gotten angry that he was dancing, she was very strict about that. *Lyle, you're teaching that girl all the wrong things.* Daddy had spanked her later, tears running down his cheeks, breathing hard as his hand came down, again and again, while she screamed and wiggled and cried for Mother. But Mother was just a shadow in the doorway.

The trailer tilted, blocking out the dizzy weak light. For a second, as she spun, she saw the house like a raw wound on the horizon. She reached out for it, closed bloody fingers around it, and tried to pull it closer.

Custer Grady's hands on her shoulders, forcing her down in the cushions, his panting behind her, never saying her name, never saying anything. When it was over she'd always believe it was her fault somehow. She hadn't pleased him enough, and she'd agree to do anything for him because at least he was *there*, he was *something* in her ugly, empty life.

The trailer was falling.

The cellar, dark as the grave around her.

Custer, dragging the woman's limp body through

the house, leaving a trail of blood on the carpet, the one brown eye open in the smashed face, blood beading like a second skin down her arms and legs. *Is she dead? Is she dead?* she'd screamed, horrified for the carpet, the smell of that sweat and fear and blood. Custer, in the kitchen, tossing a handful of scattered change and a battered gold pocketwatch on the table. *She didn't have nothing,* he'd spat. *Goddamn dog nearly bit me.*

The roof of the car was coming down, slow as a dream.

Custer, rolling the woman's body down the stairs with a shove of his foot. The sound of flesh slapping wood. Of bones breaking.

Ain't she dead? she asked breathlessly. *You can't leave her here.*

My house is full of 'em, you know that.

What if she don't die?

Custer's strong square teeth, gleaming. Eyes demon-blue. *I expect you know what to do. You done it before.*

The roof of the car brushed Abby's hair, soft as John Lee's hand.

Down in the dark, the woman howled like a dog. Not dying fast enough, not by half.

The next day, on the phone, somebody saying, *They found bodies out on Custer Grady's farm—he's going to hell, sure enough—*

Oh, Lord, the noise, howling like an animal, and she had to do it, had to do it before they came to look.

Take the shovel. Make her stop. Make her stop screaming.

The roof of the car became a club, smashing.

Make her stop.

Out of her window, as darkness fell, Abby saw John Lee standing frozen, arms outstretched.

Make it stop.

Abby

hear me?
Sir, you have to step

I love you, Abby.

Pianissimo:
December 25, 1994

There was a man sitting beside her bed, reading a battered newspaper. He had on cowboy boots, blue jeans, and a blue denim shirt. She remembered the shirt, remembered the feel of it on her skin when she'd put it on in the middle of the night . . . when? Last night? The smell of his skin rose up warm around her and made her blink back tears.

"John Lee?" Her voice sounded thready and old. The newspaper drifted to the floor and he was close, so close, hands closing warm around her fingers. Tubes stuck out of the back of her hand like exposed veins. She ached all over, persistently, in spite of a thick blanket of drugs.

"Hi." He smoothed hair back from her face. She felt the drag of adhesive tape along her cheek, reached up and plucked fretfully at a thick soft pad of bandage. "Don't do that. Just lay still."

She remembered that she was supposed to be mad at him for something, couldn't quite latch on to what. That didn't matter anymore. Nothing mattered except the concern in his eyes.

"What happened?"

"You had an accident." The way he said it made her afraid, made monitors beep somewhere near her shoulder. "You're okay, Abby. Some cuts, a good solid bang on the head. Your left arm is broken."

He said it so matter-of-factly that he must have expected it to be worse, much worse.

"Accident?" He nodded, looking down at the hand he held, tracing the palm with a gentle thumb. "Car accident?"

"You ran into a tractor-trailer," he said. After a few seconds of silence, "We thought you were dead. There was so much blood."

She had a fraction of a memory, a red semi cab coming at her, a man's stubbled face blank with terror. It seemed very distant, like a movie she'd once seen and hadn't liked.

"Guess I'll have to take defensive driving," she murmured.

"It's not funny, Abby. You . . ." He blinked hard. "Don't you remember anything about it?"

She tried. She remembered wrapping his present, green foil and silver angels. She remembered, for what seemed no reason, his package sliding under the seat of her car.

"Your Christmas present was under the seat."

"Hell, seeing you alive is my Christmas present." He smiled, but the corners of his lips had a tremble of uncertainty. "Yours is at the shop. I'll show it to you when you get out of here."

"How's my car?"

John Lee cocked an eyebrow. "What car?"

"Oh." She leaned her head back against the pillow.

Gone, just like that, a heap of twisted metal. Lucky she hadn't been buried in it. "God. I—did you see it? Where was I?"

"Highway. Yeah, I saw." His eyes flickered. "Saw it all. Abby, I never been so scared in my life. I tried to get the door open but Terry had to use a crowbar. He practically smacked me on the head with it when I tried to get you out, told me to leave you where you were. Car wasn't on fire, so he said to wait for the paramedics."

"Terry?" she repeated. "Deputy Terry?"

His smile failed, and something wary entered his face and locked the doors of his eyes. "He caught the 911."

Something about Terry, something bad. John Lee had seen . . .

Seen them together. She couldn't remember if she'd said anything to him, couldn't remember anything after . . . after . . .

After the diner, where she'd talked to Custer Grady. Terry had been there. Sheriff Hayes. Pumpkin pie she hadn't wanted. Grady, braying like a mule as he laughed about raping Evvy Doderman.

Evvy Doderman. That was important, deadly important. She'd been on her way to talk to Evvy when . . . when . . .

Make her stop.

She flinched at the jab of memory, an alien whisper in her head, rich with desperation and hate. Something about the cellar. Pearl's cellar.

Something about Pearl.

"Abby?"

She focused on John Lee's face, on the guarded concern, the tight lines around his eyes.

"I'm sorry, I'm just tired." Suddenly, as she said it, she was, so tired she could hardly hold her eyes open. Her head throbbed. "Need to sleep."

On that, they clearly agreed. He nodded and leaned over to press his lips to her forehead, and the smell of him made her dizzy. She wanted the feel of him, the security. She thought that the last time she'd felt safe had been when she'd been in his bed, next to him.

But safety wouldn't tell her anything, wouldn't help her grow. And she needed answers even more than she needed him.

She heard the chair creak as he leaned back. After a few minutes of silence she forced her eyes open and saw that he hadn't left her. He was sitting quietly, watching.

The need on his face frightened her. She shut her eyes again and let the fear drift away on the sea of painkillers. The last sensation she felt as she floated free was the remembered pressure of his lips on hers.

"Hey." A voice at the door drew her attention away from the magazine she was reading—she'd sent John Lee home to sleep. "Mind if I come in?"

Terry Bollinger hadn't brought any gifts or flowers, and he was dressed in his usual khaki uniform, badge gleaming like a grin. When she nodded, he crossed to her bedside and stood, ignoring the empty chair next to him.

"Where's your boyfriend?"

"He told me you helped get me out of the car," she said.

His eyes narrowed. "I pry a shitload of idiots out of cars. You're just lucky you didn't end up part of the goddamn semi's upholstery."

"Was he hurt? The trucker?"

"Nope. Just lost a trailer full of Sony televisions. Trucks don't usually suffer too much, this kind of tangle. How's the head?"

"Still on."

He frowned and said, "Half an inch farther down and we'd be burying you, closed casket. I wouldn't go joking about that."

"I wasn't." She turned a page on her magazine and made an effort to be pleasant. "Thanks for helping. I . . . appreciate it."

He looked uncomfortable. She wondered what had happened there on the road, whether he and John Lee had acted like rival tomcats or whether they'd actually forgotten, for a while, to hate each other. They'd probably forgotten, or he wouldn't look so uncomfortable.

"You missed your chance," he said. She blinked. "Pearl's house. Remember?"

She didn't, for a moment, and then remembered. Pearl Jordan, gone to church. An hour in her house, to search.

"No! No, I'm okay. We can still—"

"You're half dead." His tone stung. "No way I'm gonna haul you around like a sack of broken bones."

"It's just a broken arm, Terry. I'll be fine." When

he grunted disbelievingly, she said, "What's wrong? Afraid you can't keep up with me?"

"I'll be three days dead when I don't keep up with you." He turned away and pretended to look over the arrangement of daisies and roses that John Lee had brought. "I thought you were dead. You bled all over me."

A moment of weakness, from Terry? If it was, it was over in a second as he turned and pulled up the chair and took a black notebook out of his shirt pocket.

"You remember enough about the accident to give me a report?"

"I thought John Lee saw the whole thing."

Terry tapped a pen against the paper and nodded. "Wanted to hear it from you. Wanted to hear why the hell you were parked in front of Pearl Jordan's house again, like a goddamn stalker."

"I was just—"

"Don't lie."

"I'm not, I was just turning—"

"Like hell. You were sitting there watching her house like a goddamn nutcase."

"Like you watch John Lee's place?" she shot back, and saw she'd made contact. "I just stopped for a minute. I swear."

"You're a bad liar," he said, and leaned back. He snapped the book shut and shoved it back in his pocket. "You remember, I got that tape. You toe the line, and you might just get it back."

"You always attack," she said. He looked up sharply. "Whenever you start to feel anything, you attack. That's why you're always poking at John Lee, isn't it? Because otherwise you might feel something for him."

He gazed at her a long time, then tipped his hat up with one finger and said, "Whatever you say. Ma'am."

"Tomorrow," she called as he turned away. "Six p.m."

"Maybe."

The door creaked shut behind him.

She dreamed of a dog barking, distant and urgent. It sounded like Carlton trying to alert her to danger. That was the way he'd barked at Terry, she remembered. She woke up slowly to the faraway sound of someone crying but it stopped as soon as she opened her eyes. The room was dark, gray leaking in around the curtained window. A strip of yellow glowed under the door and gleamed from the metal base of the IV stand beside her bed.

What kind of person was I? It was a question she'd never bothered to ask. She'd assumed that Pearl had just been Abby with a different face. It had never occurred to her that Pearl had wanted Custer Grady, had needed him. Had been a willing accomplice.

She had stood by and watched while he dragged his victim through her house, had let him kick her down into the basement.

When she'd gone down the stairs into the dark, she'd intended to kill.

For Custer Grady's love.

The thought nauseated her, but what was worse

was that Pearl had been so deluded—Grady had never loved her, he'd raped her and used her just like he'd used Evvy Doderman and every other woman he'd found.

Pearl had been pathetic.

She had been pathetic.

She closed her eyes tight against the pain, the emptiness.

Was it worth bringing an old woman to justice for the murder of someone so worthless? So shallow?

Was it even murder if Pearl had gone into the cellar determined to kill?

"I have to know," she said aloud.

What was in that cellar would tell her the truth, once and for all.

The door creaked open. Golden light slid across the wall, was interrupted by an angular shadow. Someone's head poked cautiously in the door.

She recognized the black and white cornrows with a shock of pleasure so strong it almost brought her to tears.

"Benny?"

"Shh!" Benny eased in and let the door click shut behind her. "My ass is grass if they find me in here. They already threw me out once."

"When?"

"The other day—you were unconscious." Benny's shadow moved to the chair next to the bed. "I tried to get them to call in a decent homeopathic healer. They tossed me out."

"For the suggestion?"

"Well . . . not exactly. More because I punched out

an orderly, I guess. I would've punched out the damn nurse but she was too tall." In the dark, Benny's warm fingers found hers. They clung together so hard it hurt. "You still mad at me?"

John Lee. Abby felt a surge of sadness that had nothing to do with anger, really. Disappointment, but not anger.

"He called to ask me about you. About . . . well, if you'd been acting weird. He said you'd made threats against his mother." Benny sounded doubtful. "I told him I'd believe he was out of his head before you were. But he said . . . well . . . I remembered what happened at Miklos' shop. What you said about Pearl Jordan."

"And you decided to come and see if you could help."

"Yeah." Benny cleared her throat. "Well. It seemed like a good idea at the time. John Lee picked me up at the airport. Look, Ab, I won't say he ain't a cutie, but swear to God, it was just dinner. No dessert. He was scared to death for you. *Of* you, too."

Her voice went strange and thick at the end, and she made a snuffling sound. Abby said cautiously, "Are you crying?"

"Fuck, no." Benny snuffled again. "They got any tissue in this place, or is it fifty bucks a sheet?"

Abby felt around on the table next to the bed and tore out a handful of tissue. She passed it over. Benny honked her nose.

"Better?" she asked.

"I saw that truck hit you, Ab. My God. My *God*. I thought you were gone, I really did." She blew her nose again. "I thought you were going to kick off mad at me. You really pissed me off."

"The feeling's mutual, I guess." Abby felt tears prickling in her eyes and cleared her throat. "Did I miss a rehearsal?"

"Probably. Hell, you probably missed a concert but even an asshole conductor would have to give you sick leave for this one."

It hadn't occurred to Abby until that moment, through the drugs, that her arm was broken. Her *arm* was *broken*. She burst into tears and fumbled for tissues; Benny grabbed some for her.

"Am—am—can I still—p-p-play? Did anybody say?"

"Yeah, kiddo, you can still play, you just gotta heal. Jeez, it isn't like they cut your arm off. It's just a bone. Well, a couple of bones. If you do what they say, you'll be playing good as new in a couple of months."

They sat in silence for a while, fingers twined together.

"I've gotta go," Benny said. A smell of musky perfume, the rope-harsh brush of cornrows on her skin. Benny's lips pressed on her forehead.

" 'Bye."

The tears pushed at her harder, forced the words down in her throat. She couldn't say anything as Benny pulled away. Benny's high heels tapped across the floor, slow at first, then faster. The door squeaked open and then ate the light it had let in.

" 'Bye," she whispered to the closing door. Tears trickled hot down the sides of her face. "I love you."

Fermata:
December 27, 1994

John Lee came to pick her up when she called the next morning, and she endured the wheelchair ride out to the parking lot, carrying his roses and daisies in her lap. Her left arm felt weirdly disconnected and when she had to move it in its Velcro cast she did it gingerly. Her fingers wiggled. She thought that was heartening.

Her face was a tic-tac-toe of shallow cuts and a checkerboard of bruises. When she moved too fast she got a pounding headache. No marathons in the near future. On top of that, she'd discovered a sore knee and a pain in her foot that the doctor said cheerfully might be a broken small bone.

On the whole, she'd been lucky as hell.

"Nobody said it was going to snow," Abby said as John Lee unlocked the car door for her; she tilted her head carefully up to look at the clouds and the spirals of flakes falling. Her neck protested. She sighed as a snowflake licked her lips.

"Nobody said it wasn't, either. Here, I'm moving the seat back, let you stretch your legs out. Okay?"

He helped her into the car and brushed his hand

along her cheek before he slammed the door. As he got in the other side, she asked, "Where's Benny?"

"Ah . . . I got her a room at the Motel Six. Got her a rental car, too. She's all right."

"I need a car," she said. He shot her a stern look and put his arm over the back of the seat as he turned to back up. "I'm serious. I can drive."

"One-handed. With a bad knee and a head injury. I don't think so, Abby. I think you're going to be spending a lot of time lying flat on your back." She smiled. He caught her eye and raised his eyebrows. "Think you ought to heal up some first."

"I'm healing as fast as I can. Hey, how's Carlton? God, I feel like such a louse, it seems like all I do is leave him. He's probably forgotten all about me."

"I went and got him. Your roommate left a message she was going to be doing a trade show in Cozumel, so I figured I'd better give him a warm place until you got well enough to take him on. He's okay."

"He's at your shop?" She frowned at the thought of Carly, big clumsy Carly, romping around all that glass. John Lee shook his head.

"He's okay," he repeated, and reached over to turn on the radio as he turned the car left onto the street. He reached over and came up with a cassette tape. Before she could stop him, he slipped it in the tape player and turned up the volume.

The tape started on the third movement of the Mozart clarinet concerto. She listened to the rich, buttery notes for a few seconds and said, "Stoltzman?"

He seemed surprised as he handed her the cassette case. "He's good, right?"

"He's great," she murmured. "How'd you find it?"

"I called up the professor at UTPB. He gave me a whole list."

"I'll bet you bought them all."

"I was missing you."

She remembered what he was trying to distract her from. "Where's Carlton? Really?"

He sighed and slouched further in the seat. The snow pattered harder on the windshield as the car accelerated out onto Main.

"At my mother's house. Look, before you say anything, I took him to my place but he busted out a window and ran over there. She heard him scratching at the door and by the time I got over there he was curled up by the fire. I didn't have the heart to move him."

Carlton was in Pearl's house. Abby felt a spasm of jealous rage and swallowed hard to contain it. That was a Pearl-feeling, not an Abby-feeling. No reason for her to be upset because John Lee's mother had taken in her dog. No reason in the world.

"Fine," she said shortly. It was all she could trust herself to say. "Where are we going?"

"My house, if that's okay by you. I don't want you stuck there in your apartment all by yourself, no car, no roommate, no nothing." He kept his eyes on the road as he said, "Besides, I want you with me. Maybe that's selfish, but there you go. What the hell, it's Christmas. Call it a present to myself."

"You don't have to babysit me."

"Wasn't planning to." He was silent a few seconds as Stoltzman played light, airy, perfect notes. "Just offering a place to sleep where you won't be alone."

It was what she wanted, more than anything, but it wouldn't be honest to take it, not yet.

"I thought I'd spend some time with Benny, you know, while she was here," she said, and turned her face away to look out at the snow-softened buildings as they floated by the window. The Wal-Mart parking lot looked ghostly; she'd never seen it deserted before. Everything was closed up tight.

John Lee didn't say anything. He made a right turn at the next street, then a left. Stoltzman continued to play, oblivious.

"Want something to eat first?" he asked. "Or you just want me to drop you off?"

Up ahead, the Motel 6 sign appeared out of a forest of McDonald's arches and Texaco stars. She blinked hard and said gently, "I'm not really hungry. I'm sorry, John."

"Yeah." He nodded. "Yeah, me, too."

"You," Benny said with admiration in her voice, "are a real *bitch*, Abby. I never would have guessed it. You told him to *drop you off*? My God. That man *loves* you."

"I know." Abby picked at the plastic veneer of the headboard and watched Benny rummage in her suitcase. She pulled out a jacket that looked as if M&Ms had exploded all over it—splotches of red, green, yellow, blue. The background was hot pink.

"But if I stay with him I can't do what I need to do right now."

"What? Celebrate Christmas? Have a regular normal life?"

"Find out what really happened to Pearl Jordan."

Benny tossed her jacket on the bed and dug out a neon-purple leather vest. She stripped off her shirt and shrugged the vest on, frowning down the V-neck.

"Too low?" she asked. Abby gave her a disbelieving look. "Well, I mean, too low for a nonhooker?"

"Depends on if you're going to church or Peeping Tom's."

"Peeping Tom's? Let me guess, strip bar?"

"Their motto is that they're the home of the vertical smile," Abby said. Benny sighed and took off the vest. She hunted up a black camisole and put it on, then buttoned the vest over it. She spread her arms for Abby's approval. When she didn't get it, she shrugged on the jacket and studied the effect in the mirror.

"I thought you had the whole scoop on Pearl Jordan," Benny said as she brushed lint from her spandex pants. "What more do you have to know?"

"I have to talk to a woman named Evalyn Bollinger. I think she knows exactly what happened."

"Bollinger, Bollinger—the cop? The cop's wife?"

"Mother. I think she was there when Pearl died, or right after. And I think she knows everything."

Benny stopped in the act of adjusting her lapels to say, "I'm visiting a cop's house?"

"You might be a little overdressed," Abby said,

and in spite of her headache, had to smile. "Unless you want a date."

Benny stopped in the act of tugging her camisole higher to say, "Well, there's a thought. He *is* kinda cute, for a cowboy."

Evvy Doderman Bollinger was listed in the phone book under the one-page Fall Creek subheading. Abby clutched the address while Benny drove, swearing under her breath at the falling snow and peering at the dim, rusted street signs.

"There." Abby pointed. The Bollinger house was a small clapboard house with blue trim and twinkling Christmas lights wrapped unevenly around the porch railing and the scraggly evergreen tree. "Looks like somebody's home."

There was a sparkling new Ford Bronco parked in the driveway, blanketed with snow on top. Benny pulled the car in to the curb and waited, idling.

"Park or drive?"

"Park." Abby swallowed hard and said, "You can wait here if you want."

"Ten-four, boss. I'll defend the fort. Hey, you all right? Not sick or anything, right?"

Abby got out of the car and leaned in the doorway, fighting back a wave of dizziness with a grin. "Sick of not knowing what's going on. I'll be all right. Hey, if not, you're right out here, aren't you? I'll just yell."

"Yell loud," Benny said, and turned up the radio. AC/DC was screaming out "Highway to Hell."

Abby rang the doorbell and waited for any Pearl-memories to surface; nothing did, except the familiar dislike. She didn't think Pearl had ever been here, to Evvy's house. The porch light came on, bathing her in weak yellow light. The front door cracked open, then swung wide.

Evvy was dressed in a red dress too bright for her pale skin; it washed all the color out of her pale blue eyes and gave her silver hair a pinkish shine. She had on a Christmas tree pin that lit up in random colored flashes, battery-powered. A rush of warm air bled out around her, and with it the sound of Perry Como singing. The air smelled like pine potpourri.

"Yes?" Evvy's eyes flickered at the sight of Abby's battered face. "Can I help you?"

"I . . ." Abby cleared her throat and tried again. "My name is Abby Rhodes, I met you at Dr. Urdiales' office. Can I come in?"

Evvy's hand tightened around the door. It swung partly closed again.

"Ma'am, please—" Abby held out her good hand. She must have looked sufficiently pitiful, because the door stopped moving. "Just give me a minute. I only want to ask you some questions."

"Questions about what?"

"Please." Abby shivered. "Just a minute."

The shiver must have decided her; Evvy stepped back and left the way clear to the hallway. Abby stepped into a thick blanket of warm air and pine, smelled a sweet hint of baked cookies. The hallway was dim and close, the wallpaper a faded climbing rose pattern.

"In there." Evvy pointed down the hallway to what looked like a living room. They must have passed through some invisible screen of manners, because as Abby looked around at the big tufted sofa and artfully arranged chairs Evvy folded her hands together and said, "I'm sorry. Can I get you something hot to drink?"

"Oh. No, no, thank you. I won't take but a couple of minutes."

Evvy smiled and seated herself with brittle grace, gestured Abby to the sofa. Abby sank down into the softness and felt her arm give a twinge to remind her to be careful. She adjusted it in the sling and said, "I'm looking into something that happened thirty years ago here in Fall Creek—the day that Custer Grady was arrested."

Evvy paused in the act of straightening her skirt. She sat straighter, pulled her knees in closer together. "I'm sorry, who, dear?" She smiled widely, but the corners of her lips trembled. "Custer . . ."

"Grady," Abby finished. "I don't think you've forgotten him, Mrs. Bollinger. He's the only murderer ever arrested in Fall Creek. You knew him."

"No, I don't think I did." Evvy tilted her head, silver permed curls gleaming. "Are you sure you wouldn't like some tea? I can make some coffee for you."

"Mrs. Bollinger, I know that you went to see Pearl Jordan the day Grady was arrested. You came to tell her they'd found a body on Grady's farm. I know you and Pearl weren't friends, so maybe you didn't come to warn her, but I know you came." Abby swallowed hard. Evvy had become a statue, barely breathing, smile frozen solid on her lips. Her eyes were wide and fixed. "You didn't find her when you came in. The house was empty. And then Custer Grady showed up."

The silence that followed was long, heavy as the snow falling outside. In the kitchen a timer rang, but Evvy didn't move. A glass and gold anniversary clock spun its weights in a slow spiral, up and down, behind her.

"I know he . . ." Abby couldn't make the word come out. "He hurt you—"

Evvy's eyes glittered suddenly, and her smile jerked on her face as if somebody had pulled its string.

"Would you like to see a picture of my son? His name's Terry, he's a police officer."

"I know Terry, Mrs. Bollinger."

"His father's from Tulsa. Tulsa, Oklahoma."

Abby let the lie sit. Evvy blinked rapidly and looked away.

"I need to know what happened after Grady left. Please tell me what happened," Abby said. "Did you hear something in the cellar? Is that what happened?"

It seemed so strange to sit here in this Christmas-scented room, with Perry Como crooning in the background, and see the fragile control in Evvy's eyes breaking apart. The worst of it was to know that she was hurting this woman so terribly, and in some way was glad. That was Pearl—malicious, shallow, angry Pearl.

"Cellar?" Evvy repeated blankly. "She was crying."

Hair prickled along the back of Abby's neck, painful as needles. She felt heat climb up from her stomach, a wave that turned to dizziness when it hit her aching head.

"Who?" Abby whispered. Evvy's eyes focused on her suddenly, sharp and bright.

"Pearl. He'd beat her half to death. She was lying down there at the bottom of the steps. I called the doctor."

"He meaning Custer Grady."

"Well, who else?"

Something was wrong. It *sounded* right, but something didn't make sense. It hadn't bothered anybody else, but nobody else had known Pearl, known what Pearl knew.

Pearl had gotten a phone call before Evvy Doderman had shown up, a phone call that had warned her Grady had been found out.

Pearl had decided to kill the prisoner in her cellar. Nobody else knew there had been two women in the house.

Custer Grady had never seen Pearl that day, never beaten her, because she had gone down in the dark and never come out. So far, so good—and the woman Evvy found in the cellar was the wrong woman, beaten so badly it was an easy mistake to make, to think she was Pearl Jordan.

Only one thing.

Where was Pearl? If the woman had been beaten as badly as all that, how could she have buried Pearl's body?

"Were they both down there?" Abby asked. Evvy's face went blank again. "Both women?"

Evvy remained quiet, but her eyes widened.

"You buried Pearl. Why?"

"I think my son's coming home," Evvy said brightly. "I'm so sorry you can't stay."

Abby got up slowly, watching her. Evvy's head swiveled to follow her, but she stayed seated, hands clasped together in her lap hard enough to shake.

"I'm sorry, too," she said. "I know you did it; nobody else could have."

"You be careful going home, now," Evvy said. Abby nodded and went down the hall to the door, opened it, and breathed in cold, clean air with a feeling of relief so strong it made her dizzy. "Merry Christmas, honey."

She shut the door as Perry Como started singing "White Christmas."

In the car, Benny turned down Nine Inch Nails and asked, "So? Find out anything?"

"She didn't tell me anything," Abby said. "But, yeah, I found out anyway. And there's one more person I need to ask."

"Shit, Abby, it's the holidays!"

"We can do it from the motel. Local calls are free, right?"

Dr. Urdiales' answering service told her he was out of the office for the holidays but accepting emergency calls. Was it an emergency?

"Yes," Abby said, and read her the motel phone number. "Room 152. I'll wait for his call."

"He won't call," Benny said from the other side of the room, where she'd flopped on the other bed. Her M&M jacket made an eye-popping contrast to the floral bedspread. Her cornrows draped over the side of the bed like exhausted party streamers. "He's sitting around the tree with the kiddies, opening presents and puffing on a pipe. Hey. Is he cute?"

"He'll call."

"Jeez, Abby, he's a shrink. He makes two hundred thousand and gets three months of vacation a year. This is not a man who's going to call you back on vacation."

Abby settled herself against the headboard and opened the bag on her lap. The smell of hamburgers and fries made her mouth water.

"Cheeseburger," Benny said. "Large fries. Lots of ketchup."

"Coming right up, ma'am." Abby found a cheeseburger wrapped in orange grease paper and sailed it across the room. Benny grabbed it out of the air. When she held up the fries Benny jumped up and came to get them. "Smart girl. Want your shake hand delivery or air mail?"

"You're a lousy shot." Benny reached past her for a vanilla shake and sat cross-legged on the bed, spreading her feast out in a semicircle. She took a big bite of the cheeseburger and rolled her eyes. "Perfect. I can feel my thighs expanding already."

Abby dug her own food out of the bag and started with the french fries. Her shake was chocolate. It was watery but she didn't care, her body was screaming for calories, it seemed like days since she'd eaten—hell, it *was* days since she'd eaten.

"Can you manage?" Benny asked, in between bites. Abby chewed french fries and nodded silently. "You let me know if I need to cut your food or anything."

Abby threw a fry at her.

The phone rang. They both froze. Abby wiped greasy fingers on a napkin and twisted to grab the receiver.

"Abby? Dr. Urdiales."

It's him, she mouthed to Benny. Benny mouthed back, *Marry him.*

"Uh, hi, how are you?" She almost hit herself in the head with the receiver, would have except for the persistent headache she still had. What a stupid question. "I'm sorry to bother you today."

"It's not a problem, Abby. The question is, how are you?"

"Well, not too good. I've been in the hospital. I had an accident."

He hadn't known about it, and he seemed concerned. She told him about the broken arm, the knee, all the rest of it.

"Where were you when it happened?" he asked, too damn acute for her own good.

"Sorry?" she stalled.

"Abby, were you in Fall Creek?"

"I need to ask you about Evvy Bollinger," she said. There was a delay of about five seconds before he answered.

"I can't discuss my other patients, you know that."

"Wait a minute, this is important. Just listen, okay? You've been seeing Evvy for a long time, right?"

"Yes, a while."

"Did she ever tell you anything about Fall Creek? About Pearl Jordan? Custer Grady?"

"I can't discuss Evvy's case."

Abby adjusted the phone against her ear and said, "Evvy Bollinger told you about the rape. She also told you about burying a body in a cellar. When I came into your office and started telling you about Pearl Jordan and the cellar, you couldn't believe it, could you? Independent verification of something you weren't sure was real."

He said, "We're not discussing Evvy, we're discussing you. Were you in Fall Creek when you had your accident? Did you talk to Evvy?"

He was afraid for Evvy. The thought hit her like a bolt of lightning.

"Do you think Evvy's capable of violence?" she asked softly. "Doctor?"

"Did you talk to her?"

"I . . . went to her house. I told her I knew she'd found Pearl Jordan dead the day Custer Grady was arrested."

After a long, static-laden silence Dr. Urdiales sighed.

"Custer Grady as much as admitted to me that he'd raped her," she rushed on. "That's what it's all about, right? He raped her and left her, and she went down in the cellar and found the body—bodies. She buried one and dragged the other one upstairs and called the ambulance. She knew the difference, but she didn't tell anybody. Did she hate Pearl that much?"

"You know I can't answer you."

But he was still on the phone, still betraying anxiety. She said, "Is there something else? Something I don't know about?"

Dr. Urdiales said softly, "Perhaps you should meet me at my office. I'd like to show you the tape of our last session."

"Damn!" Benny twisted the wheel as the rental car tried to shimmy off the road, got it back under control with an effort. "Man, are you sure we have to do this *now*? Like, in the middle of a freaking *storm*?"

"You know I need to."

"Yeah, I know, I know—shit, hold on!"

Abby shut her eyes as the world slipped, fought back cold-sweat memories of the truck coming at her. When she opened her eyes they were traveling sedately down Carter Street, heading for Dr. Urdiales' office.

"I owe you one," she said. Benny laughed and shook her head.

The parking garage was cold and deserted except for a sleek-looking Lincoln parked near the elevators. The click of Benny's heels echoed for what seemed like miles as they crossed the concrete to the closed doors; the slap-drag of Abby's tennis shoes seemed to die within a few yards. Benny punched the button and tapped her foot, humming something with too many notes to be a Christmas carol.

"You sure about this?" she asked, very casually.

She picked at a loose thread on her jacket with a rainbow-painted fingernail.

"You know I am."

The elevator doors opened with a grinding wheeze. Abby limped inside, following Benny's bright comet trail. She reached across to push the button for the third floor.

" 'Cause I'm just saying we could still go shopping, here."

Abby reached out with her good hand and squeezed Benny's arm. Benny didn't look at her.

"Thanks," she said. Benny nodded. "Wait for me?"

"He better have *Playgirl* in the waiting room."

Dr. Urdiales was standing at the coffeepot in the reception area when they came in, pouring water into the reservoir. He smiled, put the pot under the spout, and flicked the brew switch before saying, "I'm Rick Urdiales. And you are . . ."

Abby punched Benny in the ribs to remind her that he was talking to her. Benny's lips were parted, her eyes sparkling. She jerked and said, "Benina Wright, Doc. Hi."

She held out her hand. Dr. Urdiales must have noticed the rainbow nail polish, the tinkling bracelets, but he didn't let any surprise show in his face. He shook firmly.

"I've heard a lot about you," he said. "Pianist, correct? I'm sure people ask you this all the time, but how do you play with those fingernails?"

"Well, for serious stuff I take them off. They're

plastic." Benny tapped them on the counter next to her, grinning. "You a piano man, Doc?"

"I play a little," he said. "Please, feel free to have coffee if you'd like—or tea; there are tea bags in the drawer. Soft drinks in the refrigerator, here. Magazines on the table."

"Cool." Benny threw herself into one of the armchairs with a bounce that made her cornrows temporarily weightless. "You guys just have fun. Don't worry about me."

Abby mouthed *Thanks* as Dr. Urdiales opened the inner door and ushered her into the womb of carpet, quiet, and memories.

He wheeled out the VCR and television once she was comfortable, chose a numbered tape from a locked cabinet, and put it in the machine. Before he pushed PLAY, he said, "Anything you need to talk about first?"

She shook her head. He sat down across from her and pointed the remote control at the set.

On the screen, her face sharpened into focus, eyes open and fixed on something in the distance. Dr. Urdiales fast-forwarded through the first part, watching the timer on the VCR. When he let it play, Abby's expression had turned guarded and strange, her eyes narrowed to slits.

". . . cellar?" he asked. She leaned forward a little, then back into focus.

"Lyin' there. Just lyin' there."

"And is there someone else with you?"

"*She's* there. Curled up at the bottom of the stairs."

"Is she still alive?"

"Rotting. rotting like old meat." Abby's—no, Pearl's—lips parted in a narrow smile. "Got bones stickin' out. Don't think she's gonna make it."

"And you, Pearl? How do you feel?"

"Sleepy. Can't feel anything."

"Can you move?"

Silence. Pearl's face twitched. The smile faded.

"Can't move my hand." Her eyes opened wide, almost all pupil. "Can't move! My arms, my legs—"

"You fell, didn't you, Pearl? Fell down the stairs when she grabbed your ankle?" His voice was so calm, so quiet. Abby tore her eyes away from the screen to look at Dr. Urdiales, but he seemed intent on the video.

"I can't move!" Pearl screamed. "Goddamn, I can't—"

"Pearl, let it go, let it pass, it can't hurt you now. Let's go on a little further. What's happening?"

"Noise. Noise upstairs."

"What kind of noise?"

"Don't know. It stopped now."

"Let's go on. Do you hear anything now?"

"She's screamin'. Must have heard the noise."

"She meaning the other woman? The one by the stairs?"

"Somebody heard. The door's openin'."

"The cellar door?" Off screen, a creak of leather as Dr. Urdiales shifted in his chair, probably to make a note. "Is anyone coming down to check?"

"Evvy."

A long, long silence. After it Dr. Urdiales asked, "Evvy Bollinger?"

"Doderman. Comin' down the stairs. Comin' down like it's her own damn house!" Suddenly Pearl's eyes rolled back in her head, whites flickering wetly. Abby gasped. Dr. Urdiales reached across the distance between them and placed a hand on her shoulder.

"Pearl? Pearl, what's wrong?"

Pearl's eyes continued to flicker, like a static-infected television. She moaned.

"Pearl, tell me what's happening."

Flicker, flicker, suddenly her eyes were back, black and strange.

"She's talkin' to me."

"Evvy? What is she saying?"

"I never knew she hated me. I never knew that." Pearl sucked in a deep breath and said, "She's pickin' up the shovel."

Off-screen, Dr. Urdiales murmured, "That's enough, Pearl, let's stop now. You want to stop now, don't you?"

Pearl said, "She's diggin' a hole in the dirt behind the stairs. She ain't very strong."

"Pearl, let's stop now. When I tell you to wake up, you will wake up as Abby and you will remember nothing—"

"She's gonna put me in the hole."

"Wake up, Abby."

"She's dragging me to the hole."

"Abby, wake up now."

Pearl screamed.

Dr. Urdiales pointed the remote control at the television and froze Abby's face in midcry. Abby, staring through a veil of tears, thought it could have been anybody's face, all mouth and eyes.

"You knew," she whispered. He let go of her shoulder and sat back, remote resting on his knee. "You knew Evvy buried Pearl alive because she told you. Pearl had a broken neck, and Evvy buried her alive."

He looked gray around the mouth, weary lines engraved around his eyes. He said, "Patients often claim extraordinary things, Abby. There is no reason to believe they are all true."

"But this was *murder*!"

"I checked. Pearl Jordan was alive and well in Fall Creek. From the pieces Evvy told me, I had no reason to suspect someone else had taken Pearl's place. It was only when you came to me and started telling me your pieces that I realized I had been mistaken."

"Mistaken?" Abby got slowly to her feet, ignoring the complaint from her knee. "Custer Grady said a girl came to see him a few years back."

Dr. Urdiales nodded. "I'm certain a lot of women came to see him. So?"

"What if her name was Marlene and she was from Fall Creek? What if she knew what I knew? What if she knew Pearl Jordan was dead and Evvy Bollinger had killed her? Terry said she wanted out of Fall Creek, always had some scheme or other. What if her road to fame and fortune was Custer Grady and Evvy Bollinger?"

"Marlene?" Dr. Urdiales frowned. "I'm afraid I don't—"

"Evvy's son had a girlfriend named Marlene. Marlene's missing." She watched his eyes. "Would she go that far?"

"I can't . . ." He sighed and shook his head. "All right. There is no mystery regarding Marlene. Mrs. Bollinger disapproved of her son's relationship with Marlene. Marlene, as you suspected, tried to blackmail Mrs. Bollinger with interviews she'd conducted with Grady in prison."

The skin tightened down Abby's back. "You *knew* that and you didn't—"

He held up his hand to stop her. "Marlene Hargist is alive and well. She is living quite comfortably in California on the proceeds of her blackmail. Mrs. Bollinger paid her, on the condition that she leave town and never return—and never exchange a word with Terry. Which Marlene did." He regarded her steadily. "Marlene was never murdered. While I have urged Mrs. Bollinger to tell her son the truth, evidently she has chosen not to do so. There is very little I can do about that."

"And about Pearl Jordan?" she said. He looked away.

She stood up and limped for the door, heard the television click off behind her. When she looked back he was still sitting where she'd left him, staring after her.

"I think you should call the police," he said.

She paused, one hand on the doorknob. "If I do, will you tell them what you know?"

He looked down at his hands and shook his head. "Not until there is conclusive proof."

She nodded and went out into the waiting room.

Benny had her feet up on the coffee table, lost in *Cosmopolitan*, but she jumped up as soon as she realized Abby was out, looking guilty as a schoolkid with a comic.

"You okay?" Benny lost her smile as she studied Abby's face. "Ab?"

"Let's go."

Molto Vivace:
December 27, 1994

"I'm not letting you do this," Benny said in the dim twilight as they lay in separate beds, watching shadows crawl across the ceiling. A television show played loudly in the next room, and from the parking lot car engines ground their teeth against the cold. "It's totally insane. You're *not* going to jail for this. I won't let you."

"You don't have a lot to say about it," Abby snapped. She ached all over, worse than before because the medications were all flushed out of her system and her muscles had the room to scream as loud as they wanted. The pain left her weak and fretful. "Just go have yourself a good dinner and I'll be back soon."

"So *you* say. I gotta tell you, I don't trust this cop guy as far as you can throw him. He's nuts, his mom's nuts, this whole town's nuts. I thought Dallas was bad. Jeez." Benny sat up and threw the covers off, shivering against the cold as she threw on a thick blaze-orange robe and green Marvin the Martian slippers. She shuffled to the bathroom and slammed the door.

Abby half slid, half fell out of bed and stood bracing herself with one hand clutching a wooden chair, waiting for the tremble to shake itself out of her legs. Her head throbbed like a heart. She reached for her purse and dumped it out on the bed, a rain of wallet, keys, tissues, plastic reed cases, coins. She grabbed up a handful of pennies and nickels and made it to the bathroom door as she heard the shower come on. Two stacked pennies weren't enough to jam the door near the hinges; she had to go with a nickel and a penny, three pennies above the hinge. That done, she tied a plastic cord around the doorknob and wrapped it around the sink faucet at the vanity.

"Abby?" Benny yelled from the bathroom over the rush of water. "Hey, Ab, hand me the shampoo, will you? It's in my suitcase."

Abby stepped into her discarded blue jeans, wincing at the ache in her knees, and dragged her sweater over her head. She didn't dare take time for anything else, just shoved her feet into her boots—discovered the broken bone in her foot with a hiss of pain—and grabbed her coat and purse. She almost forgot the rental car's keys, had to come back for them and the motel room key.

As she opened the door she heard the bathroom door rattle. Benny said "Abby?" and rattled harder.

"You'll be okay!" Abby yelled back. "Just stay there!"

"What the fuck—Abby—shit! Shit!" The door rattled even more violently. "Don't you do this!"

"I'll be back before eight," she said.

The door stopped rattling. In the sudden quiet as

she swung the front door shut she heard Benny say, "Hope the fucking hot water doesn't run out."

The roads were so slick that few cars were on the road, and those that were chugged along at no more than thirty miles an hour on the freeway. Abby passed the snow-ghosted shadows of cars and trucks in ditches along the road, some with their emergency flashers still blinking sleepily. The twilight was so gray it was hard to tell what time it was, but the rental car's digital clock said 5:53 P.M. as she shepherded it toward the broken husk of Custer Grady's farmhouse.

The road hadn't been used in years—was really just another patch of snow, fractionally lower than the rest. The rental car—thank God Benny hadn't been able to find a bright color and had been stuck with white—made it to the clear space in front of the Grady house that must have once been a yard.

Abby got out and stood for a second by the car, soaking in the heat from the engine. Grady's farmhouse was really just walls now, the roof rotted out, the windows just ragged holes. The front door had been haphazardly boarded over but half of that was gone, and the door sagged on one rusted hinge.

If Grady was going to stay in Fall Creek, he had a real fixer-upper on his hands.

Abby trudged across the uneven snowfield toward the misty shape of Pearl Jordan's house, two fields away. On the way she had time to wonder where the bodies had been found. Here, under her feet? Closer to the house? On the other side? There'd been a lot of ground to search. She wondered how many were left sleeping under the cold ground, waiting for someone with the stomach to discover the past. What was it Terry had called it? *America's dumping ground.*

Terry's police car was parked on the highway out by the road. She saw it lurking like a sleek black predator through the snow. She kept walking as the cold bit down on the back of her neck, sucking out strength and will until the only thing left was the growing shadow of the house.

There was a red ribbon tied at one corner of the house, fluttering in the wind. Abby stared at it, frowning. It was tied in a big bow around something.

She went over to it and looked down. The bow was tied around a walkie-talkie. She picked it up and brushed the snow away, untied the bow, and dropped it in the snow where it trickled away like blood.

The walkie-talkie hissed and clicked and Terry's voice said sharply, "You hear me?"

She held it to her ear, found a button to press, and said, "Yes." She turned toward the road. She couldn't see him standing by his car, but she sensed he was there, somewhere.

"Get around the side of the house, toward the back."

"Aren't you coming?" she asked. There was a short delay as static hissed and clicked.

"Nope. Go around the back."

She stared in the direction of the car for another couple of seconds, then turned and walked around to the back—where she'd tried to get in that first night. It seemed like ages ago.

"I'm at the back," she said. "What now?"

"Alarm's off. Open the back window and climb inside."

Climb was not a word she wanted to hear, but she supposed he knew that. She gritted her teeth and pushed up on the glass window; it slid up and let out a puff of warm air on the side of her face. She hesitated, looking into the gloom inside, and keyed the walkie-talkie again.

"Terry, I thought you were coming with me."

"Can't," he said. "I need to be outside the house if you find any evidence, 'cause if I'm inside it damn sure won't hold up in court. You find something, you call 911 and I'll be busting down the door inside of a minute."

She keyed the mike and said, "How the hell do I climb up here with one hand, Terry?"

"Stand on a box; I put one back there," he said. She pocketed the walkie-talkie and hunted for something to stand on—sure enough, lying just a few feet away, she found a wooden crate that looked sturdy enough to support her. She dragged it under the window and climbed.

It was not quite as painful as being yanked through a meat grinder. She stopped halfway in the window as she remembered her snow-caked boots, wiggled uncomfortably to a sitting position on the sill, and dragged them off. She let them drop into the trampled snow under the window and stepped down into the bedroom in her stockinged feet. The cold air coming in the window kissed the back of her sweaty neck like dead lips. She straightened and tugged the window closed again, took a deep breath, and looked around.

It was *her* room. Pearl's room. She remembered the smell of it, the shadows in the corners, the burled wood of the dresser with its art-deco handles. She opened the closet and saw rows of clothes, none that she remembered. In the corner on the floor was an old hatbox; she pulled it over and opened it, lifted out a faded black velvet cloche hat that her mother had bought and hidden in the box, too precious to be worn. It felt fragile as dried flowers. She smelled it and even though her mother had never worn it, it smelled of her hair, her perfume. She closed her eyes and remembered her mother saying her name.

Pearl.

At the other end of the closet was a black velvet coat, soft as fur, with big diamond-cut buttons. It had been the most elegant thing Mother had owned; she'd loved it so much she'd never worn it, afraid the sun might rot it, the rain damage it. She'd kept all her precious things locked away in the dark.

Maybe that was why Daddy had kept all the lights turned on.

She put the coat back and shut the closet, turned to the dresser.

In the second drawer she found a pair of white gloves, stiff and yellowed with age. They were too small for Abby's sturdy fingers, but she remembered Pearl's fingers sliding easily inside as she got ready for Daddy's funeral. She'd worn Mother's black velvet hat, too, and the coat.

All of Mother's precious things, dragged out into the sun.

In her pocket, a crackle of static. She fumbled it out and held it to her ear.

"Find anything?" Terry asked.

"Not yet."

"Hurry."

The static cut off in midblur. She dropped the walkie-talkie back in her pocket and opened the pale blue jewelry box on top of the dresser. It folded out wings of boxes, one holding neatly racked earrings, the other a small collection of bracelets. Pearl had some thick pearl and bead necklaces, only a few simple chains. Abby folded it all back together and turned to look at the rest of the room, the bed, the silvered old mirror.

A necklace glittered on the mirror's frame. She reached out to touch the shining gold links. It slithered off of the nail it had been draped across and filled her palm.

A gleaming gold cross. The weight of it felt heavy as blood in her hand. She put it down on the dresser top and reached for the walkie-talkie, felt the links between her fingers like the beads of a rosary.

Daddy had given this to her on her sixth birthday. She remembered the weight of it around her neck. He'd given her a little pocket Bible, too, leather cover soft as a baby's skin. She remembered the sharp, ammoniac smell of the paper.

The house breathed as a door opened. She fumbled

for the walkie-talkie, expecting Terry's warning, but nothing came. Maybe it *was* Terry coming down the hall. Maybe those were his bootheels clicking on the wood floor.

She pressed herself hard into a dim corner between the dresser and the open closet door. The footsteps echoed closer.

Why hadn't Terry called her?

John Lee came in the doorway, stopped, and looked around. He went to the bedside table and opened a drawer. She held her breath as he pulled out a bottle of pills, turned, and walked out again, never glancing in her direction. His footsteps receded again.

A volley of barking exploded from the other side of the wall where she pressed.

Carlton. Oh, God, she'd forgotten that Carlton was here.

"Hush up." John Lee's scolding voice came indistinct. "There you go. Yeah, you're a good boy, you mangy thing. You stay quiet, now. Hush."

Carlton's bark changed to a confused whine. He knew her smell, knew she was here.

She heard John Lee shut a door down the hall. Carlton's claws scratched on wood, and he whined and snuffled.

Locked in.

She dragged the walkie-talkie out, keyed the button, and whispered, "Terry! Terry, come in!"

Static and silence. If Terry was still there, he wasn't responding. She could go out the way she'd come in, put her boots on, plod across the snow, and go home. It would be the wise thing to do.

The cellar, Pearl's voice whispered. *You promised.*

In a way, she supposed she had.

John Lee and his mother were in the living room on the couch, sharing the newspaper. On the radio the choir was singing something about the mighty river Jordan.

"More coffee, hon?" John Lee's mother asked as she folded her section of the paper. He shook his head and rattled pages as she got up and limped off for the kitchen. Abby waited, shifting her weight from one chilled stockinged foot to the other. From the kitchen, the woman took up a tuneless, happy humming along with the singing choir.

She came out again with a coffee cup and a plate of small muffins. She put them carefully on the coffee table and sank down on the couch with her coffee, sighing.

Now or never. *Hurry.*

Abby crossed the ten feet of open space behind them, almost lost her balance when her sock-feet slid on well-polished wood as she turned the corner. She grabbed hold of the nearest thing she could find—a countertop—and kept herself upright. Behind her in the living room, the sofa squeaked.

"What's wrong?"

After a delay of two or three seconds, John Lee said, "Nothing, I guess. Thought I heard something."

"Don't let these muffins get cold," his mother scolded.

The kitchen had a thick smell of warm bread and

brewed coffee. The oven ticked quietly to itself as it baked, and through the glass door she saw the humped dome of a turkey. Everything quiet, everything normal.

At the far end of the kitchen, the cellar door beckoned bright as the sun. Ten more feet. She couldn't force herself to cross it.

In the living room, weight shifted on the sofa and John Lee said, "I think I'll get myself some milk. You need anything?"

The crystal doorknob was warm as flesh under her hand. The door swung open on darkness, and cool breath whispered over her face, welcoming her home.

She stepped in and closed the door behind her. As the latch clicked shut, she heard John Lee's footsteps in the kitchen.

Darkness, thick as cobwebs on her skin. She reached out for the light switch she knew would be there but didn't throw it; the light might shine under the door, might alert John Lee to her presence. She kept her hand pressed flat and trembling on the cold plastic.

From somewhere below her, there was a rustle in the dark. *Nothing.* It was *nothing.* There was nothing in the dark but her own imagination. Pearl—if Pearl was even here, if any of it was real at all—was long, long dead and buried. The dead didn't walk.

In the kitchen, water splashed. John Lee was washing out a plate, maybe, rinsing a glass. She bit her lip hard and tasted pennies on her tongue. It was hard to remember the warm bread-smell of the kitchen because everything smelled dead here in the dark, even her own skin.

Something scraped metal under the stairs.

The rusted blade of the shovel, rising and falling. Dirt falling on her face like hard rain, her mouth open but no sound coming out of it and the taste of the dirt like vomit on her tongue.

"No," she whispered. In the kitchen, water cut off. She heard John Lee open a cabinet.

Under the stairs, a sighing sound as if something dragged over the cold, moist floor.

Dirt in her mouth. She choked and spat and gagged down a breath that tasted like the grave and melted like shadow on her tongue.

Something subtle as a breath touched her foot.

She snapped on the switch, not caring anymore if John Lee found her, not caring about anything but *light*, but even though she heard the switch click, no light came on and she opened her mouth to scream but something pulled, gravity or fear or her own despair, and her legs somehow carried her down into the dark and let her fall hard to the packed earth.

As she fell, she heard John Lee slam the cabinet door.

Voices, whispering to her in the dark.

Evvy Doderman's voice whispered *Deserved it, you deserved it, now look at what you've done*, and the light patter of dirt on her face like running rats, but that was old, years and miles and lives ago. Abby shoved it to the past, where it belonged, and tried to get up.

Her muscles didn't want to work right. She rested her cheek against the cool dirt floor and tried to think but her head seemed lazy and disconnected from the pain in her arm and knee.

Somebody was calling her name in a thin, scratchy voice. She rolled over on her back, staring into the dark, and fumbled toward the voice in her pocket.

The walkie-talkie was almost too heavy to lift. She braced it against her chest and heard the voice say "Abby?" again just as she found the switch and pressed it.

"I'm here," she whispered. The reply was a long time coming.

"Get out," Terry's voice said. It should have been loud, it was all there was in the dark, but he sounded so very far away, so weak. Some of his words disappeared into static. ". . . my gun. In the house."

"What?" Some of the buzz was leaving her head, and as it went, a headache filled the space left behind. "Terry, what?"

Empty, rapid clicks, as if he couldn't hold the button down to transmit.

"Terry!" She forced her stomach muscles to get her upright and had to grab the rough wood of the stairs for support to keep herself there. "Terry, are you okay?"

Static hissed, soft as winter snow. Through it, Terry whispered, "He's in the house. Get out, Abby."

He, she thought. *Custer Grady.*

In the house.

More voices, and these weren't ghosts from the past, they were from above, from the top of the stairs.

The cellar door creaked open, spilling light down the steps. Abby flinched back into the shadows.

"Stay here," John Lee said; his voice was a ragged whisper, thin with pain. He was a black hole of shadow in the doorway. As he moved aside, his mother limped down one step, two, then turned and held out a trembling hand toward him as he started to ease the door shut.

"No, honey, I can't—not down here—"

"Stay down here, Mom! Please!" He didn't give her time to argue. The dark slammed down. Abby heard the other woman give a breathless moan, heard a rustle of cloth as she shrank against the wall or sank down on the stairs. In the kitchen, silence. The normal creaks and groans of an old house in the winter.

The old woman's breathing sounded shallow and labored. Abby listened to it with her eyes closed and heard a Pearl-memory of the same labored, hoarse, choking sound. It had been Pearl on the stairs, then, terrified.

Just the two of them alone in the dark again, close as lovers.

Go ahead, Pearl's voice whispered in her head. *Go ahead. Say something. Listen to her scream. Maybe she'll fall and break her goddamn skinny neck, too. Then you can pick up that rusty old shovel and bury her, too, bury her while her eyes are open and she's screamin' inside. Go ahead.*

Abby slowly stood up. Her coat brushed wood with a nylon whisper, and she heard the other woman's breathing stop, bottled up with a scream. One word, and it would be done. She was an old woman.

Her heart might give out, her legs fail. She'd tumble down the steps. Her neck would snap like a dry stick.

That was justice, wasn't it? Abby wouldn't even have to lay a hand on her.

Go on, then, Pearl said, insistent as a prodding finger. *She never meant nothing anyway.*

She was John Lee's mother, and he loved her. She was a woman who'd survived Custer Grady's rapes and beatings, survived broken bones and shattered dreams.

Her only real crime was survival. *That* was why Pearl hated her so much—because even crippled and alone, even beaten and broken, this woman had taken over Pearl's life and made it worth something.

Made it a life instead of a life sentence.

She means something, Abby thought.

No, she don't, Pearl snapped. *I'll show you. I'll show you how easy it is.*

To Abby's surprise, her hand lifted, stretched out toward the warm space where the woman waited, trembling. She couldn't do this. She *wouldn't*. Pearl might have been this way but she was different, she *was*.

Her hand kept moving. She tugged hard on her own muscles but Pearl wouldn't let go.

Scream, why don't you? Pearl's sly laughter in her head. *Course that'd scare the old biddy right down the stairs, wouldn't it? Don't scream. Just reach on up and grab that skinny ankle, just like she grabbed mine.*

"Is somebody there?" the woman whispered. "Please. Please don't."

Abby's fingers brushed the nubby fabric of the woman's pants.

Upstairs, in the kitchen, pots clanged. Wood splintered. The old woman cried out "John Lee!" and toppled into Abby's outstretched hand. Abby grabbed her reflexively and pulled her in tight, breaking her fall.

"It's okay," she said when she felt the woman's body tense in panic. "It's okay, I'm here to help you."

"Abby?"

"Yeah, it's okay now. Just hush. Come over here and sit down."

She smelled of rose-scented soap and baby powder, something fresh and clean in the dark waiting death of the cellar. Abby let her go with reluctance and helped her limp to one wall, settled her on what felt like a wooden crate in the corner.

Feet scuffled upstairs. In the distance, Carlton's barking reached a frenzied pitch. They both froze, and the woman's hand tightened on Abby's with surprising strength.

"It's Custer Grady, isn't it?" she said. "I always knew he'd come back. He said he would."

Abby said "Pearl—" but the woman interrupted.

"No, honey. You know. You always did know, the first moment I laid eyes on you. I've been Pearl a long time, but I was born Ruth Ann."

"Ruth Ann," Abby repeated. "I'm sorry. This is all my fault."

"You didn't start it, honey. You sure didn't start it." Ruth Ann's body shook, and Abby knew she was crying. "Maybe I did. I just gave up that day, on the road, and it was like he could feel that. I didn't have anything left inside."

Upstairs, Abby heard a distant crash of glass from

some other part of the house. Carlton had stopped barking. From the kitchen, silence.

Then, stealthily, a jiggle of the cellar doorknob. Ruth Ann drew in a sharp breath.

Abby squeezed her hand and let her go. She stood up and put her hand flat on the moist concrete wall, found glass jars and wooden shelves, cool whispery spiderwebs, an empty box.

Where was it?

Another corner. She tried to move faster but the dark seemed to push on her, hold her back.

At the top of the stairs, the doorknob turned. The door creaked open an inch.

There was a shadow behind it.

"Hey, Pearl," Custer Grady said. "Hey, there. You come on out now."

Abby's elbow bumped something that grated metallically in the silence. She flailed out and found it hanging on the wall, gritty under her fingers. The wooden handle felt cool and hard as marble.

Grady opened the door wide and started down the steps, quick birdlike steps, Terry's black service revolver leading the way like a flashlight. He tried the switch, squinted up at the dark light bulb when it failed to come on.

The shovel was surprisingly heavy, hard to lift off the nail with her one good hand. Her left arm ached fiercely now, from cold and vibration and the tumble she'd taken down the steps. She held the shovel one-handed and stepped to the bottom of the stairs. Stood between Grady and his long-ago victim.

Grady's eyes caught the motion, even in the shadows, and he peered over the rail at her. His white teeth showed in a horsey grin.

"Hey, there, missy. Thought you were dead." He came another step down. The gun eyed her with interest. "I got no quarrel with you."

"Liar," she whispered.

"Naw, I'm telling the truth. Hell, you was the one that told me about *her*." He twitched the gun to indicate Ruth Ann, half hidden behind her. "Kept calling her Pearl, but I knew it wasn't Pearl. I figure, this one and Pearl came down here, and only this one came out. She's a killer, just like you said."

Abby tightened her grip on the shovel. Her arm trembled with the strain, ache gnawing her shoulder.

"She's the last," he said. "The very last one. See, we got history together. You ain't no part of this."

"Yes, I am." Abby took a deep breath. "Last time I didn't stop you, Custer. Last time I let you do just whatever you wanted, but that won't happen again. This is what I'm here for now. You want her, you're coming through me."

Grady stared at her, head slightly cocked, and grinned. "You're a tough one, ain't you? Tougher than Pearl. She never was much."

He was going to fire, she saw it staring out of his eyes. She lunged, shovel scything down toward his forearm hard enough to break bones.

She was too slow. He moved back from the whispering downswing, and the shovel thudded hard into wood, numbing her bruised arm with the impact. Grady said, "If that's how you want it, I don't mind a bit."

She saw the lazy pleasure in his eyes as he took aim.

A scrabble of claws in the kitchen, a shadow in the doorway. A blur of motion, teeth, and claws.

Carlton hit Grady squarely in the back, snarling and biting. Grady's shot went wild. He tumbled down the stairs, tangled with Carlton, and slammed into the dirt.

Carlton snarled once more, stood up, and backed off. He stood stiff-legged, head down, lips curled, as Grady twitched and moaned and coughed out a bright red stream of blood. His head lolled at an unnatural angle.

"Well, shit," he said pitifully, and convulsed, heels digging into the earth, head rolling loosely.

When he relaxed, the blue eyes were empty and surprised.

Abby crouched down beside her dog, one hand on his warm heaving side. He had glass cuts again, streaked red down his back and sides, and one foot looked badly cut. She hugged him carefully and blinked back tears as he butted his head against her chest and licked her cheek.

When she let him go, he whined and picked his way carefully around Grady's body to where Ruth Ann sat. He put his head in her lap and closed his eyes while she petted him.

"He killed my dog, you know," Ruth Ann said. Her voice sounded rusty and tired. "Killed him on the side of the road when he first took me."

"I know." Abby hung her head, tasted blood and death and Pearl's thwarted, empty rage, and said, "Good boy, Carlton."

Decrescendo:
December 27, 1994

John Lee was sitting against a wall in the living room, both arms wrapped around his stomach. He lifted his head as Abby limped toward him, and she was terrified by the putty-gray color of his skin, the blankness in his eyes.

"Is she okay?" he asked. "Mom?"

Blood on his fingers—not much blood, not rivers of it, but enough. She stared fixedly at the smear of color, so bright against his skin, and felt as if the world were falling away under her feet, collapsing into the cellar.

Grady still had the power to do that, even dead.

She crossed the room in a daze, aware of dry hot air stirring her hair against her neck as she passed a vent, aware of the burned-out smell of gunpowder hanging like an invisible circle around him. His hand, when she took it in hers, was shockingly cool, slick on the palm.

"Let me see," she said. He lifted his other hand away.

A neat little hole in his shirt, a neat little bubbling spring of red underneath it. She gasped and stripped off her coat, held it hard against the wound, and heard him wince.

"Mom?" he asked again. She glanced back toward the kitchen, where she could hear Ruth Ann's dragging limp coming toward them.

"Ruth Ann, call the ambulance!" she yelled. "Tell them John Lee's been shot!"

"Shot!" Ruth Ann's voice was muffled. Abby looked up to see her standing in the kitchen doorway, so bent, so fragile, both hands wrapped over her mouth to trap in a scream. "Oh, dear God."

"Please," Abby said. "Please call."

Ruth Ann turned, stumbled, caught herself, and reached for the telephone.

"Where is he?" John Lee was breathing rapidly, shallowly, little huffs of breath like a train coming up a hill. Abby did the only thing she could, pressed with the coat, bit back her tears, and tried not to think about the damage the bullet could have done, internal bleeding, seconds ticking away.

"He's dead, John. It's all right now."

He stared at her, brown eyes wide, and she recognized the lines of Custer Grady's face in his, but the eyes were pure Ruth Ann, mild and strong. She leaned in to kiss his forehead, cradling him close, giving him what heat she had in her body. He was trembling, very slightly, a fine vibration against her skin like a hum.

"You find what you were looking for?" he asked.

"I found you."

"I mean, did you find what you were looking for in the cellar?"

The silence stretched between them, strangely comfortable. She kissed his hair, smoothed it with her cheek.

"Yes," she said. "Yes, I think I did."

"Ruth Ann." She felt his breathing stop, then start up again with a hitch. Fear made her strangely calm. She closed her eyes and listened to his lungs fill and empty, fill and empty. "You called her Ruth Ann."

"Yes."

After a long silence he said, "I guess I knew all along her name wasn't Pearl Jordan. Seems like no surprise at all."

"She's still your mother."

His body trembled again. His breathing hitched.

"And he's my father." His hand tightened on hers. "Wonder if he knew when he shot me. Wonder if he cared."

In the distance an ambulance wailed, screaming louder as it pulled closer.

"It's goddamn cold, Abby."

"I know."

"Think we need a good hot shower."

"Yes."

A shadow fell over them—Ruth Ann. She'd come up so quietly Abby hadn't noticed, but she wordlessly made room for Ruth Ann to kneel stiffly down next to her son. Ruth Ann stroked his face gently.

"You're going to be just fine," she said. Tears dripped from her cheeks to rain on the hardwood floor; one fell on his leg and soaked into the thick denim blue jeans. "Oh, honey, you shouldn't have done this."

He looked up at her, brown eyes wide and full of pain. "Couldn't let him get you again, Mom. I had to do something."

The door vibrated under a fist. Abby got up and went to let in the paramedics; they ignored her and rushed to John Lee, displaced Ruth Ann with boxes and bandages.

Abby looked out at the snow and saw Terry's black-and-white cruiser, a dark shadow still parked on the highway. Her lips parted in horror as Ruth Ann said, "They got here awful fast, didn't they? I just hung up the phone."

"Terry," Abby said, and flung open the screen door, limped breathlessly down the steps. Snow, drifting cold and silent. "Terry!"

Her shout drifted, too, lazy on the wind. She saw a flash of red spilled on the snow.

Terry Bollinger lay on his back, staring up at the sky. The snow around him was a vivid cherry-red. His lips had turned a pale, delicate blue, almost the shade of his eyes.

The walkie-talkie was on the ground next to him, hissing static. In his hand he held a black cellular phone. The circuit was still open; she could hear voices distant and ghostly coming from the speaker; *"Sir, if you're still there, try to signal the paramedics, they should be coming anytime now—sir, can you hear me?"*

There was a neat black hole in his cheek, and a huge gaping one on the right side of his head. He looked so terribly young.

Abby knelt in the snow next to him and bowed her head and said, "I'm so sorry." She stayed there, listening to the quiet and the snow and, when she thought Terry would have liked her to go, she went back to the house and told the paramedics that the man who'd called them was lying dead in the snow outside.

Coda:
December 30, 1994

Abby unlocked the door to John Lee's workshop and hurried inside to punch in the alarm code he'd given her. Behind her, Benny stamped snow from her boots—not snow boots, of course, Benny didn't own anything practical—and moaned about the state of the suede.

"You're lucky you didn't break your neck in those," Abby said as she unzipped her jacket. "Well, here we are. Now what?"

"Well, now you go in a small smelly bathroom and I jam pennies in the door and lock you in," Benny said. "You know, there's just way too much snow out here for my peace of mind. It's like living in a jar of Liquid Paper."

"Seriously." Abby tucked the keys back in her pocket and turned toward her friend—Benny had dressed down today in a thick green and blue striped sweater, an orange vest, and black and white leggings. A zebra in a state of terminal confusion. "What're we doing here?"

"Giving you your Christmas present." Benny grinned. "John Lee swore me to secrecy, so you're just going to have to play along."

"I don't have to—"

"Ah, ah, ah—who was sitting on a rickety toilet seat for three hours while you were playing Annie Oakley?"

Abby spread her hands in defeat. Benny motioned for her to stay there, stepped into John Lee's workroom, and turned on the lights.

The glitter of crystal was as beautiful as she remembered it, and it brought back the memory of his voice, his touch, his smell. She blinked back tears as Benny crossed to a plain black telephone and dialed a number she'd written on the back of her hand.

"Hey," she said into the receiver. "That you? Okay, hold on. Here."

She held the receiver out to Abby. Abby stepped over and took it, tucked it in the crook of her neck as she watched Benny teeter away in her high-heeled boots, heading for something round in the center of the workroom. It was covered with a drop cloth.

"Abby?" John Lee's voice on the other end, drowsy and slow. "Are you watching Benny?"

"Yeah, I'm watching. Shouldn't you be asleep?" she asked.

He chuckled. "Sure. Are you watching her?"

"Yes, I'm watching." Benny reached the drop cloth, took hold of the edges, and peeked underneath. She grinned and waved. "She's doing something."

Benny yanked the drop cloth away with a magician's flourish.

The stained-glass window. The woman still

reached up for the sun with an expression of love and awe—but the face . . .

The face was hers. Abby's. She felt an instant's complete disorientation, and then another instant's panic. Was this how he saw her, so perfect? So beautiful? How could he see that in the imperfect face she saw in the mirror every day?

Her throat burned and she had to swallow hard not to burst into tears.

Behind Abby's kneeling figure in the glass was another one, so delicate it was just a shadow, a ghost in glass. Abby's breath caught painfully in her throat. *Pearl.* But this Pearl was free of pain now, free to go.

"I didn't want to sell it," John Lee's voice said softly. "Told him I'd make him another one, but this one I had to keep. It's yours, Abby. If you want it."

She took a deep, unsteady breath and said, "I do."

Dr. Urdiales said quietly, "How do you feel?"

Abby looked down at her right hand, folded neatly in her lap, and said, "Better. Isn't that terrible? Terry's dead and I feel better. John Lee was shot and I feel better."

"John Lee's going to be all right."

"Yes."

"Do you think you're to blame for everything that happened?"

She blinked and looked up. "Well, I am, aren't I? I had to know. I let Pearl take over and Pearl didn't care about anything but revenge. We always have the choice, don't we? To walk away?"

Dr. Urdiales leaned back in his leather chair, studying her. He wore a new sweater the color of a soft summer sky; she decided she liked it. The office still smelled of pine and, faintly, Polo cologne.

"If you'd walked away, Ruth Ann would be dead now. Custer Grady might have continued on out of town, just as he was planning to. John Lee would probably be dead as well. You needed resolution, Abby. There's nothing wrong in that."

"Yeah." She glanced over at the clock, ticking reassuringly in the corner. Even in here, time passed. "I need to visit John Lee."

"Of course." He nodded and stood, polite as always. She gathered her purse one-handed—they'd had to reset the bone in her left arm, but the ache was going away now—and was almost to the door before a pink corner of paper sticking out of her purse reminded her of something.

"Oh. Here." She handed him a printed flyer. He studied it, eyebrows rising.

"A memorial concert for Terry Bollinger?"

"Yeah. I'm going to play the Mozart concerto as soon as my arm heals."

He smiled and offered her his hand. When she took it, he said "I thought you had a fear of performing," and she smiled and then laughed out loud.

"I'm not afraid of anything."